THE
MAN WHO
UNDERSTOOD
CATS

THE MAN WHO UNDERSTOOD CATS

Michael Allen Dymmoch

St. Martin's Press
New York

Production Editor: David Stanford Burr

Library of Congress Cataloging-in-Publication Data

Dymmoch, Michael Allen.
    The man who understood cats / Michael Allen Dymmoch.
       p. cm.
    "A Thomas Dunne book."
    ISBN 0-312-09332-2
    I. Title.
  PS3554.Y6M36 1993
  813'.54—dc20   93-10060
                                                CIP

First Edition: May 1993

10 9 8 7 6 5 4 3 2 1

for
Peter Brogno

The author wishes to thank Carol Fitzsimmons, M.S.W., A.C.S.W., for answers to psychological questions; literary agent Ray Powers for advice on plotting; Oakton Community College Instructor Gary Deters, M.S., for general information on law enforcement; U.S. Customs Public Affairs Officer Cherise Mayberry for answers about Customs; N. Craig Luttig, CPA, for answers to financial questions; and the following members and former members of the Chicago Police Department for their answers to questions about the department: Sergeant Philip Derring, Neighborhood Relations Officer Michael Barone, Commander Hugh Holton, and Director of News Affairs Tina Vacini. I have taken liberties with the information given me. Any errors are my own.

Thanks also to the reference librarians of the Northbrook Public Library; Janice Irvine, The Book Bin, Northbrook, Illinois; Judy Duhl, Scotland Yard Books, Winnetka, Illinois; Nancy of the U.S. Post Office, Northbrook, Illinois; Megan T. Blake and to readers Doug Cummings, Barb D'Amato, Morton Hartman, Hugh Holton, Ron Levitsky, Marilee Luttig, Mary Ann Rosberg, and the Red Herrings.

mad

THE MAN WHO UNDERSTOOD CATS

ONE

The arena beneath the forest canopy was black, though a moon shone through the foliage with a strange luminosity— like a giant firefly on a tapestry. Pale daylight, caught in the understory leaves by day, refined and filtered free of heat, glowed in the moonlight from the faces of orchids and the fingers of epiphytes. A path sloped gently downward through the undergrowth like C. S. Lewis's gradual road to Hell, through air flavored by black locust blooms and redolent of jasmine. Old-Tarzan-movie jungle sounds crescendoed and decrescendoed, and a glass-chime trickle of water perfused the darkness. There were no thorns. No snakes. No insects.

Caleb ran.

Night things fell silent as he passed. Tiny eddies in the fluid air stroked his damp skin with lover's fingers, and the attenuated grasses of the forest floor stroked his long thighs. Cool kidskin leaves whipped his naked shoulders, leaving bloodless welts on his sensation. Damp humus cushioned his bare feet, and the rhythm of his breathing seemed to echo back to him from the smooth surfaces of leaves. As did the soft thuds of his footfalls. And the pulses of his heart.

Then something sinister added snarls to the jungle music, and Caleb's enjoyment was interrupted by the ominous, distant crashing through vegetation of something invisible in the darkness behind him. Suddenly a cougar screamed. Suddenly Caleb was sweating profusely, in terror and quite out of breath.

His terror intensified. His heartbeats became the downstrokes of a pile driver, the open path a maze of exposed

1

roots. Low branches reached out for him. The path widened onto a steep bank below which shallow water mirrored the green-gold light. Indecision froze him. Run or make a stand? Upriver or down? He turned to face the terror behind him. Twin yellow reflections of the moon peered back at him from the black jungle-patterned brocade. Caleb scrambled backward onto the brink. Then, as a fluid mass of darkness detached itself from the deeper black of jungle, the earth gave way beneath his feet and he was falling, tumbling, sliding in an avalanche of damp soil to the river's edge.

His pursuer launched itself into the shallow river. Briefly it was silhouetted against a neon flash of watery moonlight. The mirrored moon shattered, and its shards cut a cat's silhouette of sinister darkness between Caleb and the far bank. Caleb pressed himself against the embankment, into the soft earth, and squeezed his eyes shut as the cat whipped its tail against the shallow water. It crouched lower. As it sprang, it screamed, and as it screamed, a second cry echoed. He threw his arms up and braced himself for the blow. Just then, a second cat—white in the moonlight—launched itself at the first and bore the attacker earthward. The deadlocked bodies struck his chest with force enough to knock the scream from his throat. The shock sucked air into his lungs.

Then the gravity of the situation lessened. The oppressive weight crushing him was transmuted, and a roiling mass of claws and needle teeth and small furred bodies churned across his chest, a yin-yang of black and amber. The monster paws pounding him became the hammering of his own heart, and the pummeling of tiny heels and elbows. The scream that lodged in his throat deepened and was amplified by rage.

"God damn it, cats!"

Caleb's eyes snapped open; confusion glazed them momentarily. As he sat upright, his eyes stretched wider with rage. The furred turmoil on his chest disintegrated as two small bodies scattered. He stared down at himself, expecting blood and flayed flesh, but saw instead a naked man, gleaming with sweat, moderately hirsute, not in bad shape for forty-two. He turned to stare at his

2

image in the mirror covering the door of the closet next to the bed. A long, flat face with high cheekbones stared back at him, with pale eyes and brown hair that was not as thick as formerly.

He glared around. Daylight transformed the jungle to a ficus scraping the ceiling, a large Boston fern in the north window, a hanging philodendron, and abstract art. The river embankment had become his bed; the undergrowth, silk leaf-patterned batik sheets and oriental carpets. Two house cats, black and orange, paced opposite sides of the room with diminished ferocity.

Freud and Skinner.

He willed his heart rate back to normal and glared from orange to black. "One of you bastards is going," he told them fiercely. The cats regarded his hostility with well-rehearsed indifference. B. F. Skinner jumped back on the bed, staring as if to say, "Were you addressing me?"

Caleb laughed and scratched the cat along his jawline. "Just as soon as I can sucker someone into taking you."

TWO

He bounded from the king-size bed onto the parquet floor and pushed between the luxuriant dieffenbachia screening his view of the lake to inspect the morning from his balcony. The first edges of daylight squeezed between clouds piled over the water, tinting them the colors of the age—pastel pink and lavender. Intense humidity, visible as a thin haze shrouding distant landmarks, promised to make the day unbearable, but this early, the air was still cool enough to be intoxicating.

Caleb felt as if he was at the center of the universe. Chicago, not Easter Island, was the world's navel. Heart of the heartland. Drug and air trafficker to the nation.

He ran five miles every morning, six days a week, weather permitting. When it was too hot or cold outside, he ran or swam at the health club. Usually he headed north along the lakeshore and ran through Lincoln Park. Sometimes he drove to Evanston and ran through the Northwestern campus; occasionally he'd follow the Green Bay Trail as far as Ravinia in Highland Park. This morning he went south along the shoreline, trying to keep his mind in the present, thinking of nothing but the perfect placement of each footfall. Zen and the Art of Jogging. Actually secondhand Zen; like most Americans, he hadn't the time or the patience for the real thing. He stopped on the Ohio Street Beach to stretch and skip a flat stone across the water. He trotted through Olive Park, out to the end of Navy Pier and back. Further south, he stretched again as he inspected the flotilla of sailboats ranked artlessly on the gray wash of the harbor. The sky would have sent his beloved scrambling for a paintbox. Ah, well. The agony had subsided—even

4

compound fractures of the soul heal, given time—leaving him a little empty, a little melancholy, victim of a pervasive malaise. It would be easy to become depressed.

Of course, there was still the question; why? But there was no reason. The clichés that came to mind were anesthetic: *Those whom the gods love die young; God has His reasons;* etc. Perhaps He does. Perhaps the foremost is to make us value life.

"You're getting maudlin, Jack," he told himself, "How about this one—Physician, heal thyself."

He sprinted across the Drive, dodging early commuters, and shook the mood off by pushing himself to his limits through Grant Park. He went almost to the Field Museum before heading back north. One of the advantages of keeping your body fit was that you had control of it.

B. F. Skinner watched him shave and peered into the shower as he adjusted the water. Caleb's cats were less pets than symbionts. He gave them space, vaccinations and regular meals; and received, in return, companionship and a sort of aesthetic experience. It wasn't just that they were beautiful and amusing, though their forms were satisfying, their behavior fascinating; they embodied the same balance and grace as certain works of art—no wonder the Egyptians worshiped them. There was no logic to it, no way to explain it to non–lovers of cats.

The shower was a ritual. He stepped under the water, soaped and rinsed off quickly, then stood with his back to the stream, concentrating on the sensation as heated fingers of water massaged his neck. He gradually turned up the temperature to as hot as he could stand it, shifting from foot to foot, then forward and back, so that the fingers played across his shoulders, back and buttocks, and up and down his legs. He turned the temperature down a little before he turned around to get his front. When he finally stepped out, his skin tingled. He took inventory as he toweled off and found little with which to be dissatisfied.

Back in his room, he selected an expensive suit from a closet full of expensive suits and coordinating ties, shirts, and shoes. He had invested a great deal of money and time in his wardrobe, taking care to choose each suit for the particular sensations it aroused, the subtle differences that made it quite unlike the others. He had gone back for fittings as many times as necessary to insure that each suit was as comfortable as skin. He chose a pale gray summer wool by instinct, the correct weight for the weather, the right color for his scheduled clients. Considering his clientele, exquisite taste had a definite survival value.

He entered the living room, noting—with almost subliminal satisfaction—the mossy support of the Bidjar Herati beneath his shoes. The elements of his environment—the oil portrait over the fireplace, the wall of walnut bookshelves, the stereo system—gave him great comfort and pleasure, though he took only cursory notice of them now. Before leaving, he checked his reflection in a gilt-framed mirror by the door and patted Sigmund Freud, who was perched on a nearby chair-back. Then he set the security system controls and let himself out.

He took the Jaguar so he could stop in at the hospital at lunch without wasting time trying to get a cab. Though he wouldn't get it out of third gear in the short hop between garages, the look and feel of the silver-blue vehicle gave him the same sense of pleasure he felt for his cats, and a lion tamer's delight in its power.

At the Grant Park garage, he angled it into his usual space—next to the attendant's car—and locked it. He gave Matt the keys and a five and asked, "How's your family?" As he listened while the man thanked him and told of tribulations that would have vexed Job, he knew Matt's gratitude was more for the question than the money. For two minutes of concern, Matt would guard the car as carefully as he would have for fifty dollars. Caleb wondered where the manipulation left off. Was what he did with words different from what others do with money? What harm did it do? Yet, can a man see things clearly if he has his eyes on his own interest?

Caleb walked to his North Michigan Avenue office building and took the stairs to the third floor. As he unlocked the door, he read the sign on it autonomically—NORTH MICHIGAN AVENUE ASSOCIATES—and noted that the FM beyond it was set for elevator music.

The doctors' private office doors stood closed on opposite sides of the waiting room, which was decorated with soothing colors and comfortable furniture, a variety of plants, windows with a view of Grant Park, prints on the walls, and a tank full of tropical fish. An L-shaped reception desk near the entrance isolated clients psychologically from the receptionist and kept the more restless ones from playing with the copier or the computer.

The receptionist, Mrs. Sleighton, was watering the plants, and she hurried to turn the radio down to barely audible as he came through the door. Irene—so Caleb thought of her, though he was careful to keep their relationship formal—was in her late forties, and fierce or motherly, as necessary. Because she was cheerful and punctual, exceptionally discreet, and didn't file her nails or chew gum in the office, Caleb was inclined to overlook her propensity for tabloid news and Muzak.

She said, "Good Morning, Dr. Caleb."

"Good morning, Mrs. Sleighton." He looked around. "Did Mr. Finley cancel?"

"No. It's not like him, is it?"

It wasn't, Caleb agreed. Allan was always punctual. As he went into his inner office, Irene turned up the odious Muzak and took out a copy of the *Star*.

The furnishings in Caleb's office were similar to those in the reception room. A large desk stood opposite the door, with comfortable chairs on both sides; the wall behind it was covered with shelves of impressive tomes and built-in cabinets. A bank of windows—to Caleb's right as he entered—provided a priceless view of Grant Park to the conversation area, with its couch and armchairs, and tables bearing ashtrays and designer Kleenex. The wall opposite the windows displayed a clock and the Jason Rogue lithograph of a cat. Caleb sat down in one of the armchairs and lost track of the time as he stared at the view and pondered the liberating and enslaving nature of habit. Until the intercom buzzed on his desk. He crossed the room and pressed a button.

Irene's voice came from the machine. "Mrs. Gates is here, Doctor."

"Thank you. Did Mr. Finley call?"

"No. Shall I call and reschedule?"

"Please. If you can't get him at home, try his office, but if he's not there, don't say who's calling." He shut off the intercom and smiled as Mrs. Gates came in.

"Good morning, Dorothy. . . . "

Three fifty-minute hours later, Caleb's eyes had nearly glazed over with boredom as his third client meandered on. The man was a self-described VIP, the president of a small manufacturing company, who'd inherited a patent that was making money faster than he could spend it. He was a man who couldn't be wrong, and he couldn't understand why he was snubbed by Chicago's "beautiful people." Caleb listened to his troubles with part of his attention, noted contradictions and discrepancies, and filed away details for reference. But he had heard most of it before. Waiting for the man to get to the *real* point was testing Caleb's endurance. Caleb would have found him intolerable had his unhappiness been less obvious or his defenses less transparent.

Caleb had diagnosed him a dog man. He tended to classify everyone as either dog people or cat people; he'd even considered submitting a paper on the subject. The former were those for whom social approval was the goal of existence. Dog people couldn't function without constant reassurance that they were loved and admired. They were creatures who needed to fill every moment with sound or activity, to make friends with everyone they met. Cat people, on the other hand, were more discriminating. More independent. More self-possessed. Less concerned with public opinion. He had met cat people from whom he'd managed, after several years' acquaintance, to elicit no more than hello or good morning. With some people, as with some cats, that was the best one could hope for. On the whole he found cat people more interesting.

" . . . and then she had the nerve—I don't know why I married that bitch—to tell me I bore her."

"What exactly did you expect to get from coming to me?"

"Just what I *do* get. I get to say I support one of the most expensive shrinks on the North Shore."

"I'd say you're getting a rather poor return on your investment."

8

That got him. "You kissing me off?"

"I'm telling you I can't write a prescription for what's troubling you."

"What makes you think I want . . . "

Caleb waited.

"They say the one who dies with the most toys, wins."

Caleb raised an eyebrow.

"I want to know *what*?"

Caleb nodded and glanced at his desk clock. "We'll work on that next time. In the meantime, I'd like you to think about what changes you'd like to make in yourself. Just yourself. You can't change anyone else."

"It's not enough I gotta pay you a fortune, I gotta work too?"

Gotcha! Caleb stood, smiling. "You pay me to make you work."

The VIP nodded as he got up, and Caleb ushered him out. When he'd closed the outer office door on the man, Caleb turned to look questioningly at Irene.

"Mr. Questor canceled. He said his grandfather died."

Caleb smiled humorlessly. "That's the fourth grandfather in six months. You'd better call his parole officer. And bill him for the missed appointment."

"Very well. And Mrs. Reston called. An emergency. She *has* to see you."

He smiled wryly. "If it's a genuine emergency, Dr. Fenwick can see her. Did you get hold of Mr. Finley?"

"No. His office said he didn't come in today. They presume he'll be in tomorrow. I left a message on his answering machine at home."

"Thank you. The next appointment's at one?"

"That's right. *Ms.* Goodwin."

Caleb let the implied disapproval pass, knowing Ms. Goodwin would never hear it. "I'll be back by then."

He used the car phone to call his answering service. They usually relayed messages from patients to Irene, but he'd check anyway. He said, "This is Dr. Caleb. Did you have a message for me from a Mr. Finley?" No. "No one took a message for a Mr. Finley from Dr. Caleb?" Messages had been scrambled that way before, but not this time it seemed. It was very strange. In three years Allan hadn't missed an appointment.

On impulse, Caleb changed his plans for lunch. Instead of turning east on Superior, he continued north, onto the Drive.

THREE

Thinnes always drove. As senior dick, he could have had Crowne do it, but he didn't trust Crowne's judgment or his over-reliance on the brakes. And Thinnes preferred to be in control of things.

They were headed south on Lincoln. He kept his eyes moving, noticing things he was no longer paid to concern himself with—a car parked in a fire lane, an expired tag, traffic violators. You still go through the motions, he thought. Today his mood matched the weather. It seemed like half of Lake Michigan had boiled into the sky and hung over the city like a climax that wouldn't come. His skin and nerves and muscles, even his attention span seemed stretched too tight. He knew he wasn't really with it. He felt as if he'd slept too long, or waked right after nodding off; everything looked and sounded slightly out of focus. He wished he'd had less to drink last night, but Christ, he'd only had three beers! He hadn't slept well.

At thirty-eight, he'd seen too many homicides. Too many weird incidents. Too much Chicago politics. His outlook had gotten gray as the industrial atmosphere hanging over the city, his hopes as thin as his lank frame. The need to build an airtight, *closed* case for every incident, to fill out a rap sheet on everyone he met had gone beyond habit, had become obsessive. And exhausting. The burned-out cop syndrome. The mid-life crisis. Boring. He wished he could flip a switch in his head and turn it all off.

You're a cliché, Thinnes, he told himself as he turned onto Webster and took in Grant Hospital on his left without really noticing it, slowing automatically to maneuver around the double-parked cars and the pedestrians. He took one of the two polysty-rene cups from the dash and watched his partner watching him.

11

Crowne knew better than to talk before Thinnes had his coffee. The junior detective was twenty-nine, average height, weight, looks, and intelligence. And above average cynicism. Weren't all cops?

Thinnes slugged down the coffee. It was too hot, and he swallowed fast to get it out of his mouth. It burned all the way down. He put the cup back on the dash and made himself say, "What've we got?"

Crowne pulled the notebook from his breast pocket and flipped it open. "Twenty-one twenty-three Cleveland, apartment three-B. Death investigation; one A. Finley; male cauc; probable suicide." He snapped the book shut. "They said step on it 'cause Bendix is there already and they want the coppers back on the street. This ought to be a cinch."

Thinnes kept his eyes on the street. Cleveland was the next corner. "You volunteer?" Even without looking directly, he could see Crowne's annoyance.

"If you'd be on time for work," Crowne said, "you could volunteer us for *your* idea of easy duty."

Thinnes let it pass, but Crowne wasn't going to let it drop. "How do you get away with it? Evanger's got to know."

Thinnes stopped for the sign at Cleveland. "I've got a partner who covers for me."

"Right."

Thinnes glanced sideways and noted Crowne had gone beyond annoyed. "Evanger's button is the bottom line," Thinnes said. "You want to push it, just give him lots of good busts and keep your nose clean—he'll let you do anything."

He turned right. Cleveland was a quiet, tree-lined street. A block down, they could see a marked squad and the crime lab van. Twenty-one twenty-three was a modern three-story apartment building in an area of exclusive rehabbed yuppie residences. Thinnes double-parked their unmarked squad in front of the door, allowing just enough room for cars to squeeze by if no one parked in the empty space by the fire hydrant. They took their cups from the dash and went inside the building.

The coffee was starting to do its work by the time the elevator doors opened on the third floor. As Thinnes stepped into the hallway outside Finley's apartment, he felt more alert. He kept his eyes moving, taking in details—the last of which was the familiar personnel. He nodded as he flashed his star at the two uniform coppers. He noted that the male officer's paunch hung over his belt and he stood with the careless authority old street cops have. The female had it to an extent lessened by her shorter tenure. She rested her fist on her hip, near her piece, but casually and out of habit. Thinnes observed these things the way a professional driver takes in traffic signals—almost without noticing.

A. Finley's L-shaped front room was expensively furnished—regulation Yuppie decor—but there was a slickness about it that suggested a lack of imagination, as if Finley had bought the furniture store display. There was almost no personal stamp. The only things that were not perfectly coordinated were in the dining room: a very businesslike office desk and a blood-spattered lithograph on the wall to its left. At the far left-hand corner of the desk there was a checkbook, a book of stamps, and a neat pile of addressed, sealed envelopes. Finley himself lay slumped on the floor near the desk, with a .38 caliber revolver and a gold pen just beyond reach of his empty hand.

Something about the scene was a little off, and Thinnes tried to define just what. It wasn't simply the fact of death—apparent suicide, or the corpse with its head blown half away, or the gross spray of blood and brain tissue on the wall and picture.

The body was being photographed by a pimply-faced junior evidence technician supervised by Bendix, the senior tech. Bendix spotted Thinnes and groaned to his colleague. "Christ! They sent Thinnes. Might as well send out dinner orders now." He was fiftyish, balding, out of shape, congenitally insensitive and professionally cheerful. His nod at Thinnes wasn't cordial; his nod to Crowne was friendlier. He jerked his thumb to indicate Thinnes. "Why'd they send him?"

"Just your lucky day," Crowne told him sourly. He stayed where he didn't have to look at the body.

As he walked over for a closer look at the corpse, Thinnes ignored Bendix. He sipped his coffee thoughtfully while he studied the body, then squatted and used a pen from his pocket to pick up the gun by its trigger guard so he could examine it without damaging latent prints. He looked up at Bendix. "Pretty heavy artillery for a civilian, wouldn't you say?"

Bendix shrugged. Thinnes put the gun back. "This guy live alone?"

"Landlord said he did."

Thinnes looked around the room. Except for the bloody spray pattern on the wall, the apartment was unusually clean and orderly. "Maid service?"

"Landlord said no. Compulsive neatnik."

"Gay?"

"Not the sort of thing you put on a lease application," Bendix said. Thinnes gave him a moderately disgusted look. "If he was," Bendix added, "he was discreet." He very deliberately took out a cigar and lit it, putting the spent match carefully in his pocket and creating a toxic haze.

Thinnes pointed to the door. "Out with that."

Bendix went to the doorway and stood just inside, holding the cigar out in the hall, flicking the ash against the wall, where it wouldn't be tracked into the apartment. "What's the difference?" he said. "The stiff has a gun in his hand, gunshot residue in the right places, and all the doors were locked from the inside. So why are you asking questions like it was homicide?"

Thinnes ignored him and turned to Bendix's assistant. "You get pictures in the other rooms?" The technician shook his head. "Do it."

As the tech left, Thinnes pulled a pair of latex gloves from his pocket, put them on, and started poking through the pile of bills. They were addressed to American Express, the Blessing Realty Company, Commonwealth Edison, North Michigan Avenue Associates, Northern Illinois Gas, Visa. Bills.

Bendix said, "Jesus Christ, Thinnes, you been at it too long. You fried your wires—you're seein' murder in everything. If he'd had a heart attack, you'd probably try to make it out someone scared him to death."

"Take a look at this, Bendix." Thinnes indicated the entire scene. "What do you see?"

Bendix looked at the corpse. "Just a poor SOB who blew his brains out."

Thinnes shook his head. He said wearily, "Who's got the data?"

Bendix hitched his thumb toward the hall behind him. "Copper."

Thinnes didn't try to hide his annoyance. "Which one?"

"The pretty one. You're gettin' nuts, Thinnes. You need six months in New Zealand or someplace they don't have homicides."

"Doesn't it bother you that we don't have a clue he was suicidal? No note, no motive. Nothing."

"Guy kills himself, he's crazy. Crazy people don't *need* motives. Or if *you* need a motive, how's his lover left him, or his stocks just bottomed out, or how's his laundry put too much starch in his shorts?"

Thinnes wasn't listening. "Ray," he said to Crowne, "go see what the coppers have and send them back to work."

As Thinnes left the room to follow the technician, he could hear Bendix ask Crowne, "How do you stand that?"

"You want to give me odds he's wrong?"

The bedroom looked brand new. Unused. Like a setup at Wickes or Homemakers. Everything was too well coordinated to have been bought piecemeal. One each: masculine bedroom set, with matching drapes, and bedspread. The plush, chocolate brown carpet still showed marks from the vacuum cleaner. Thinnes stared, as if he could flush some clue or motive out of hiding. He looked at the tech, who shrugged as if to say, what's to shoot?

"Just a couple of angles for reference," Thinnes told him. When the tech'd shot the dresser, Thinnes sorted through it. He found what you'd expect to find—socks and shirts and Jockeys, only folded neater than they'd come from the factory. He checked behind the color-coordinated starving-artist's-sale still life and the mirror over the dresser. Not even cobwebs. The only personal item in the room was a framed photo of Finley standing with his arms around a woman who had to be his sister.

When the tech had photographed the bed, Thinnes stripped it, finding only clean sheets. There was nothing under it but more vacuum tracks. The closet had sliding doors. Thinnes opened one side, then the other, standing back to let the tech shoot the contents. The clothes were on the low end of the high-price category, not Perry Ellis, but out of Thinnes's range. Finley seemed to have had a suit for every occasion. None of the shirts looked like they'd been worn since they came from the laundry. The shoes were all expensive, carefully polished and lined up like marines, prompting the technician to remark, "This guy wasn't real." Thinnes went through every shoe and the pocket of every piece of clothing but found nothing. Not even lint.

The utility closet between the bedroom and the bathroom was a wonder. Crammed onto its narrow shelves was every cleaning product available in the city. Brushes and rags, mops and pails and rubber cleaning gloves hung from hooks below the shelves. There was a dust mop and a broom, and both upright and canister vacuums filled the floor space. Thinnes squeezed the dust bag on the upright. It was empty. When he opened the top of the canister, he wasn't surprised to find an unused liner.

He half expected to find a paper strip on the toilet—the can was cleaner than the ritziest hotel john he'd ever been in. There wasn't a spot on the mirror or a drip on the counter. There was a single hair in the brush—red, like the victim's. The wastebasket had been emptied and rinsed out. There was a single change of clothes in the hamper, used but not dirty, as far as he could see. After the technician photographed the open medicine cabinet, Thinnes rummaged through it: toothpaste, squeezed and rolled from the end, Maalox, Excedrin, a razor with a virgin blade and not a trace of soap scum, shaving cream and aftershave, deodorant—the usual things, and a prescription vial half full of pumpkin orange capsules. Thinnes noted the particulars on the label and told the tech, "After you dust and log these, make sure it is what it says."

When Thinnes returned to the dining room with the technician, Bendix had gone out into the hall, and Crowne was looking aimlessly around.

"Well?" Thinnes demanded.

Crowne consulted his notebook. "According to the officer, the building manager signed for a UPS shipment for this guy around ten A.M., then let himself into the apartment to leave the package so it wouldn't get ripped off. When he opened the door and saw the blood, he dropped the box, backed out fast, and dialed nine-one-one. Said he didn't know Finley personally, but he was a good

16

tenant—paid his rent and didn't make noise or complain. End of story."

Thinnes pointed out more shots he wanted the tech to get, then went into the kitchen. Crowne followed, looking around indifferently as Thinnes studied the room. It was clean enough to be pronounced sterile, with matching appliances and few gadgets. The refrigerator appeared to have been cleaned recently and contained only unopened packages of perishables and domestic beer. With so little to see, they finished quickly and started back into the dining room. Thinnes went ahead, looking back at Crowne to say, "It wasn't suicide."

Crowne stiffened subtly, looking into the dining room beyond Thinnes. Thinnes turned to see a tall man staring with a strange, sad expression, at the wall above Finley and at the blood-spattered print.

"Who are you?" Thinnes demanded.

The man's eyes dropped to the remains of Finley, and he answered without looking up. "I was Allan's therapist. . . . " He looked at Thinnes with obvious dismay. "And I agree. He wasn't suicidal."

Thinnes studied him. He was a big man, very fit, six two or three, with a bland face, thinning brown hair, and mild blue eyes, a man who—if he got fat—would be ugly, since fat would blur the masculine features of his face and figure. His suit had been made for him and was such a definite if modest statement about his income that Thinnes was surprised he didn't also wear jewelry. He seemed easygoing enough, but—Thinnes wasn't prejudiced in these matters—he *was* a big man, and size brought advantages in life and fights, advantages often concealed for further gain.

"How'd you get in here?" Thinnes demanded. "Bendix!" he shouted, then said to the intruder, "Let's see some ID."

The man took out his wallet and removed his driver's license. Thinnes glanced at it, read JAMES A. CALEB, and handed it to Crowne, who recorded the particulars in his notebook.

Bendix entered with his cigar, no longer lit, in his mouth. "Yeah?"

Thinnes indicated Caleb. "Why'd you let *him* in?"

"Isn't he . . . ? I thought he was the new *department* shrink."

17

Thinnes turned to Caleb. "You touch anything in here?"

Caleb appeared flustered. "I . . . ah . . . don't know."

"Would you wait out in the hall?"

Caleb nodded and stepped past Bendix, who started to retreat. Thinnes said, "Hold it Bendix." Bendix stopped. "Where's your print man?"

"I sent him out for coffee." Bendix took out matches to relight his cigar, then looked at Thinnes and changed his mind.

"Then *you* get your box of tricks and get printing."

"Five'll get you ten they're all the victim's."

Thinnes was inclined to agree. Anyone smart enough to make murder look so much like suicide wouldn't destroy the victim's prints or leave any of his own. The only hope in such a case was based on the huge number of things to overlook. With luck the murderer had overlooked one. Thinnes gestured with his thumb toward the hall door. "Start with the shrink's."

When Bendix had gone, and Thinnes was trying to get his thoughts back to where they'd been before the interruption, Crowne quietly announced, "The medical examiner's here."

They ended up interviewing Dr. Caleb in the rental office, a cramped cubbyhole of a room adjoining the manager's apartment on the first floor.

"Tell me about Allan Finley, Dr. Caleb."

"He was a CPA, a very controlled, meticulous man, with a passion for order that served him well in his work. He liked things black and white, unambiguous, all lined up facing the same direction. And he liked puzzles, especially mathematical ones. Anything with a discrete solution. He found human interactions frustrating in their ambiguity. He wasn't suicidal."

"Mightn't the ambiguity have gotten to be too much?"

"When it did, he would bring it to me."

"He have any enemies?"

"None that I know of."

"What exactly was he seeing you for?"

"I suppose, under the circumstances, he wouldn't mind my telling. My diagnosis was a mild form of obsessive-compulsive disorder. Allan's overwhelming need for order and cleanliness was

18

interfering with his life and his relationships. I was helping him loosen up a bit."

"He was on medication?"

"Tofranil-PM, seventy-five milligrams daily, to be taken at bedtime. That's a minimum dose for an adult."

Thinnes checked his notebook. Caleb might have been reading from Finley's prescription label. But then according to the label, he'd written the prescription. Thinnes said, "What does it do?"

"It's a tricyclic antidepressant."

"I thought you said he wasn't depressed."

"I said he wasn't suicidal. OCD—obsessive-compulsive disorder—is thought to result from a chemical imbalance in the brain that causes the sufferer extreme anxiety if he doesn't repeat certain habitual behavior patterns, sometimes for hours at a time. Tofranil seems to restore the balance, enabling the victim to refrain from his compulsion."

"Judging by his apartment, I'd say he was still pretty compulsive about cleaning."

"The drug doesn't change the basic personality. Allan was a very fastidious man."

"Was he gay?"

"No."

"Female friends?"

Caleb answered slowly. Trying to put the answer diplomatically, Thinnes guessed. "One. Someone he'd known professionally for some time and was just getting to know socially."

"Sleeping with her?"

"He was working up to it, but he said they'd just gotten as far as dating."

That would explain the lack of feminine traces in the apartment, Thinnes thought. "The lady's name?"

"Alicia Baynes."

"Where did Finley work?"

"Wilson, Reynolds and Close, an accounting firm."

"What about the people at work?"

"Miss Baynes is one of them," Caleb said. "He respected her talent, though he said she was lacking in self-confidence—professionally, that is. She didn't seem to doubt herself as a woman."

Thinnes nodded; Crowne scribbled furiously. Caleb went on. "Allan's relationship with Marshall Close, his employer, was strictly professional. He'd been invited to Close's house on a few occasions recently. Close was grooming him for a partnership."

"What about Wilson and Reynolds?"

"Close bought Wilson out five or six years ago. Reynolds has been dead for ten years."

"Go on."

"Allan mentioned that he thought the office manager—I can't remember her name—was insecure, but since rumors started going around about the partnership, she'd been quite obsequious."

"What?" Crowne said.

Thinnes translated. "Sucking up to him."

Crowne nodded and went on writing.

Because of his problem, Finley had been a private person, not getting close to anyone until just recently. As a result, he'd had sort of an outsider's view of the staff at WR&C. Caleb gave a brief rundown on each of Finley's coworkers, based on what he could recall of what Finley'd said about them over the years. "There could be things I've forgotten," he added. "I'll look over Allan's file this afternoon and call you if I find anything else that seems important."

"Maybe I could stop by your office and have a look for myself," Thinnes suggested.

"Not without a subpoena."

He said it quietly. Thinnes couldn't detect any attitude behind the words. No defiance. No fear. It was nonnegotiable. There was no way to tell whether he was safeguarding his client privilege or covering his ass. And without probable cause, there wasn't a snowball's chance in hell of getting a subpoena.

Thinnes decided to try another tack. "Tell me about Finley's work."

"The one area where Allen's compulsivity paid off was his job. It required discretion and perfect accuracy, and scrupulous attention to detail."

"He ever mention any clients?"

"Only once. He recognized that a print in my office was from the Margolis Gallery and said the gallery was a client."

"So what'd he do for kicks? How'd he spend his free time? Was

20

he a virgin? Did he have any vices?" Finley seemed so curiously vague that if they hadn't had a corpse, Thinnes would have been willing to believe he hadn't existed.

"People with obsessive-compulsive disorder often don't *have* a life," Caleb said. "Their compulsions take up so much of their time, they can't develop relationships or interests, even hobbies. Often they can't read or go out to dinner or travel or relax."

Thinnes waited. Caleb seemed strangely detached about what he was saying. Thinnes wondered if he often lost patients. And if he was always so unmoved. Or maybe he was just real good at keeping it close to the vest.

"The irony," Caleb was saying, "is that he was finally getting his personal demon under control, just beginning to come alive."

Thinnes decided to try and shake Caleb up a little, get an off-the-cuff reaction. He winked at Crowne and said to Caleb, "You must've liked Finley a whole lot to make a house call." Before the doctor could respond, he asked Crowne, "Doesn't it seem a little strange that a high-powered shrink would take such an interest in a client?"

"Queer as Clark and Diversy."

Caleb froze at the crude reference to the City's gay center, then seemed to catch on to the ploy and relax.

"You ever have clients you don't like, Doctor?"

"I try to encourage people I don't feel I can work with to find another therapist."

"Ever have one who wouldn't go along with that?"

"Once."

"What'd you do about it?"

"I charged him three times as much."

"And he paid it?"

"He did."

"Why?"

"Why do people camp out for days to get tickets for perform-ances given by boors with no talent and obvious contempt for their audiences?"

Thinnes shook his head.

"May I go?" Caleb asked with impatience Thinnes was sure he feigned.

"You want to give us your number? In case we need anything else."

It was too easy, Thinnes thought after the doctor left. Caleb's interest in one nebbish of a client was too suspicious. Or maybe just weird. Weren't shrinks supposed to be as goofy as their clients? And a rich shrink. A fat-cat doctor, insulated from the real world by his thousand-dollar suits and Gold Coast address. If he wasn't returning to the scene of the crime—What crime? Maybe Finley *did* off himself!—what the hell was he doing here? Thinnes sighed. Rhonda, his wife, never understood why he wouldn't help her with her jigsaw puzzles. Life's already a puzzle. Actually, more like the results of a tornado in a puzzle factory. Thousands of puzzles. With all the pieces scrambled.

FOUR

The offices of Wilson, Reynolds and Close were typical high-power accounting-firm offices designed to set people at ease. The name was lettered on the plate glass entryway in gold leaf. The carpets were deep, the furniture pricey, the lighting subdued. Thinnes showed his star to the receptionist, who picked up her phone.

Marshall Close's inner office had the same aura of money and success as the outer office, but with all the little touches of comfort that mark a head honcho's perks. Smooth and confidence-inspiring, Close stood to shake hands with Crowne and Thinnes and offer them chairs.

Close sat down. "What can I do for you, gentlemen?" he asked when they were seated.

Male cauc, Thinnes thought, five ten or so, one seventy maybe. Black hair, gray at the temples. Blue eyes. Figure him for about fifty. "We're inquiring into the death of Allan Finley," he said. "What can you tell us about him?"

"We heard on the news. A horrible tragedy! I can't believe it." Thinnes nodded; Crowne got ready to put any relevant data in his notebook. "He was a person of the utmost integrity. I could cite numerous examples—but that would violate confidences. Just let me say that of all my employees, Allan was the most principled."

"Had he found irregularities in any of his clients' books lately?"

Close managed to look shocked. "Not to my knowledge. What is this leading up to? What have some hypothetical irregularities to do with Allan's death?"

"I'm trying to find out why he died," Thinnes said, "and I'm not going to overlook any possibility. Was he depressed lately? Had you noticed any changes in his behavior?"

23

"Actually, he'd been more cheerful lately than I've ever seen him. I was going to take him on as a partner. He was elated."

"Did you know he was seeing a psychiatrist?"

"No, but it would explain a great deal."

"Would you have considered him for a partnership if you'd known?"

"Inspector, my company handles the business and personal accounts of some of the most successful people in the world. You'd be amazed at how many of them see psychiatrists."

"Whose books was he working on Thursday?"

"That would be Margolis Enterprises, in Marina City. I believe he spent the entire day there."

"Did he come back here afterward?"

"No."

"Have you ever found any irregularities in Margolis's books?"

"Of course not!" Close thought about it and added, "A few minor errors, now and then. Not everyone who's worked on them has Allan's accuracy."

Personnel confirmed Thinnes's guess about a sister. Adrianna Finley was on file as the person to notify in case of emergency. She lived in New York City.

Finley's desk was in a huge room divided into identical cubicles by panels of sound-deadening material. The ceiling alternated between plastic-grilled fluorescent lighting and acoustical paneling. The floor was deeply carpeted. Each of the dozen or so employees of the firm had a cubicle with a desk, two chairs, and a desktop computer and phone, and each seemed to have tried hard to personalize the space.

Except Finley. Finley's desk was as tidy as his apartment. Only the walnut name plate with its incised gold-plated lettering gave any sign the desk had belonged to anyone. Thinnes found nothing of interest in or on the desk except the appointment calendar, which he confiscated and signed for after allowing the office manager to note upcoming appointments.

Bettina Calder was a tall trim black woman in her forties who seemed genuinely disturbed by Finley's death. Thinnes recalled Caleb's comments as he questioned her.

"He was good?"

"Allan was almost overqualified."

"He have any enemies?"

"None that I know of. I wouldn't say everyone liked Allan, but I don't believe anyone *disliked* him. Ms. Baynes probably knew him as well as anyone. Ah . . . " she hesitated. "She called in sick today."

"Can you give me her home address and phone number?"

"Certainly."

"Just one more thing, Ms. Calder. Was Finley right-handed or left-handed?"

"Left-handed, I believe."

The other interviews were similar. Crowne noted the particulars. Thinnes asked the questions and compared each subject with Dr. Caleb's assessment, wondering how much of what Caleb had told him was straight. Finley hadn't seemed to inspire any strong emotions in anyone during his life. In death, he seemed mainly to have produced the feeling *this can't have happened to someone I know.*

"Despondent? Quite the contrary. In the last few weeks, he was as optimistic as I've ever seen him."

"And was he right-handed or left-handed?"

"To be honest, I can't say for sure."

"There may have been a few who were jealous, but I can't think he had any enemies."

"Was he right-handed?"

"No, I think he may have been left-handed."

"I can't say I knew him as a friend. He was a very private person—nice, but hard to get close to."

"Was he left-handed or right-handed?"

"I'm sure he was right-handed."

" . . . extremely versatile. He could do almost anything, any job."

"Was he right- or left-handed?"

"Left-handed."

Left-handed seemed to be the consensus.

25

Alicia Baynes lived on Wayne, north of Addison. The building was larger than Finley's, but similar in nature and price. Thinnes found the listing and pushed the button beside her name. He waited. No one answered.

"Sick, huh?" Crowne said. He pushed the button marked BUILD-ING SUPERINTENDENT.

After a while a man appeared who looked more like a janitor than a super. He was wearing Levi's and a sleeveless tee-shirt that showed off his tattoos. He opened the door cautiously. "Yeah?"

Crowne showed him his badge. "We'd like to talk to one of your tenants. Baynes."

"She ain't here."

"We know that. You know where she is?"

"What'd she do?"

"We'd just like to ask her some questions," Thinnes said.

The super shrugged. "I don't want no trouble with the cops." Thinnes nodded. "Said she was going' away for the weekend to visit her folks. Said if anyone called from her job, to say she went to the doctor's. Should be back Monday."

"Yeah," Crowne said.

Thinnes said, "What can you tell us about Miss Baynes?"

The super shrugged. "Not much. Not my type." When he didn't get a reaction to this, he added, "Pays her rent on time, doesn't put grease down the drain. No pets."

FIVE

By the time Thinnes and Crowne headed back to the office, the city's infamous humidity had thickened to a serious overcast, threatening rain. They took their coats off before getting in the car, but even with the AC, their shirts were soon soaked.

Thinnes planned ahead as he drove. "I'll call New York and see if I can get someone to break the news in person to the sister. And ask her a few questions. You call around and see if he owed any money."

Crowne made a note in his notebook and Thinnes asked, "You ever do anything off the top of your head?"

Rumor had it Crowne had made detective in spite of a lousy score on the exam because of his political connections. He had no particular talent for detecting and none of the natural curiosity that makes a great detective. Still, in exchange for his doing much of the boring, routine work, Thinnes had taught him a basic line of questioning that served—sort of a who-what-where-when-how-and-why of detective work so that he'd been able to make out all right on performance reviews. They worked well enough together, though they didn't hang out after work. Different ages; different aims. And Crowne was still single.

Crowne ignored the dig. "You're gonna make a federal case outta this." He wasn't asking.

They came up on Western. Thinnes got a green and pulled through the intersection to turn into the Belmont entrance of the parking lot flanking the modern two-story dark brick building—headquarters for both Area Six and Police District Nineteen, and home of Cook County's First Municipal District Circuit Court. Thinnes couldn't find a parking space near the door and was forced to leave the car in the far northwest corner of the cops' lot, near where the car buffs angled their new or rehabbed classic vehicles into two spaces each to avoid dents. He toted Finley's check and appointment books and the UPS package, all smudged with black fingerprint powder and carefully packed in numbered Ziploc bags; Crowne carried their jackets. They passed through the building's plate glass doors into the cool cave of the lobby, and nodded at the desk sergeant in the square stone ring that was the reception desk.

The Area Six squad room was on the second floor, a large, square room with standard commercial overhead lighting, yellow-painted cement block walls, and a red ceramic tile floor. North-south rows of tables and chairs filled the center of the room. On each was a phone, and on some, old manual typewriters. A small table off to one side held a thirty-gallon coffee maker, plastic cups, sugar, and nondairy cream. The three outer walls of the room were interrupted by the doors and Levolor-blind-covered one-way windows of the interview rooms, and by the doors of small offices—the Area Six commander's and Property Crimes on the north, Karsch's on the east, Violent Crimes on the south. The operations desk took up the whole west wall.

Detectives Viernes and Swann were at work at the two tables nearest the Violent Crimes office—Lieutenant Evanger's—when Thinnes and Crowne came in and hung their jackets on the row of hooks near the door. Viernes, one of the area's three Latino detectives, was questioning a woman in Spanish, typing her answers on a form; Swann was on the phone. Crowne carried a soft drink and the *Sun-Times* to a table, where he spread the paper out and started skimming through it.

Thinnes put the stuff he was carrying down near Crowne and went to get coffee. "God bless Karsch," he remarked to no one in particular.

"You think he's the only one makes coffee around here?" Swann said with a grin that emphasized his resemblance to the late beloved mayor.

"The rest of us have work to do."

Viernes added his two-cents' worth without looking up from the typewriter. "How long's it take to get a Ph.D.?"

28

"In coffee making?" Swann asked.

Thinnes and Viernes laughed. The woman Viernes was questioning seemed bewildered.

"Hey, Thinnes," Crowne interrupted, "our accountant made the afternoon edition."

Thinnes walked over to read over Crowne's shoulder. The story was captioned ACCOUNTANT SUICIDE.

"The reporter must have talked to Bendix," Thinnes said dryly.

Later, Crowne and Swann had wandered off, and Viernes was talking on the phone when Thinnes pulled the report sheet from his typewriter, signed it, and said to no one in particular, "Read all about it." He walked over to hand the sheet to the sergeant behind the operations desk. After he'd helped himself to more coffee, he tapped on Jeffrey Karsch's door, which was partly open.

Karsch's voice said, "Enter." Thinnes pushed the door wider and walked in.

Dr. Jeffrey Karsch, Ph.D., was sitting at his desk in the uniform of his profession—a suit no honest cop could afford, a crisp, unrumpled shirt and civilized tie. He was a civilian—though word was out that he fancied playing cop—part of an experiment aimed at bringing mental hygiene to the police department. On the theory that since Mohammed wouldn't go to the mountain, the mountain must be brought to Mohammed, the department had put shrinks right inside some of the area headquarters and attached them to Homicide and Violent Crimes divisions, where it was assumed that both officers and crime victims would be in greatest need of their services. The psychologists were recruited from among the professionals the department had previously referred the walking wounded to. The National Institute of Mental Health was picking up the tab. Karsch happened to get an office because the space available at Area Six was the object of dispute between rival lieutenants. The area commander had been happy to resolve the conflict by assigning the office to a neutral third party. Karsch had decorated it with his own money. The comfortable chairs, plants, drapes and artwork—actually posters of city buildings—gave it a more civilized feeling than the no-frills squad room it was attached to. And to show he was just a regular guy, Karsch had the obliga-

29

tory picture of himself with his wife, standing in front of the old ragtop T-bird he'd restored and drove to work on nice days.

Karsch made it clear he would meet with anyone, any time, anywhere, and he'd go to whatever lengths necessary to keep things confidential. Only *he* knew if this'd done much for business. Thinnes didn't know anyone who consulted him—or to be accurate, he didn't know anyone who'd admit needing to. Karsch's chief function, aside from keeping the coffee maker filled, seemed to be answering questions about the murky motives of criminal suspects.

"I need a refresher," Thinnes said. Karsch waited, looking interested. "Besides drugs and depression, what would make a young man kill himself?"

Karsch's dark eyes narrowed as he thought. "Psychotics do it."

Thinnes shook his head. Karsch pointed to a chair, and Thinnes sat down.

"Accidents are probably the next biggest category."

"Accidental suicide? You mean the sickos who get their kicks by half strangling themselves and don't always stop in time?"

Karsch nodded. "And there's a fairly amazing number—sometimes referred to as type Ts—who're addicted to excitement and put themselves in dangerous situations for kicks. Sometimes they miscalculate."

"Russian-roulette players?"

"Mm-hm."

"What else?"

"Losses—loss of a loved one, loss of status or self-esteem, loss of health. Rape victims, especially victims of forcible or drug-related homosexual rape, often kill themselves, as do bankrupts." He paused to reflect further. "And white-collar types caught in crimes likely to result in disgrace or prison. People diagnosed with incurable disease sometimes kill themselves, though not as often as you'd expect."

"Compulsives?"

Karsch nodded. "Sometimes. You have something that would interest me?"

"Don't know yet. I have to see the autopsy report." He stood up. "It may turn out to be an ordinary homicide."

30

Thinnes was back in the squad room, thinking about Allan Finley when Crowne came back.

"Do me a favor, will you, Ray?"

"What's that?"

Thinnes handed Caleb's card to Crowne. "Tail Dr. Caleb when he leaves his office this afternoon. See if you can get some idea of what sort of man he is."

"You mean a stakeout, for cryin' out loud? All night?"

"No, just till he goes home. I'll pick him up in the morning."

"Jesus! What if he doesn't *go* home?"

"He has to go somewhere."

"Yeah? Well what's wrong with you tailin' him? As far as I'm concerned, this whole homicide idea's a crock."

"My wife's ready to walk out if I don't show for dinner tonight. Anyway, you owe me for that hooker I ran down for you. I'm still catchin' shit about the blond hair."

"Yeah, okay. All right, I'll do it—but then we're square."

"Thanks, Ray."

SIX

Even for a man skilled at unraveling peculiar events and motives, it had been a strange day. Stressful. Allan's death brought
back all the feelings Caleb thought he'd done with. Not the undi-
minished anguish, but the gray depression and the paralyzing outrage. The appalling waste. Dispassionately, Caleb noted his own
symptoms of anxiety. He found—to his immense dismay—that he
was unable to picture Allan clearly. After three years of weekly
visits, his only vivid impression was of the bloody remains. And the
irony. Such an innocuous man; such a brutal end.

Caleb willed his thoughts into other channels and noted with
sardonic amusement how he used repression when it suited. After
his last client left, he performed all the appeasing rituals, searching
his memory and Finley's file for clues to the tragedy. But Allan had
been tediously innocent, and—even knowing the chaotic and libid-
inous drives motivating the man's compulsivity—Caleb would
have predicted he'd die of boredom. Not suicide. Certainly not
murder.

Allan's death was a police matter. In the few moments he'd
observed the detective, Thinnes, Caleb had been intrigued and
impressed. He'd noticed his flattened affect, his subtle twitchiness,
the tired lines in his face. As he'd watched Thinnes deal with the
medical examiner, he thought he'd detected the retarded re-
sponses, the general irritability and reluctance to expend energy
that were characteristic of depression.

But there'd been a sharpness there, too, a cunning, a quickening
of interest over the exchange like a cat awakening to the possibili-
ties of a mousehole. If he could resist the ennui, Thinnes would
give Allan's killer an uneasy time.

He decided to consult Margaret.

She lived in Evanston, west of the Northwestern campus, in a huge old house with a tree-shaded yard in front and a garden in the back. There were parking spaces on the street, and Caleb didn't feel uncomfortable leaving the Jaguar in one of them. It didn't seem conspicuous. As he went up the steps to the spacious porch, Margaret's golden retriever greeted him with a wag of her entire body. Caleb took a moment to pat the dog, then told her, "Enough, Anna."

The door was opened by Margaret's teenage daughter, Lisa, who threw herself at him like an exuberant toddler. "Jack, it's *great* to see you!" She gave him a huge hug and a grin that displayed voluminous hardware. "You're staying for dinner, of course." Almost as an afterthought, she added, "Mom's in the study."

The study, Margaret's office away from the office, was warm and small and quiet, sort of a brightly lit womb, with comforting chairs and cheerful artwork. Margaret had decorated it herself, over years, so that everything about it expressed her personality and amplified her intense empathy. Only her most trusted clients and oldest friends were invited in.

Margaret was a slim woman, fifty-three, clear-eyed—figuratively and literally—and ladylike in the old-fashioned sense of the word. Though she wasn't shocked by profanity, Caleb had never, even under the most trying circumstances, heard her use it, and he'd never seen, in fact couldn't imagine, Margaret wearing pants. Her dress today was silk, flattering without being flashy, and she'd recently cut her salt-and-pepper hair.

"Margaret, how are you?"

"Fine, thanks. Coffee?"

"No, thank you. You changed your hair. Very becoming."

"*You* would notice. Sit down and tell me what's on your mind."

He took one of the comforting chairs and she sat down across from him. "It's been a hell of a day. I woke up this morning dreaming I was being attacked by cougars."

"Some aspect of your life getting the better of you?"

"Nothing so Freudian. The cats were slugging it out for possession of the bed. They fight all the time."

She laughed. "Why don't you just get rid of one?"

"I will if I find someone I can trust to take care of him."

She smiled and waited.

"Celibacy is the pits."

"I know. Have you considered starting with just friendship?"

"Not recently."

"When was the last time you had a relationship?"

He gave her a rueful smile and a self-deprecating shrug.

"Good Lord, Jack, five years ago?"

"I know. I still haven't worked it all out."

"I've heard that before. What's special about today?"

"One of my clients was found dead."

"Oh Jack, I'm so sorry. A special friend?"

"Just 'a bit of the continent.' "

"Then? You've had clients die before."

"Not by murder. He didn't show up for his appointment this morning—the first time. So I went round to his apartment on my lunch hour. The police were there. . . . I almost lost it, Margaret."

"What, Jack?"

"That subtle complex of behaviors we call control."

"What would happen if you lost control?

"The last time it happened, I killed a man."

She was unperturbed. She'd heard the story before. "Do you want to talk about that?"

"No. It's old business."

"Tell me about your client."

"He was a nice, a decent man, a man of integrity. And he's dead. I gather the police think he killed himself, though he wasn't suicidal. They found him in his apartment with his head blown half away."

SEVEN

It was finally raining. Traffic was snarled and crawly. The radio announced fifty-five minutes—Kennedy to the Junction, equal delays on the Eisenhower, the Dan Ryan, and the Drive. Thinnes took side roads. In among the visual garbage that littered the commercial streets he spotted a billboard: SAY IT WITH FLOWERS. Not a bad idea. He signaled a turn and headed south. He'd stopped for a red light half a block from the florist's when the old street-copper autopilot kicked in.

There were several cars parked in the lot of a liquor-convenience store across the intersection. One particularly caught his eye, the one in front of the plate glass door, with its engine running and the driver's door open.

He fidgeted with impatience. As he waited for the green, he looked around for a blue-and-white. He stared daggers at the retarded traffic signal. Still red. His eyes kept moving, from light to car, to traffic, to street. Through the plate glass he could see the pantomime of what *might* be a robbery in progress. He reached for his .38 and slipped it half out of its holster, let it settle back in place.

Suddenly a gunman exited the store and stepped to the car. Thinnes started forward, then hit the brakes to avoid tail-ending the car in front. The light hadn't changed. He leaned on the horn. The gunman heard and stopped. The light changed. The car in front of Thinnes took off. He floored it, heading for the gunman. He leaned on his horn and hit the brights.

Instead of running, the gunman took careful aim and fired, just missing Thinnes, but crazing his windshield. Thinnes slammed on the brakes and cut right to avoid killing him. The brake pedal went to the floor. The car spun sideways. The gunman fired again, then was struck by the side of the car as the Chevy skidded out of control on the wet pavement. The gunman sailed into the center of the lot. Hit the blacktop. Bounced. Thinnes pumped the brake, but the car spun around until Thinnes's door slammed the rear of the gunman's vehicle.

As he drew his .38, Thinnes let out the breath he'd been holding. He couldn't see through the spiderweb of cracked glass on the windshield or open his crumpled door. He scrambled across the seat and out the passenger side door and ran to cover the gunman.

At that moment, squad cars with Mars lights flashing blue squealed into the parking lot from every direction, and uniformed officers swarmed out with guns drawn.

Thinnes felt an overwhelming panic as the coppers closed in. He quickly raised his hands and shifted his hold on the gun so he was holding it by the cylinder, not the grip. He was breathing and sweating as if he'd just run the Chicago Marathon. "I'm a police officer." He tried to reduce his adrenaline level by taking deep breaths. Two of the cops covered him while a third approached from the rear and took his revolver. The cop who'd arrived first reached down and relieved the unconscious gunman of the weapon he was still clutching.

A man hurried cautiously from the store. "He's not the one!" he told the cops.

Thinnes told the cop behind him, "Left inside pocket."

The copper extracted Thinnes's star, glanced at it, and showed it to the others. He relaxed. "Sorry, Detective."

Thinnes let his breath out slowly as he put his arms down. "It's all right."

The officer gave Thinnes back his gun and star, and Thinnes put them away. He bent and felt the gunman's throat and was relieved to feel blood pulsing beneath the skin. Behind him somewhere he could hear one of the cops calling for an ambulance. He thought of the paperwork that would occupy the next few hours of the arresting officer's time. He turned to the first cop on the scene and said, "The suspect fired on an off-duty police officer on the scene, causing him to skid and lose control of his car and strike the suspect, throwing same to the ground. At that point, the first patrol officer on the scene, Officer . . ." He looked at the copper's name tag. " . . . Officer Selkirk, disarmed the suspect and placed him under arrest. Nice bust, Selkirk."

Selkirk started to protest, then shrugged. It wasn't anywhere near shift change, Thinnes could see him thinking, and the arrest wouldn't look bad on his record.

Selkirk's partner laughed. "The dumb fuck. Six thousand off-duty cops in this city, and he has to pull a gun on Dirty Harry."

Thinnes stepped into the speaker's personal space and pointed at the suspect. "This son of a bitch is gonna live!" As he turned away, he added, "And Selkirk made the bust."

Later when the truck had his car in tow and was about to pull away with it, Thinnes felt the letdown, the depression that sets in when the adrenaline rush has passed. Time to go home.

He approached the coppers still talking to the store manager. "You guys going by HQ?"

"We'll give you a lift."

"Thanks. May as well get my share of the paperwork over with."

Thinnes lived near the Northeastern campus. Sauganash was a quiet North Side neighborhood of single-family homes, with a suburban feel. It was close to midnight when the blue-and-white pulled up the drive and dropped him in front of the two-story brick and frame house. The porch light was on. Rhonda's car wasn't in the drive.

He got out and thanked the coppers, and the squad pulled away as he trudged up the walk. He checked his watch and shook his head. When he went inside, he left the porch light on.

EIGHT

Thinnes stood in the doorway and inventoried the room. Middle-class kitchen with standard equipment: appliances, oak cabinets and wainscoting, white Formica counters, bright curtains and cheery wallpaper. It was morning; the table was set for three, with place mats and a single rose in the bud vase. Rhonda's touch was evident, too, in the potted herbs and hanging plants.

Rhonda.

She was cooking, slamming pots and dishes, slapping the faucet. She was a tall woman, almost blond, thirty-seven and fit. The sunlight slanting through the window over the sink accented every line and furrow of her face, making it look tired or cruel. Or unhappy. She didn't look at Thinnes when he slid into one of the chairs at the table. They had said their curt good mornings in the bedroom. Each was reluctant to say more for fear of starting something ugly.

He understood. They'd been friends in high school, before the revolution of the sixties, and long before that kind of friendship between men and women was "in." They hadn't been political in those days. She hadn't protested when he was drafted, when he'd chosen to go—or rather, had chosen not to protest or run. But corresponding with him, she'd become political, awakened, as she put it. She joined the protest, though she'd never blamed *him*. After the war they were lovers, and when he become a rookie among Chicago's finest and signed up to study law enforcement nights, she'd studied and become a teacher. They'd married. Thinnes's indifference to politics became an active distaste as he worked his way up to detective. Rhonda taught third grade and commiserated with other coppers' wives as her husband developed his workaholic tendencies. She had't complained early or often enough. She endured the moody silences and occasional drunks as Thinnes spared her the terrors of his job, the disgusting events, the atrocities. She hadn't wanted to undermine his morale, she told him later. Too late. His silence had, by then, become a habit that came between them like bulletproof glass, and all her efforts to shatter it reinforced the wall. Thinnes couldn't help. Sometimes it seemed only habit held them together. Habit and Rob, the one thing in their lives about which they had no disagreement. But Rob was nearly fifteen . . .

Thinnes studied his son as he slipped into his place with the *Sun-Times* and a nervous smile for each of them. The boy had Rhonda's hair and clear blue eyes, Thinnes's lank frame, and a promise of height one day soon.

Rhonda put a plate down, carefully, in front of Thinnes without looking at him or speaking. Rob, also, didn't look at him. After the first uncertain grin, he studied the paper as if it contained all the secrets of the universe.

Thinnes ventured, "What time did you get in last night, hon?"

She didn't bother to look at him. "You really give a damn?"

"No, I just asked to make conversation."

"If you'd been here when I left, you'd have heard me say when I'd be back." She glared at him. "Damn it, if you'd been here, I wouldn't have gone out. Where were *you?*"

Thinnes looked at her but she faced away. "Working late."

Rhonda glared at him. "Working late! Working on a blonde, I'll bet! When I called at seven, your office said you left at five."

"So they screwed up. They got seventy people to keep track of, and I don't always say where I'm going."

"You son-of-a-bitch," she said, advancing on him.

Thinnes stared at his eggs. He wouldn't argue. There was no point. There was no winning, even if she agreed.

"Mom, you better look at this," Rob said. He pushed the paper across in front of where she stood over Thinnes, waiting for him to react.

"Don't try to get him off, Rob."

"But you need to look at this!"

The urgency in his tone got her attention, and she turned

sharply away, taking the paper to the neutral territory beyond the stove. Thinnes picked at the eggs while she skimmed the article. Out of the corner of his eye, he watched her anger build as she read. She threw the paper down next to his plate. He glanced at it. The headline read OFFICER HITS, GUNMAN DOESN'T RUN.

"Like I said, I was working late."

"You couldn't bother to tell me! You let me go on and on about some—"

"For chrissake, Ronnie, if you don't know me better than that, what's the point?" He looked at Rob, who'd grabbed the paper and was studying it with desperate concentration. "Rob shouldn't have to hear us argue."

Rhonda glanced at him, then looked at the ceiling. "You're right, John. You're almost always right."

Thinnes looked up at her and, when she wouldn't return his look, pushed his chair away from the table. He carried his plate to the sink, and stood there, looking at his hands, trying to see—through a gray fog of misery—what he'd meant to do with them. He wanted to put them on Ronnie's shoulders and hug her and apologize, because this was the point where—in the movies—the estranged lovers kiss and make up. He knew it would just make her more angry. He let his hands drop.

He said, "Good breakfast, hon. Sorry I don't have much appetite."

Rhonda said nothing.

NINE

Crowne and Ferris were at tables near Evanger's office and Karsch was getting coffee when Thinnes came in. Crowne was reading a report. Ferris was reading the *Sun-Times*; a half smoked cigarette burned in the ashtray next to his coffee cup.

Thinnes thought it was disillusionment with his Catholic upbringing that made Ferris more cynical than most cops. And middle age had lowered his center of gravity as well as his expectations. He was a short, auburn-haired, round-cheeked South Sider of Irish extraction—puckish, Rhonda'd called him. A grandstander, master of the cheap shot. Evanger tolerated him because he had the highest clearance record on the shift, but they were all aware that many of his cases were thrown out of court. He worked hard enough to get evidence for probable cause but didn't bother with the more strenuous proof required for beyond a reasonable doubt. Sheer laziness, Thinnes'd decided long ago.

"Hey Thinnes, you lose your piece?" Ferris demanded.

Thinnes wasn't really listening. "No. Why?"

Ferris drowned the cigarette in his coffee cup and threw the cup in the wastebasket beside his desk. "Hear you're shootin' perps down with your car."

"What?"

Ferris laughed. Thinnes realized he'd been had.

"If you don't have enough to do . . . "

Ignoring Ferris, Crowne shook the paper he'd been reading at Thinnes. "Preliminary autopsy report." He paused to find something on the page. "Says here Finley died from 'a gunshot wound to the head' roughly twelve to fifteen hours before the super found him. 'No other marks of violence, no drugs, no apparent pathol-

41

ogy.' His fingerprints were on the gun and he had gunshot residue on his right hand. Thinnes, you don't have a case."

"Right. So what did you find out about Dr. Caleb?"

"You had your hearing tested lately?"

Thinnes waited. Crowne finally took out his notebook.

"Subject drove up to Evanston. Went into a house on Orrington belonging to a Margaret Linsey. He was greeted at the door by a female cauc—"

"Girlfriend?"

"I doubt it. Looked like jailbait to me. And an older woman—also cauc—saw him out. Very friendly."

"Coulda been the younger one's mother. Anyway, he apparently had dinner there—was there about two hours. He left at six fifty-eight and drove to Northwestern Memorial Hospital—he drives a Jag, by the way. He remained at Northwestern until seven forty-five, when he drove into Uptown, to a Spaulding House, on Wilson. Parked inside—"

"What's this Spaulding House?"

Crowne shrugged. "Anyway, he was in there about four and a half hours. Then he drove home. If he went anywhere else last night, he didn't take his car. I checked the odometer this morning—after I heard the news I figured you wouldn't . . . Car hadn't been moved."

Thinnes pick up the autopsy report. "Thanks, Ray." He started to read and, without looking up, said, "Find out about this Spaulding House, would you?"

"You're wasting the taxpayers' money, Thinnes."

Thinnes glanced up from the report but didn't say anything.

Crowne shrugged, picked up the phone, and pushed a button. "We got a narc in the building? We need one up here. Tell him I got a hot tip." He listened for a moment then said, "Thanks."

The operations sergeant walked up to Thinnes with a telephone message slip and a coffee mug. "New York called. They couldn't get hold of the sister in the Finley case." Thinnes looked up at him. "She's out of the country. They gathered she's got the kind of job where they'd call you if you were in the hospital with appendicitis, so she was real vague about letting them know her travel plans.

Sposed to be back a week from Monday. NYPD left word with the landlady to have her call." He dropped the slip on the table in front of Thinnes and headed for the coffee maker.

Crowne tipped his chair back against the edge of table behind him and laced his fingers behind his head. He nudged Thinnes's chair with his foot. "Finley'll keep."

Thinnes picked up the slip and waved it. "Looks like this lets the sister off the hook."

"Unless it was a contract hit."

"There's a frightening thought." Thinnes dragged out his wallet and shuffled through it for the insurance card that had the phone number he wanted scribbled on the back. He punched the number on his phone and when the call was answered, said, "Mike? John Thinnes."

Mike said, "Not ready."

"So?"

"Good news is, your windshield's in. An' I got you a door." He hesitated.

Thinnes said, "Something's wrong."

"Who'd you have workin' on it?" There was hurt in his tone.

"What?"

"Cheap brake job's worth what you pay . . ."

"You did the brakes. Last month," Thinnes interrupted. "Check your books."

"No way!"

"What the hell are you talking about?"

"Bleeder screw loose. 'S why your brakes went. Bone dry."

He meant the master cylinder. Thinnes didn't ask if he was sure. Brakes were not something Mike would screw up. "It must've worked loose."

"Shit!"

"You didn't work on them yourself."

"Naw. But my guys . . . I'd watch my back."

"I'll keep it in mind. What was the bad news?"

"Door's maroon."

"So, paint it."

"Yeah, yeah, yeah. Reminds me. Kid you sent me's A-OK."

"Are you keeping a close watch on your parts room?"

"Told 'im if I caught 'im stealing from me, I'd have Guido break his hands."

"He believed you?"

Mike laughed. "Gives 'im an excuse to tell his sticky-fingered bros to get lost. Anyway, 's too busy to get in trouble. Put 'im in charge of the body shop."

"Maybe you weren't listening when I told you where he worked last."

"Yeah, I was. An' he put Stop 'n' Chop an' Midnight Auto Parts on his ap. But I swear he's forgotten more'n most ever knew about bodywork. An' he's got a regular girlfriend, nice little Catholic chick from Guadalajara. Think he's gonna keep his nose clean. Fact, I'm bettin' in five years he'll have three kids an' a mortgage an' enough clean money in the bank to buy me out."

Thinnes heard someone yell "Mike!" in the background and Mike didn't give him a chance to respond to the prediction. He said, "Gotta go. Tomorrow. After eight," and hung up.

Thinnes put down the receiver and went over the 211 in his mind. He hadn't thought about the brakes when he'd nearly tail-ended the car at the light. But now that he thought about it, the pedal had gone to the floor when he'd braked to avoid killing the gunman. So the brakes were dry. A loose bleeder screw was more likely to be negligence than . . . What? Attempted murder? Why? He hadn't busted anyone special lately, wasn't scheduled to testify against anyone big. Still . . .

He tipped his chair back and turned to Ferris. "Ferris, what was the name of that insurance hit guy?"

"The one who always made it look like an accident?"

"Yeah."

"Russo."

"What happened to him?"

"He's doing life plus a hundred years at Menard. Why?"

"Thinnes was thinking of hiring him to do you, Ferris," Crowne said. He thought for a minute, then told Thinnes, "I was just kiddin' about Finley being a contract job. And anyway, Finley's death wasn't an accident."

"Yeah," Thinnes said. Mike hasn't been watching his crew close enough, he thought. And he's been watching too much TV.

Five minutes later, Thinnes was going over the paperwork on the Finley case. Ferris was playing with his phone. Karsch was standing in his doorway, coffee cup in hand. Crowne was at the coffee maker when a peculiar-looking man with a shaved head and Salvation Army–reject clothes wandered into the squad room. He had a regulation ID clipped to his jacket. "Somebody call for narcotics?" he asked.

"Hey, Crowne," Ferris called, "there's something here asking for you." He pointed to Crowne's chair, and the narc ambled over to perch on the edge of the table next to it. Crowne hurried back with two plastic cups. He handed one to his visitor. "Abbot, isn't it?"

"Yeah." Abbot wiped his hand on his pants and shoved it at Crowne. They shook. "What's up?"

Thinnes answered. "You ever bust the Spaulding House?"

Abbot turned to Thinnes. "Spaulding House. Spaulding House. On Wilson?" Thinnes nodded. "Ah, no."

"You mean it's clean?" Crowne asked.

"In a manner of speaking."

"What manner?"

"They're not dealing to the neighborhood, and nobody's made any complaints."

"When's that ever stopped you makin' a bust?"

"You really don't know?"

"Enlighten me."

"It's where queers go to die. They could be up to their crotches in crack—nobody gives a damn. They're all corpses already."

"You mean it's a hospice?" Thinnes asked.

"Yeah. And they're not dealin' the streets, so we leave 'em alone. Got better things to do than roust stiffs."

"He means there's not a narc on the force with the balls to walk in there," Ferris gibed.

Crowne told Ferris, "Fuck off!"

Ferris looked around for ammunition and spotted Karsch. "Hey, Karsch, s'there some kind of weirdness test these guys take to get in narcotics?" Karsch shook his head as if confounded by Ferris's immaturity. "Look at you, Abbot," Ferris continued. "There's no street people dress as weird as narcs. How can you call yourselves undercover?"

Abbot didn't seem upset. "You just ask me up here to insult me?"

"Naw," Ferris said. He crumpled his coffee cup and walked over to press the resulting mess into Abbot's hand. "We called you up to present you with this award: best costume design by an undercover team."

"She-it!" Abbot said. He threw the cup at Ferris, then turned to Crowne. "What's this hot tip you got?"

Thinnes answered. "Next time one of these clowns has a hot tip, make 'em come down to you with it."

Lieutenant Evanger's door opened, and Evanger stuck his head out. "Thinnes, come in here, and bring what you have on the Finley shooting."

Evanger's office was the workplace of a man with modern ideas, from the PC on his desktop to the fax machine next to it. The wife and children pictured on his desk might have been models for *Ebony*. Evanger, himself, was a man in his fifties, a light-skinned black with a large, beaklike nose and a wide, stern mouth. He wore his hair in a neat natural and had a trim mustache. He'd come up through the ranks, but somewhere along the line he'd learned to dress like an attorney, and—even in August—he wore three-piece suits. A man on his way to the top, distinguished and ambitious.

Thinnes had heard rumors that Evanger's reputation was cleaner than he was, though he thought the rumors were mostly sour grapes. What *wasn't* just a rumor was the lieutenant's fondness for local politics, though there, too, he kept his record clean.

Evanger took the supplementary report from Thinnes and waved it at a chair. Thinnes sat down. Evanger hitched his rear up on his desk and glanced at the report, then at Thinnes.

"For the record, the department takes a dim view of unorthodox methods."

"Noted." Thinnes paused. "For the record."

"Off the record, that was a nice piece of work last night. Even if you didn't take credit for the bust."

"That mean I get to use a car till mine's out of the shop?"

Evanger laughed. He glanced at the report again. "Bottom line on this Finley thing: what have we got here?"

"Finley was murdered, but I can't prove it yet."

"What *have* you got?"

"The psychology's all wrong." He paused to get it in order. "Here's a guy's such a compulsive neatnik, you can't find dust on the tops of his doors—I checked—blows his brains out all over his designer walls. And right-handed, when half a dozen people swear he was a southpaw. It doesn't make sense."

Evanger picked up his phone and pushed several buttons. Into the phone he said, "Karsch, have you got a minute?" He put down the phone and studied the report until Karsch came in.

Karsch said, "Lieutenant?"

"You read the report on the Finley death?" Karsch nodded. "What do you think?"

"An interesting situation."

"You need a Ph.D. to tell me that?"

"It's possible Finley killed himself. People often behave compulsively to control their unacceptable impulses towards violence or disorder. If those impulses break through the control, the compulsive can do things apparently quite out of character."

"Like shoot himself with his right hand when he was left-handed?"

"Not quite. But I'd say that without more data, there's no way to know with certainty. And without evidence, there's nothing you could do even if you knew for certain."

Evanger nodded. "Fair enough. Thinnes, you got *any* evidence?"

"Not yet, but if I stir things up enough, something'll surface."

"Well, file your report, and stir 'em on a back burner. We've got plenty of cases pending for which we *do* have evidence."

Thinnes nodded. As he left he heard Karsch ask, "Why don't you just tell him to forget it?" and Evanger answer, "There's no point. He won't. He'll work it on his own time if he has to."

TEN

Thinnes lay next to Rhonda, watching her sleep, feeling longing and regret he couldn't express. For some time he'd had the feeling she was lost to him. He knew better than to ask or accuse her—which would be to lose her instantly. He feared she might have taken a lover, though not greatly. On some level, Rhonda was the last person in the world Thinnes trusted. What she *had* taken was almost impossible to fight: what she'd taken was a career job, the first step toward independence. A maggot of uneasiness gnawed at his insides.

He reached over to gently touch her cheek, and she wakened, giving him a smile that faded as she remembered how things were between them. Before he could say anything, she rolled on her back, staring at the ceiling. "I have to work today. We've got three people out sick."

He shrugged, resigned. He wished she was still teaching. He hadn't felt threatened when she was teaching. It was a woman's job, so in some respects, not really a job, not full time. The men she'd come in contact with were mostly wimps, or older—no competition for a half decent husband, and anyway, too worried about appearances to fool around. But she'd had the sense to quit teaching when she burned out. She liked the office she managed now. Thinnes thought she even liked the long hours.

He said, "So we'll see dad next weekend."

"You could go by yourself. Or take Rob."

And give the old man more proof he and Ronnie were heading for the rocks. No way. He had enough to worry about without that.

"Rob's got plans." He propped his head on his hand and

48

watched her reaction as he added, "I have to work Wednesday night—pickpocket detail at some society function. So we're even."

"Wanna trade?" she said dryly. She threw back the covers and stretched to give him a perfunctory kiss that blocked any move on his part toward real reconciliation. Clutching the covers with white knuckles, he watched her cross the room and disappear into the bathroom.

ELEVEN

Mike's place was a converted auto dealership on West Fullerton. Mike had turned the showroom into a body shop that ran with the speed and efficiency of an outfit chop shop. And why not? Half Mike's employees were ex-cons. He was *very* popular with the John Howard Association.

Stealing and shoddy work were about the only things Mike wouldn't put up with. His tolerance for variations in race, creed, work history, and standards of personal hygiene extended to allowing people between leases to crash in the shop, so Thinnes wasn't surprised to find the place open at six A.M.; convenience was one of Mike's selling points. Thinnes *was* surprised when Mike himself popped out of the office with the bill.

"It's Sunday," Thinnes said, shaking hands.

Mike said, "Wife's outta town," as if that explained everything. He handed Thinnes the bill.

Thinnes looked it over. Mike had charged him fifteen dollars to refill and readjust the brakes. If he'd been more sure of his ground, he would've charged twice that. Thinnes didn't argue though. Even taking into account that one questionable item, the price was very reasonable. As he pulled out his wallet, Mike said, "Russo."

Thinnes shook his head. "He's in Menard. Anyway, if he didn't go after the cop that busted him, why would he bother with me?"

The mechanic shook his head, pulled the bill out of Thinnes's hand, and scribbled over the fifteen-dollar charge, adding NC in the column above it and deducting fifteen dollars from the total. He handed the paper back to Thinnes.

"I wasn't arguing," Thinnes said. He extracted bills to cover the new total and waved a don't-bother when Mike reached in his pocket for change. Mike shrugged and gestured toward the Chevy. The newly painted door made the rest of the car look shabby.

Mike must've been thinking the same thing. "Bring it back when you got time. We'll paint it."

"Thanks, I'll do that."

Mike nodded and stood watching critically as Thinnes backed the car out of the shop.

No charge. That was as close as Mike would get to admitting one of his guys had made a mistake. Funny thing about coincidence—you couldn't buy it in a movie, but in reality, it happened all the time. If he hadn't been suckered into driving to that Maine East game, sophomore year of high school, he wouldn't have met Rhonda, who'd never gone to a basketball game before in her life. And the one time one of Mike's guys screwed up a brake job, it had to be a cop's car.

TWELVE

Caleb's silver-blue Jaguar pulled out of the underground garage and down the street. As it turned the corner, Thinnes eased his Chevy away from the curb in front of the building.

Traffic was light—standard for early Sunday. Caleb took the Drive north. He drove a constant sixty-five, signaling to change lanes and changing smoothly and often to maintain his speed. Thinnes figured he must be driving a half mile ahead. He was impressed; most owners of yuppie cars couldn't plan as far ahead as the next light.

So maybe this Dr. Caleb had something going for him. Maybe he had enough upstairs to kill Finley. But why would he? It didn't take any brains to be a murderer. And to get away with it, all you needed to do—most of the time—was keep your mouth shut. Something—Thinnes was grateful—most killers didn't think of.

He kept Caleb's Jag in sight reflexively. Tailing was something he had done so long he could do it on autopilot—like walking. It left him free to think.

He wondered what it would be like to consult a psychiatrist. Like an annual physical? Did they stretch you out on the couch and say, "Where does it hurt?" Did they do something like blood and urine tests, or a kind of "chest x-ray" for your skull? Karsch had offered his services on occasion, and Thinnes had been tempted— just to go in and talk—but something held him back. Just a hunch, like the hunch that Finley had been murdered. Some instinct of self-preservation. After all, talking to a shrink about your personal problems was an admission of losing it—the beginning of the end of your active-duty days. *Nobody trusts his life to a frayed rope.* And he was fairly certain only another cop would understand the problems. Karsch wasn't a real cop.

Caleb got off the Drive at Irving Park. Traffic was heavier, and Thinnes had to work at keeping him in sight on Irving Park without being seen. At Clark Street he signaled a right and, to Thinnes's surprise, turned into Graceland, the cemetery that stretches like a park from Irving to Montrose between the Howard-North El line and Clark Street.

Thinnes swore. The cemetery covers more than twenty blocks and is a maze of interconnecting roads. Caleb must've spotted the tail. A red light gave Thinnes a minute to think, but apart from recalling that Graceland had only one entrance, he drew a blank. The light changed. The cars at the front of the line took off, and those behind Thinnes started to honk as he sat making up his mind. He shrugged and turned through the gates. Caleb's Jaguar had disappeared; the only vehicle in sight was a security agency's car. Thinnes pulled into the lot next to the memorial chapel office and got out.

A security guard in a white uniform shirt and dark pants got out of the car and came to meet him in the center of the entrance drive. He eyed Thinnes the way a cop would and asked, "Help you?" in a cautious tone.

Thinnes flashed his star and said, "You notice a silver-blue Jaguar come in here?"

The guard nodded, leering. "He rob a bank?"

Thinnes hid his annoyance. "He's a material witness in a murder investigation."

The leer disappeared. "No shit!"

"You could be of assistance in this investigation." The guard nodded eagerly. "Stall him a bit when he leaves. Don't let him know he's being followed, just ask if he spotted any dogs in here. Or tell him you've had a problem with graffiti and ask if he's seen any kids."

"Sure thing. By the way, he took the fork to the right." The guard pointed.

Thinnes said, "Thanks," and went back to his car.

As he snaked around the winding access road, the cemetery seemed like one of the city's parks, peaceful and green, and almost wild in the few places where the landscapers hadn't gotten to the grass. It was a historical treasure, too. A list of its residents read like a Chicago directory—most having streets named after them. And there was the elevator Otis, Pullman of railroad fame, and J. P. Getty. This early in the morning, it was nearly empty of living souls. Another time Thinnes would have liked to get out and read the headstones and look into the crypts, many of which had elaborate carvings or unusual architecture and stained glass windows. He spotted Caleb's car parked in the shade on the east side. He pulled past it and parked. He fished his binoculars out of the glove box before getting out for a better look.

In the distance, he could see Caleb, dressed as for church, standing in front of the black granite bulk of Lorado Taft's statue, *The Crusader,* that marks the resting place of Victor Lawson. Caleb gazed at the statue before stepping south of it and stooping to free a marker from the long grass there. He straightened up and stared long and reverently at the stone, then looked around—not searching for a tail, Thinnes would have bet—just taking in the scenery. He seemed to study each tree around the grave as if trying to remember what kind it was or commit it to memory. He stared at nearby monuments the same way. Then he went slowly back to his car and drove off.

Thinnes hurried over to the Lawson monument, which he'd seen before in pictures, and was brought up short by its inscription:

ABOVE ALL THINGS TRUTH BEARETH AWAY THE VICTORY

He walked around the statue to read the headstone Caleb'd freed from the grass. The legend, CHRISTOPHER MARGOLIS 1963–1988, was not what he'd expected.

The silver-blue Jag was fairly easy to keep tabs on as it spun back onto the Drive, northbound, and continued up Sheridan Road. Thinnes dropped back in the sparse traffic to avoid being seen and followed the doctor past the art deco facade of Mundelein College and the south entrance of Loyola University's north campus, around Calvary Cemetery and north through Evanston and the Northwestern campus, and past Dyche Stadium on Central Street. At Green Bay Road he turned north again and eventually into the parking lot of Walker Brothers Original Pancake House in south Wilmette.

Thinnes stayed in the car, munching the sandwich he'd brought for lunch, recalling the times he'd been there with Rhonda.

As teenagers, they'd often gone with their friends to concerts at Ravinia, had sat on the lawn and passed a joint around while they listened to Zappa and Joplin and B.B. King. Sometimes they'd stop at Walker Brothers beforehand. Every once in a while he'd taken Rhonda there for breakfast on a Sunday. They'd talked for hours, taking their time over the rich apple pancakes that were a meal for two. They'd been able, in those days, to talk about anything. Before he'd joined the force. Before his job had come between them. Before he'd retreated into the silence of his own counsel. Over the years, their conversations had floated to the surface of their life together. Somewhere along the line, she'd stopped trying to reach him. The thought made Thinnes shudder.

He tapped one of the four large coffees, long cold, that he'd bought at McDonald's before setting out and wondered if Caleb, too, was given to long conversations over apple pancakes. He hoped not and rather doubted that the management would allow it, with the waiting line winding around the building.

Thinnes was right. Caleb came out shortly afterward with a yuppie couple, whose license plate Thinnes noted. He got into his car without looking around and made good time back to the city.

When he left his apartment again Thinnes almost missed him. He was wearing a nondescript sports jacket and ordinary slacks. He came out the front door and walked over to Michigan Avenue, where he boarded a 151 bus.

There is no inconspicuous way to tail a bus. Thinnes was certain he'd been made. Nevertheless, he got in line behind it and searched the sidewalk crowds for the doctor's tall form after each stop.

Caleb got off in Lincoln Park and walked west, along Dickens. He stopped in front of a three-flat to shake hands with another man, and they went into the building together. Thinnes parked and walked up to read the sign on the door: VIETNAM SUPPORT GROUP, 2ND FLOOR, VETERANS WELCOME.

THIRTEEN

The caption on the chalkboard spelled out POST TRAUMATIC STRESS DISORDER—PTSD, and underneath it was a list of symptoms: anxiety, nightmares, instant replays, emotional anesthesia, insomnia, decreased libido, depression, irritability, extreme sensitivity to noise, decreased tolerance for frustration, paranoia.

The group leader, the therapist, was short and heavyset with straight, thinning blond hair and a curly red beard. Arthur. He wore wire-rimmed glasses that made him look wimpy, but he had forearms like Popeye's and biceps half a yard around. He wore Levi's and a casual shirt open at the neck, and with sleeves rolled to the elbows.

His clients were an odd lot: Ragman, the lone black, had been laying the grounds for a plea of insanity all his life. Nam hadn't improved his condition. He was currently on probation after a stretch in Joliet for assault: he'd chased a motorist who'd cut him off in traffic half a mile down the Stevenson with a hunting knife. At times during the sessions he held on to the arms of his chair as if to prevent himself from repeating the offense.

Ed, the soft-spoken, balding accountant, didn't suffer from PTSD, but he felt that he should and he suffered remorseless guilt because he didn't.

Maharis had been discharged on a section eight. Most of his life—like most reactive schizophrenics—he'd been a little unsure of his boundaries. In Nam, he'd lost them altogether.

Erik retold his story, of *having* to commit atrocities, in a voice so soft they had to strain to hear it. Caleb dispassionately noted his flattened affect and his restlessness, the signs of sleep loss, the paranoia. Erik insisted that his actions were inevitable and that everyone who'd seen combat had done the same. They had all heard the argument before.

"That's not how it was!" Ragman insisted. Their discussion was also a rerun, and it was getting old.

"Maybe that's how it was for him," Ed said mildly.

"You tell 'em, Jack. Tell 'em that's not the way it was."

"I can't speak for him," Caleb said. "That's not the way it was for my unit, but it may have been that way for his."

"Bull*shit*!"

Maharis, who was enjoying a period of relative lucidity thanks to the miracles of modern pharmacology, said, "Just how *was* it for you, Jack? You sit there, week after week, like some big happy Buddha, not saying' nothing'. What're *you* doin' here?"

What indeed. Caleb took several deep breaths. This was, after all, a group therapy session, and he was a participant. And he *had* sat immobile, session after session, closed like a secret. Like a cat whose small size made it vulnerable and whose vulnerability made it timid. Caleb was aware of his vulnerability. He'd left Nam with few scars and no new hangups. The old ones were enough. He constantly checked himself to be sure he wasn't projecting the aggression of which he knew he was capable. It was a professional habit. But it was more than habit. He was obsessed, even with the possibility of losing control again. He knew that repression made the id monsters ever more powerful and fearsome, but he couldn't take the chance of loosing them again, or rather of loosing *the* monster. He knew the name of his enemy, though he couldn't face it. His nemesis was Rage.

They were not about to let him off the hot seat today. Arthur said, "Well, Jack?" and waited. They all waited. They had all been outwaited by the group in sessions past. They all knew that their silence would force the story from him.

"I lost my temper once," he began as if making a confession. "And killed a man. In Nam."

They waited. Arthur said, "Tell us the details."

"That's it?" Ragman demanded. "That's your *big secret*? You went to war *and killed a guy*?" Ragman started to laugh.

"You don't understand," Caleb told him. "I was a CO. I don't *kill people*. It was wrong!"

57

They were all laughing except Arthur. Arthur was watching like a big orange tabby, like a psychiatrist. He said, "What were you feeling when you killed him?"

How very like a shrink! Ragman's questions were more to the point, though. "You were a CO; that mean you didn't carry a gun? What'd you kill him with, your bare hands?"

"I killed him with a gun. I grabbed an M-sixteen and blew him away." He looked at Arthur. "I was feeling overpowering rage."

Perhaps they could relate to uncontrollable anger, perhaps it was something in Caleb's tone of voice. The others didn't laugh.

Arthur nodded as if he understood. "You ever felt that way since Nam?"

"No."

"You ever have flashbacks?"

"No."

"Nightmares?"

Caleb hesitated. "Not that I recall." He could see that Arthur wasn't convinced. The others were like kids watching a new video game.

"Let's have some details, Jack," Maharis said. "Was he one of ours?"

Caleb felt his shock showing. "One of ours?"

"Yeah, you know—an officer or something."

"He was a sniper. NVA, I think." He thought of the permanence of it. The loss. The waste! The sniper had been very young. *Chris* had been as young! He looked around and saw Erik and Ragman and Maharis slavering for details, and he felt his annoyance swelling, taking a murderous shape. He said, "What's the difference? He's dead. I killed him." He made himself count to fifteen and breathe deeply. He tried to make himself feel small and innocuous. He tried to think lovely, wonderful thoughts.

"So what are you crybabying about? They ought to give you a medal."

"You're still feeling guilty," Arthur said gently.

Caleb shrugged.

"You're not going to forgive yourself?"

"It's not that. It scares me that I could be so crazy."

"Out of control?"

Caleb nodded.

"You always control everything?"

"Only my own behavior."

"Just your behavior?"

Caleb smiled wryly. No wonder I was able to help Allan, he thought. We were so alike in ways. Then he remembered how it was with Allan and his smile faded. He said, "No."

"Let me see if I have this straight," Arthur said. "You lost control and killed a man once, and now you're afraid it might happen again?"

"Yes."

"What would you tell a client in your situation?"

The others all pricked up their ears. Caleb had never told them his profession.

"But I don't know how to get just a little angry."

"You never get irritated or annoyed?"

"I've convinced myself there's nothing worth getting really angry about."

"You deal with AIDS patients."

"Professionally."

They were talking to each other now; the others had been left behind. Arthur said, "Didn't you tell me you'd lost a close friend a few years ago?" Caleb nodded. "How did you deal with your rage?"

"Conversion reaction."

Arthur tilted his head quizzically.

"A year and a half of migraines."

"What's conversion reaction?" Ragman demanded.

Arthur said, "Jack?"

"A physical illness or impairment that the mind creates to distract itself from a reality that's too horrible to contemplate, something too awful or frightening to face or remember."

"You a doctor?" Maharis asked.

"Yes."

"And you know the prescription, don't you?" Arthur persisted.

"Yes. I have to let myself get angry and accept what happens next."

FOURTEEN

Thinnes almost missed Caleb again when he came out of the meeting. A short blond fat man gave the psychiatrist a lift back to his apartment in an ancient Nova. The guy drove like a maniac, but he was still easier to tail than a bus.

Caleb emerged from his garage about a half hour later, in his Jaguar and in good clothes. He took the Drive north to Addison. As he followed the car through the Sunday afternoon traffic, Thinnes was grateful that the Cubs were out of town. Caleb eventually turned north on Wayne and took the only empty space on the street. The building he went into was familiar. Thinnes pulled past the door and parked next to a hydrant, where he could watch his quarry in the rearview, and he checked the address in his notebook to be sure. After Caleb disappeared through the inner, security door, Thinnes walked up and peered with disgust through the glass door into the now empty lobby of Alicia Baynes's building.

Much later he pulled into the doctors' parking lot at Northwestern Memorial Hospital and parked where he could keep an eye on the Jaguar. He took the lid off the last plastic coffee cup and threw it on the dashboard, where there were already three others. On the floor there were two empty fast-food bags and the three empty cups. Thinnes sipped his coffee and yawned.

What a hell of a way for a man to spend his working hours, he thought, sitting on the base of his spine, staring at the only sign in the city that motorists paid any attention to: LINCOLN TOWING.

He wondered when, exactly, it had started to go all gray. He'd used to use the time he spent on stakeouts putting the case together. It still went together, somehow, but now he spent most of the time fighting off the sandman. Cops called it burnout; he wondered how a shrink would classify it.

The restaurant's plush waiting area had a long line and a bar to pacify the waiting diners. A uniformed bartender presided at the bar, and an officious maître d' guarded the restaurant proper. Through the doorway, Thinnes could see Caleb sitting with friends at a very good table.

Doors near the bar were labeled MEN and LADIES. As Thinnes made a beeline for the men's room, the maître d' hurried to head him off. Thinnes flashed his star; the maître d' backed off, allowing him to dodge into the restroom.

FIFTEEN

Uptown. Dumping ground for the lighter-skinned unwanted—dispossessed Native Americans, Hispanic and Asian immigrants, the elderly poor, alcoholics and other addicts, the mentally and physically handicapped. It is an area of seedy bars, cheap stores, trashy streets and weedy empty lots, a few short light years from the Gold Coast.

Caleb only half noticed the surroundings as he negotiated Wilson Avenue, until he had to brake to avoid a thin black man in jogging attire who dodged from behind a double-parked van to run in place while he waited for a break in oncoming traffic. Bright letters on his shirt proclaimed NAPA VALLEY WINO—LIFE IS TOO SHORT TO DRINK CHEAP CHAMPAGNE.

Caleb grinned and mentally told the man, you got that right. He caught the fellow's eye, and the man flashed a peace sign and a smile that showed a gap between his top front incisors.

Serendipity Street, Caleb thought, but as he read the come-ons that cluttered the storefronts in English and Spanish on either side of Broadway, he sobered. Life in Uptown is too cheap for the good stuff. Buy a piece of the American dream, ten dollars down, ten dollars a month. And if you end up paying five hundred dollars for a two-hundred-dollar TV, nobody gives a damn. *Caveat emptor.* But how're you gonna keep 'em south of the border after they've seen VCRs?

He turned left onto a side street, then right into the alley behind the hospice.

Spaulding House had been a mansion in the twenties. Over the years, its wide lawns had been subdivided, its white stone walls blackened with grime, its ornate wrought iron fence had been scrapped, replaced with chain link. The former home of the wealthy had become a place for some of the city's most wretched poor to live, where some came to die. The house was home to AIDS victims who had nowhere else to go.

Caleb worked there four nights a week. He'd volunteered to treat their heads but gradually discovered that they needed more: jobs, housing, nursing care, help with housework and shopping and meals. He'd been revolted at first—they were an unlovely bunch with their purple Kaposi's blotches, open, suppurating herpes sores, and concentration-camp emaciation—but he'd gotten past the surface features to the human persons, and he found their care rewarding. He'd started small, emptying bedpans, changing sheets. Now, he did what was needed, gave them rides, advice, a shoulder to cry on, sometimes a hug, occasionally money.

He found that no matter what he did for them, they were always testing. They had to see if he'd abandon them, as their friends and families had. To that end, they were always needling.

"What about you, Jack? How long before you come in here and say, 'Fellow lepers?' "

"Don't hold your breath, Jack's a saint. Saint Damien. You *know* none of them has a sex life."

"You'll make someone a great wife someday, Jack."

"I'm still trying to figure your angle, Jack. This some kind of research project?"

"He's a masochist, that's it."

Very few—only Manny, really—had come to terms with it. Even the suicidal ones feared it and spoke of it with euphemisms: the Undertoad, the Green Ripper, the Big Sleep, or "having your number pulled." He thought of Finley. Young. Healthy. Dead. He wished he could get them to stop wasting their lives grieving for what they'd lost and get on with them, stop pushing the river.

This evening no one was home except Rafe, the house mother, a huge black man, silent and belligerent, who'd come two years earlier with a wife dying of the disease. After he'd buried her, he'd stayed. He smiled when he called them fags and gave them excellent care. Caleb never touched him. Rafe hated to be touched, except by the sickest and most feeble. The well ones respected his wishes—those who didn't got decked. He had on several occasions been found harboring stray animals in the basement, and he had twice brought home human strays. "Jus' pickin' up bizniz," he'd said, to which Brian retorted, "You and Jack!"

Brian was the neediest of the lot, the most sarcastic and the most defensive. He was also probably the healthiest. Brian was out for the evening with Paul and Bill and Lenny.

Rafe was putting the dishes in the dishwasher when Caleb came in. He said, "Donald's gone again," without taking his eyes off the twelve-inch TV next to the sink.

"I know," Caleb told him. "I saw him earlier at the hospital, when I did rounds." He studied him. He wasn't really watching TV. "You look tired. Why don't you take the night off?"

Rafe yawned. "I am tired. But who's gonna put these chumps to bed? Briggs din' show. An' Maria's got a sick kid."

"I think we could manage without you for one night. Where are they, anyway?"

"Went to a film." He looked at Caleb out of the corner of his eye. "Think Donald's comin' back this time?"

"I don't think so."

Rafe was silent for a moment—fighting his emotions, Caleb suspected. Finally he got himself in hand enough to say, "I thought, after Leona died, I wouldn't let no one get close again. 'Specially no fag." He swallowed. Caleb waited. Rafe sounded angry as he continued, "But that boy . . ." He shook his head and looked at Caleb as if defying him to comment on his lack of self-control.

Caleb gave him a bleak smile. "Welcome to the human condition." Rafe glared suspiciously. "Do you feel like talking about it?"

"No!" He must have realized how defensive it sounded because he added, more casually, "Maybe I'll just go out for a beer."

"You might want to stop in and talk to Donald."

Rafe shook his head. "Wouldn't know what to say."

"You don't have to say anything. Just hold his hand. Or say good-bye. This may be your last chance." Rafe looked at him sharply. Caleb continued. "His mother finally came by. She was terrified, but even more afraid he'd die before she saw him."

"You didn't have nothin' to do with that, I bet."

Caleb gave him a half blank who-me? look, and Rafe laughed. As he was going out, Caleb said, "Don't let them give you any BS about keeping visiting hours."

He spent the hour, after Rafe left and before the others returned, playing orderly. He changed Manny's sheets again and wrote a letter for him and gave him his medication, noting it on his chart. He kept his mind strictly in the present. Some things you practice in your head, rehearse, but certain things it didn't pay to think about too much. The dreary and the dreaded things. Thinking ahead was like going through them twice. Manny's future would be awful enough when it arrived, but being with him in the present was pleasant enough. He hadn't let anything destroy his joie de vivre. He seemed to count every trifle a gift, from the crystal prism Rafe'd hung in his window to catch the sun to clean sheets when he was too weak to make it to the bathroom. He'd explained it to Caleb once.

"There isn't any *real* time out there. For us there's only our subjective time that's sometimes slower but usually faster than that of healthy people. And this death sentence—for that's what the diagnosis of AIDS has come to mean—is what puts us out of sync with the rest of world. Each of us has a dream, or a picture of himself in the future—doing things, having a life—that's threatened by the disease. That's what's so frightening—that there's not enough time. And *they*—the healthy ones—seem to have more of it than we. The inequity paralyzes us with rage. We get so angry, so afraid of losing that mythical future that we can't live in the time we do have."

As Caleb had suspected.

Manny had discovered how to stop time by living in the present.

Caleb stayed with him until he fell asleep. When he came downstairs the others had returned.

Brian greeted him characteristically. "Hey Jack, don't you know there's no future treating fags? No money in it either."

"Ah, but it keeps me out of bars."

"You *must* be getting hard up." Brian shot a look at the two young men sitting together on the couch. "But around here that's safer than getting a hard-on."

Caleb understood. The two young men, Bill and Lenny, were in love, a situation made more poignant, desperate, melodramatic by their disease. Most of the others were jealous, especially Brian.

Paul said so, indirectly. "Brian, why do you have to be such an asshole!"

"Someone has to keep all you butt-fuckers from getting too smug."

Paul made a gesture of exasperation and stalked out.

As Brian watched him go he raised his voice to ask, "Jack, if Paul asked you to help him go straight, would you?" Paul slammed the door behind him.

Caleb responded in a normal tone. "Why are *you* asking?"

Brian gave him a grin that said plainly he was asking to make trouble. Caleb got up and followed Paul into the kitchen. Paul was leaning over the sink, sobbing. Caleb walked over and put an arm around him.

Paul said, "Donald's dying. Donald's dying and that asshole's making jokes!"

"Everyone deals with it in his own way."

"Don't give me that crap. He doesn't give a damn."

Caleb gently steered him to a chair and sat him down, massaging his neck and shoulders, listening, not talking. Paul gradually began to relax. His sobs trailed off, though tears kept leaking down his face.

"I don't know why I'm so upset. I hardly know him," he said finally. Caleb kept working on his shoulders. "Sometimes I'm not sure I know me. I mean, who am I?"

"Who do you feel like?"

"I don't know. Sometimes I feel like I'm a freak—just a walking disease. Whoever I was died when I got—when I found out I had it."

"We could talk about it."

Paul looked grateful and relieved but shook his head. "Maybe some other time. I can't deal with anything more tonight."

Caleb nodded.

When he went back in the other room, Brian raised his eyebrows and said, "What would *Fraud* say, Jack?"

"What do you think Freud would say, Brian?"

SIXTEEN

The rear of Spaulding House had an eight-foot cyclone fence around it with barbed wire on top. A sign next to the gate said PRIVATE PROPERTY—TRESPASSERS WILL BE PROSECUTED. Inside the fence, near a back door lit by a single bulb, Caleb's Jaguar had been parked for several hours. And Thinnes had been parked in the alley behind the fence, where he could see the rear and one side of the building, for just as long. From time to time he searched the windows with binoculars. For variety, he amused himself by counting rats in the ally and scouting uncurtained windows in the area for exhibitionists.

Suddenly a police patrol car turned up the alley, shining its spotlight on Thinnes's car, and one of its occupants used the loudspeaker to tell Thinnes: "Get out of the car and keep your hands where we can see them."

Thinnes obeyed cautiously, leaving his car door open, keeping one eye on the squad, the other on the hospice. The two officers got out and approached him with hands on their guns. The cop who'd been driving said, "See some ID?"

Thinnes carefully took out his wallet and flashed his star.

The cop said, "Sorry, Detective."

"What's up?" his partner demanded.

At that moment, Caleb came out of the building with another man. Thinnes turned quickly, putting his head down and his hands on the hood of the car and spreading his feet. "Guy just came out of the building's the one I'm tailing," he said tersely, "and I don't want him to make me. Make like arresting officers."

The driver said, "What . . . ?"

The other cop got the idea and quickly but unobtrusively pulled

67

his gun, pointing it at Thinnes. "Frisk him," he told his partner as Caleb and his companion watched. The driver caught on and did a creditable job of patting Thinnes down without "finding" his gun. When he finished, his partner told him, "Okay. Cuff him."

He cuffed Thinnes's hands behind his back, then closed the Chevy's door, and the two officers bundled him into the back of the squad, keeping themselves between Thinnes and their two observers. Then they got in the squad and backed it out of the alley and pulled past the building on the corner. Thinnes shifted around and presented his cuffed hands to the cop in the passenger's seat before the car stopped, and as soon as the cuffs dropped, he was pushing the door. "Take it easy," the driver told Thinnes as he got out to open the door. "If your perp takes off, we can pull him over for you."

"My suspect. He's still just a suspect. And thanks, but that would make him suspicious."

Signaling the coppers to wait, Thinnes peered cautiously around the building in time to see Caleb get into the Jag. The man with him opened the gate, and after Caleb drove away, he closed it and went back in the building. Thinnes turned to the squad and told the driver, "I owe you guys one. Thanks." Then he hurried back to his car to resume the chase.

The tail ended where it began. As Caleb pulled his Jaguar into his garage, Thinnes continued past the building to avoid being obvious and waited half a block down, next to a hydrant. But it seemed Caleb was done for the day. Thinnes waited another hour, then went home.

Rhonda was asleep when Thinnes came in. He started to undress and paused to look at her longingly. If he'd had to describe the way she made him feel, he would have said light-headed. The way you feel hyperventilating. She'd always had that effect on him, and he'd never been unfaithful, never wanted another woman.

He sighed and wondered how they'd separated so completely. She'd been his best friend when he was writing home from Nam. She'd been the beacon to sight on for the way back. Her letters were little packages of sunlight keeping the darkness away. (He'd read Conrad; he understood—better after years of police work—

about the darkness within.) But he'd had more time then, and no close buddies. Now there was the police fraternity and the customary silence.

Thinnes finished undressing and crawled into bed without waking her.

SEVENTEEN

Thinnes stood in front of Miss Baynes' door, holding his I.D. up for inspection through the security peephole. The door opened on *Ms.* Alicia Baynes, Caucasian, five seven, 130 pounds, blond. Typical yuppie career woman in her twenties with a CPA, working on a M.R.S. She'd been crying. Her face was puffy, her eyes swollen as she stood aside to let him in.

"You heard about Allan Finley?" he asked.

"Dr. Caleb, Allan's psychiatrist, told me last night." She paused to fight back tears. "That's why I called in sick again today. I couldn't face . . . " She swallowed, getting herself together. She pointed to a chair and sat on the edge of the couch.

Thinnes took the chair. "Did he seem upset or depressed lately?"

"No! Allan didn't kill himself."

"Dr. Caleb told you that?"

"No, but he *did* say Allan wasn't suicidal. He said you were investigating his death. I mean, the police were."

"Did Finley have any enemies?"

"No." She paused, then added, "He wasn't very outgoing—he didn't make friends terribly easily—but no one *hated* him."

"Why did you call in sick Friday?"

She blushed. "We had a date Thursday night. When he didn't show up, I thought he'd stood me up. I was embarrassed to face him at the office."

"You and he were close?"

"We went out sometimes."

"He have any other girlfriends?"

"I don't know. We were just friends."

"Did he ever moonlight?"

"I don't think so."

"Did he own a gun?"

"Oh, no. Allan would be the last—"

"What did he tell you about Dr. Caleb?"

"Just that he was helping him learn to relax around people. Allan's always been a bit uptight." She remembered Finley was dead and almost sobbed. "*Was* uptight. I just can't believe it!"

"Do you know what accounts he'd been working on lately?"

"Allan never discussed his accounts," she said sharply, then added sheepishly, "but I know he was working on the Margolis books Thursday because he had to go to Marina City."

"Anything else you can think of I should know about?"

She shook her head.

"One last question: was he right- or left-handed?"

She sniffed and almost smiled. "He was nearly ambidexterous, but basically left-handed. He used to tease that because the right half of the brain controls the left side of the body, only southpaws were in their right minds."

EIGHTEEN

Thinnes and Crowne pulled into the canyon between the Marina City Office Building and the twin corn cobs of Marina Towers, and Thinnes parked the unmarked car in the no-parking zone in front of the doors. He flipped an OFFICIAL POLICE BUSINESS sign onto the dash, and as they entered the building, Crowne filled him in on Margolis from information in his notebook.

"Vincent Margolis. Forty-eight. Moved here fifteen years ago from the East Coast. Millionaire real estate mogul, philanthropist, art collector. Contributes heavily to local politicians. Never been in trouble with the law—at least since he came here." He put the notebook away and looked at Thinnes. "Another thing. Besides his office suite here, he has a condo."

"I wonder what *that* costs?"

"If you have to ask . . . "

" . . . you can't afford it," Thinnes finished with him.

They waited in front of the bank of stainless steel elevators. One of them opened. Thinnes and Crowne entered; Crowne pushed the appropriate button. "Oh yeah," he added as the doors closed them in, "guy in traffic said Margolis isn't above getting tickets fixed."

The office of Margolis Enterprises was very plush, with glossy, expensive brochures on the tables and contemporary art on the walls. The receptionist was also glossy and expensive, and her expression said plainly that Crowne and Thinnes were not her idea of prospective clients. She said, "May I help you?" Her tone was disapproving.

Thinnes handed her his card. "We'd like to speak with Mr. Margolis."

She was startled by what she read on the card and gave Thinnes another look, then picked up her phone. "Mr. Margolis, there's a . . ." she read from the card, "Detective John Thinnes, Chicago Police Department, Area Six—Violent Crimes division, here." After listening to Margolis, she said, "Yes, sir," and told Thinnes, "You can go right in." She pointed to a doorway behind her. Thinnes and Crowne went through.

Margolis's inner office had an outstanding view of the river, expensive wood paneling, deep carpets, and more art. Margolis was seated behind a mile-wide walnut desk, with his fingers laced in front of him. Everything about him was smooth, urbane, professionally civilized, from his expensive suit and diamond cuff links, to his carefully manicured hands. His thick dark hair, a distinguished gray at the temples, was conservatively cut. His face was unlined—carefully lifted, Thinnes would've bet. He had a plastic-perfect nose and a mouth that gave the impression of sincerity and confidence. Success was the expensive perfume that covered up his natural odors. But he wore designer glasses through which no distortion showed when he turned his head; they were camouflage, designed to disguise his eyes, like the tinted glass of car windows that is outlawed in Illinois because it hides the occupants from view.

He didn't stand to greet them but sat looking at a point in space between them. "Detective Thinnes." He indicated Crowne. "And this is . . . ?"

"Crowne," Crowne said tersely.

Thinnes felt his back-hairs rising. This was a man it would be easy to dislike. It wasn't that he resented Margolis being rich. He just hated the attitude that seemed to go with having money—that it made you God's gift to the world, put the title to the road in your glove box, and made your shit cleaner than anybody else's. Some of 'em, like Dr. Caleb, managed to hide it pretty well, but it always seemed to leak out under pressure. Thinnes didn't think it would take much pressure to squeeze it out of Margolis. How much pressure would it take to get Caleb to show his true colors?

Margolis brought Thinnes's thoughts back to the issue by indicating chairs on the other side of the desk. "Won't you sit down?" They sat. Crowne took out his pen and notebook. Margolis asked, "What can I do for you?"

Thinnes answered. "We're inquiring into the death of Allan Finley."

"The name is familiar, but I don't . . . "

"Your accountant?"

"My accountant is the *firm* of Wilson, Reynolds and Close."

"And one of their senior accountants—who worked on your books the day he died—was Allan Finley."

"I see. Then of course you would want to speak with someone here. Unfortunately, I can't help you; I never met Finley. But you're free to speak with my office manager." Margolis picked up his phone and said into it, "Miss Ellis, these gentlemen would like to speak to Mr. Winters. Would you find him for them?" He put the phone down. "Winters will have dealt with him."

"I came here to speak to you," Thinnes said.

Margolis was amused. "Really, Detective. What an absurd waste of time—mine and yours. I didn't know Finley so can't tell you why he might want to kill himself. What possible reason can you have for wanting to speak to me?"

"I don't recall saying he killed himself."

"I read the papers. But you investigate murders."

"Among other things," Thinnes said.

"Well, that being the case, you're looking for someone far more subtle than myself. Someone with a taste for the bizarre. Like my ex-wife, for instance." Thinnes raised an eyebrow. "Anita Margolis, Margolis Gallery. Wilson, Reynolds and Close also does her accounting. Miss Ellis will give you the address." Margolis got up and opened the door for them. "If you'll excuse me, I have a meeting."

Crowne looked ready to stay all month, but Thinnes shrugged and got up. As they went past Margolis, Crowne couldn't resist saying, "We'll be in touch."

"Winters was a lot of help," Crowne said as they came out of the building. "Yeah," Thinnes said. They got in the car and Thinnes pulled into traffic.

"Evanger made it pretty clear he doesn't want us making a federal case of this, so we'd better not both talk to this Margolis woman."

"She's all yours. This isn't my type of people." Crowne had another thought. "Close told you he *never* found any irregularities in Margolis's books?"

"Hard to believe, isn't it? But you know and I know, and Close undoubtedly knows, that there's no law that he has to tell us the truth unless he's under oath."

NINETEEN

The Margolis Gallery on North Michigan Avenue catered to the Gold Coast, wealthy people of expensive tastes and nearly unlimited means. Thinnes felt underdressed just walking in the door, but it gave him a delicious feeling of thumbing his nose at the gentry. He hadn't gotten far when an artsy saleswoman, with a severe hair style and fashionable but ugly clothes, intercepted him. "May I help you?" she said haughtily.

Thinnes flashed his star. "Ms. Margolis?"

Only a blink revealed the woman's surprise. She shook her head and pointed to the rear of the gallery. "Back there. On the ladder."

The showroom—he was not naive enough to think they called it that—was broken by fabric-covered panels into small display areas containing pieces Thinnes didn't understand. No prices were evident. He made his way through the maze to the rear, where a petite brunette stood on a ladder, adjusting a painting suspended from the ceiling. She moved—and from behind, looked—like a teenager. About thirty-three, Thinnes guessed, five two, dressed in designer jeans and sweatshirt.

She was being helped by a young black man, five eleven and clean-shaven, with a neat natural and amateur tatoos on biceps as big around as Anita Margolis's thighs. He had the large hands and still-thin frame of adolescence, with a promise of future size. He was dressed in stone-washed jeans and a sleeveless tee shirt that made his shoulders broader.

Thinnes had been—from his first awareness of sex—unequivocally and inalterably straight. His first reaction to homosexuality had been bewilderment—why'd anyone want to do that? Terms like cock-sucker, butt-fucker, and faggot had never held for him the rage and loathing they have for the sexually insecure. They'd had no more meaning than mother-fucker or son of a bitch, and were less satisfying as insults than asshole. He'd been a child of the Aquarian age, at least intellectually openminded, and if his later biases had been formed by the police culture and the scum he'd encountered as a cop, the first "guppie" he arrested in flagrante delicto had been an education. The man had been polite, articulate, and indistinguishable from the dozens of johns he'd busted hustling females. Except for the young pains in the ass with the log-size chips on their shoulders, Thinnes didn't have anything against gays. Still, when Anita Margolis's assistant moved to the other side of the ladder, the diamond Thinnes spotted in his right ear surprised him.

He watched them for several minutes without announcing himself. After a final adjustment, Anita said, "What do you think, Mark?"

Mark shrugged. "You could hang this honkey shit backward— it'd pro'ly look better."

Anita Margolis laughed without looking at him and swung her foot sideways against his chest. "Seriously!" Mark shook his head.

Keeping her eyes on the picture, she jumped off the ladder and backed up until she bumped into Thinnes. She was startled, but said, "I'm sorry!" like a reflex. "Where did you come from?"

Thinnes showed her his star, and her eyes widened. "Are you with customs?"

"No. Homicide. I'd like to ask you a few questions."

She sighed. "Well, I haven't murdered anyone lately, so ask away."

"Is there somewhere we can talk privately?"

Her office at the back of the gallery was a large room with two desks, one supporting a personal computer system, the other devoted to traditional paperwork. On a table against the wall were coffee supplies and a copy machine; crates had been shoved underneath. Papers and junk covered every flat surface, and paintings and wall hangings covered the walls. Post-its were stuck on everything, including the PC. Thinnes followed as Anita swept into the room, waiting while she cleared two of the chairs.

"How may I help you, Detective Thinnes?" she asked when they were seated.

She was Gigi or Audrey Hepburn or Marlo Thomas as the girl next door. Effervescent wasn't the word—that brought Alka-Seltzer to mind. Everything about her reminded Thinnes of the best champagne, the expensive kind that could make you very drunk without making you sick. She raised his blood pressure at least a dozen points.

He took an unobtrusive deep breath and said, "Is the name Allan Finley familiar?"

"Yes but . . ." She looked away, trying to remember, then shook her head and looked back at Thinnes.

"Wilson, Reynolds and Close?"

"Oh yes. The very serious young man with the red hair." Thinnes nodded. "Is he in trouble?"

"When did you see him last?"

"Exactly?" He nodded. "I'll have to look it up." She walked over to turn on the computer. At the prompt, she typed in several words, and the name FINLEY, ALLAN came on the screen, along with WILSON, REYNOLDS & CLOSE; "WATER FOWL #37"; LITHOGRAPH; JASON ROGUE; $3700 (EMP DISC), and a date.

Thinnes read over her shoulder. "What's EMP DISC?"

"Employee discount. I gave him ten percent off because he works for my accounting firm. The last time I saw him was . . ." She pointed to the date on the screen. ". . . the day he bought that print."

Thinnes pointed to WILSON, REYNOLDS & CLOSE on the screen. "When was the last time they worked on your books?"

She made a face. "Last week."

Thinnes responded to the face. "What?"

"My ex-husband's idea. He owns forty percent—just enough to demand an audit when he wants to annoy me."

"The gallery pays for that?"

"Just the first one each year. Vincent pays for any subsequent, unscheduled work, but he's the sort who'll spare no expense for revenge." She looked very directly at him. "What's this about?"

"Do you know a Dr. James Caleb?"

She seemed mildly alarmed. "Jack? Of course."

"That's his nickname?" Thinnes figured out the answer before he finished asking the question. "Of course—from his initials."

Anita nodded. "He's a close friend, and one of my best customers. Why?"

"Dr. Caleb's a collector too?"

"Too?"

"I understand Mr. Margolis collects art."

"If you can call it that," she said dryly. Thinnes raised an eyebrow and waited for an explanation. "He has me import oils for him by a dreadfully inept expatriate American who lives on the *Rive gauche* and plays at being a bohemian."

Thinnes smiled in spite of himself. He found her very attractive. She responded, subtly, in kind. "Honestly, this man's paintings are so awful, I wouldn't hang them in an outhouse."

"So why does your ex buy them?"

"I have no idea. I've never seen him display one—what *is* this all about?"

Thinnes sobered. "Allan Finley was found dead in his apartment Friday."

Her face registered dismay. She started to say something, paused, then asked quietly and deliberately, "What has that to do with Jack?"

"Caleb was Finley's psychiatrist."

"Poor Jack. . . . "

Thinnes responded by waiting for an explanation.

"To have lost a patient. Did he kill himself?"

"What makes you ask that?"

"Jack's specialty, and he was—*Finley* was young and seemed healthy. If he was seeing a psychiatrist . . . "

"What can you tell me about him?"

She shrugged. "He had to save for the print. He put down a deposit to hold it and paid cash for it three months later."

Thinnes looked at the PC screen. "Thirty-seven hundred dollars. Is that a lot?"

"Not for a Jason Rogue. It's really a good investment."

"Was Finley your regular bookkeeper?"

"Wilson, Reynolds and Close usually sent whoever was available. Once Mr. Close came himself." She gave him a dazzling smile; he took another subtle deep breath. She giggled and continued, "Vincent insisted on an immediate audit, and they were shorthanded."

"Have you ever had any trouble with the firm?"

She was startled by the suggestion. "No."

"One more question." "Do you know if Dr. Caleb uses Wilson, Reynolds and Close?"

She seemed astonished by the question but answered with apparent honesty. "I haven't the faintest idea."

TWENTY

Crowne and Ferris were hard at work on reports when Thinnes got back to Area Six. Crowne was using a department-issue manual typewriter, Ferris his own electric portable. Karsch came out of his office, heading for the coffee pot, and Ferris raised his voice enough for Karsch to hear.

"Hey Crowne, what's the difference between a psychologist and a psychiatrist?"

"I don't know, but I'm sure you're going to tell us," Crowne said without looking up.

"About forty grand a year."

Thinnes glanced at Ferris, who grinned, then at his intended victim. Karsch looked moderately annoyed. Thinnes wondered if it was the remark about money that hurt or if Ferris had finally succeeded in getting Karsch's goat.

The psychologist disguised his irritation and ambled over to stand near Ferris. To aggravate him, Thinnes guessed. Ferris didn't like having anyone who wasn't a cop in on things.

"You'd make more in private practice, Karsch," Ferris told him. "You'll never get rich working here."

"Oh, working here has its compensations," Karsch said. "How would I ever meet someone like you in private practice?"

However Ferris interpreted it—either that he was uniquely weird or too poor to pay the going rates—it was an insult. Thinnes chuckled.

Crown laughed explosively and said, "Yeah Ferris, he's probably writing a paper about you."

It seemed to Thinnes that Karsch looked smug as Ferris changed the subject. "Thinnes," he said, "Marshall Close called. He's ar-

81

ranging a memorial service for Finley, and he wants the names out of Finley's address book so he can notify any interested parties. Is that what you call a *Close call*?"

Thinnes and Crowne looked at him; neither bothered to hide his annoyance. Crowne said, "Why doesn't he just put a notice in the obituary pages?"

"Either *he* killed Finley," Ferris said, "and he wants the names of his associates, or . . . "

"Or he thinks Finley's friends are too young to read obits," Crowne finished.

"It'd be a hell of a wake if nobody showed."

"Finley'll be there," Crowne said. "The ME just signed him off as a suicide."

Thinnes laughed humorlessly. "There goes your hit-man theory, Ray. Insurance won't pay off on suicide, so odds are it wasn't the sister."

"*Finley* did it, Thinnes."

"If you say so."

" 'Least somebody'll be at the wake, Crowne." Ferris snapped the typewriter case shut and gathered up his paperwork. "Thinnes'll be there."

Ignoring Ferris, Thinnes looked around the squad room. Half a dozen detectives were doing their respective things. Karsch walked into the property crimes office and looked out at the parking lot below. Ferris handed his report to the operations sergeant and did a little two-step as he left to avoid hitting a visitor coming through the doorway.

"Well, well, well," Crowne said as he recognized the visitor; Thinnes stood as he approached.

"Good afternoon, Dr. Caleb."

Caleb said, "My receptionist said you were looking for me."

Thinnes sat down and pointed to the chair next to his. "Have a seat, Doctor."

Caleb sat. To Thinnes's surprise, he wasn't the least nervous. Thinnes waited, but finally had to come to the point. "You've been playing detective. One of Allan Finley's neighbors called to complain about all the people asking questions, so I checked and found you talked to the super and half the tenants in the building. And Alicia Baynes said you talked to her."

"I've been trying to find out what I can about Allan's death."

"My job. It makes it more difficult if the people I have to question are prepared for me. It gives them time to think up alibis."

"I'm sorry. My impression, from the news, was that you were treating his death as a suicide."

"It sometimes helps our investigations to let people jump to their own conclusions."

"I see. I hope my amateur efforts haven't muddled things too badly."

Thinnes gave a noncommital shrug. "Where did you get Miss Baynes's address?" He'd checked; she wasn't in the book.

"She was one of Allan's few friends, the only one I had an address for."

"Was Finley right- or left-handed?"

"Left-handed."

Thinnes nodded; he'd expected as much.

Caleb said, "Was there anything else?"

"Not unless Miss Baynes told you something incriminating."

"She said she'd had a date with Allan the night he died, and she thought he'd stood her up."

Thinnes nodded again. "Well, thanks for coming in, Doctor."

"My pleasure. I've always wanted to see the inside of a police station—voluntarily, of course." He stood up to go.

Thinnes stood too. "Maybe you'd like to spend a day with us sometime—see how it's done."

"I'd like that very much. When?"

"You doing anything tonight? We're just coming on. You're welcome to join us." Thinnes pointed to his tailored suit. "You got any, ah, more *casual* clothes?"

Caleb smiled wryly. "It'll take me a while to go home and change."

"How 'bout we pick you up at your place in an hour?"

"Fine."

After Thinnes watched Caleb disappear, he turned to find Crowne seething.

"What was *that,* Thinnes?"

"We've got nothing so far, and he's the closest thing we have to a suspect. If we can get him off guard, he may let something slip."

"You can't even prove you've got a homicide. Personally, I think Bendix has you pegged: you finally flipped out! You oughta go have a nice long talk with Karsch." He got up and stalked out of the squad room.

TWENTY-ONE

Thinnes pulled the unmarked police car over in front of the Gold Coast skyscraper, and Caleb emerged, dressed casually. He got in the back seat and nodded to Crowne, who'd cooled off. As Thinnes pulled into traffic, Crowne handed Caleb a release form to sign.

Thinnes filled him in. "You missed roll call. That's where if we don't have a case of our own pending, we get our assignments—lists of people to question, suspects or prospective witnesses for whatever cases are still open."

"Tonight, we got a good twenty," Crowne added, "mostly people who're unavailable during the day or weren't home when the detectives stopped by earlier. It can be tough sometimes."

"People are under no legal obligation to tell us the truth unless they're under oath." Thinnes looked back at Caleb. "Moral obligations don't have any weight. It makes working up a case more of a challenge."

"Yeah," Crowne said, "but it's a bad idea to lie to us. When we get lied to, we get *really* nosy." He looked sharply at Caleb to see if he was listening and had understood. "And we usually know when somebody's lying."

Mutt and Jeff. All dicks played the game. Crowne wasn't as good at it as Frank Flynn, Thinnes's former partner, but he was okay for the less than subtle stuff. Thinnes watched Caleb carefully in the rearview as Crowne said, "Thinnes, you can't make a case for murder. Finley's fingerprints were on the gun, and he had gunshot residue in the right places. Somebody pointed a gun at him and said, 'Shoot yourself or I'll do it for you.' "

Caleb's expression told Thinnes only that the doctor was good at disguising his feelings. Thinnes kept his eyes on Caleb as he told Crowne, "The killer used a bullet to kill him and a blank to dust his hand afterwards."

Caleb seemed interested, nothing more.

"The gun was only fired once," Crowne said.

"Maybe. But who said there was only one gun?"

Still Caleb gave nothing away. But then the murderer was likely to be a cool SOB.

"Gimme a break. A killer that carries two guns so he can make it look like suicide?"

"But Allan wasn't killed in the heat of passion," Caleb interrupted. "If you plan to get away with murder, you plan."

Their first stop was The Wise Fools Pub. They were looking for a blues player who may or may not have seen the fatal beating of a possible witness to a probable drug buy. "One of those real solid leads," as Crowne put it. It was early; there were few patrons. Crowne and Caleb waited while Thinnes questioned the bartender, who shook his head a lot and told him not to bother the musicians. The musicians, as it turned out, were delighted to be bothered—when Caleb offered to buy them a round—but none of them had ever heard of the blues player.

They had to question the driver of a hackney cab who'd witnessed a violent assault earlier in the evening. They tracked her down at the cab stand north of the Water Tower information center. The driver told her story with gestures and much pointing; the horse waited patiently, looking bored. Thinnes asked the questions as Crowne took notes.

Why, Caleb wondered, as he watched Thinnes work, do I want to get close to a cop? It's a danger—cops have their own agendas, their own rules.

It came to him like a déjà vu, like the feeling his grandmother had described as "someone walking on your grave": Thinnes had that something Chris'd had, the same sort of attitude toward the truth—that it *must* be known.

* * *

They flagged an old Buick down on Division Street and followed it into an alley, letting it pull several car-lengths ahead. Thinnes and Caleb stayed in the car. Thinnes filled Caleb in on the case, while Crowne got out and walked up to lean against the Buick and talk to the driver, a former gang member in his twenties, who sometimes gave them useful information. As they watched, Thinnes asked Caleb, "What does a psychiatrist actually do?"

"If he's successful," Caleb said, "he helps people solve their personal problems."

A Karsch kind of answer, if ever there was one, Thinnes thought. "Yeah, but how? What *exactly* do you do?"

"There's nothing exact about it. When a client asks me to help, I have him describe the problem. I listen to what he says. I study his body language for discrepancies. I try to notice what he doesn't say."

He paused as they watched Crowne take out a cigarette and then hand the pack to his informant. Crowne lit up with a green plastic lighter, which he also handed over. The informant took a cigarette, lit it, and put both pack and lighter in his pocket.

Thinnes could read neither approval nor disapproval on Caleb's face as he continued. "If there's any suggestion of organic impairment, I send him to his physician for a thorough physical, and I test him myself for drugs and anything I think his doctor may have missed."

Down the alley, Crowne walked around the informant's car and got in the front seat. His gestures became mildly threatening, and he leaned toward the informant as the man spoke.

Caleb waited, perhaps for Thinnes to comment, then went on. "If I don't find drugs or any physical cause for the problem, I dig into his family history and try to determine what purpose the problem serves, either for the client or for significant others in his life."

In the informant's car, Crowne shook his head vigorously, almost as if disagreeing with Caleb. He listened to the informant for a moment, then shrugged.

"Motive, opportunity, and method," Thinnes said. "Basic detective work, huh?"

"That, and a bit more. A detective's finished when he's discovered who did it and presented his evidence. At that point in the investigation, a therapist still has to determine if his subject really wants to change, and if he's serious, how to help him do it."

"Sort of a one-man criminal justice system."

"That's one way to put it, although it's more frequently described by critics as playing God."

Crown got out of the Buick and started back toward them, poker-faced, but Thinnes could tell he'd struck out. Thinnes kept his eyes on Caleb and said, "What do you think, Doctor. Did he score?"

"I doubt it."

Then Crowne opened the door and threw himself into the passenger seat with a resounding "Damn!"

A little while later, Thinnes cruised slowly down Rush Street on autopilot, watching the activity as he kept up his end of the conversation. The subject was baseball, and he found he had the Cubs in common with Caleb; Crowne was a South Sider. As the car passed one of the half dozen bars on the strip, Thinnes spotted something suspicious in the alley next to it. He stopped, backed up fast, and pulled down the alley. He and Crowne were out of the car almost before it quit moving.

Two large bouncers were holding a drunk up against the building wall. The drunk was a male cauc, mid twenties, a yuppie type, too far gone to stand without help. Thinnes showed the bouncers his star.

"What's the story?"

"Guy came in D and D. We were just trying to sober him up enough to pour him into a cab."

A likely story.

"We'll take him. You want to press?"

"Hell no. We just want him gone."

Crowne glared at Thinnes but didn't complain in front of the civilians about the extra paperwork they'd have to do. He hitched his thumb toward the car. The bouncers pulled the drunk away from the wall, and he almost collapsed. They backed him up to the car, where he sagged onto the hood like a water balloon.

* * *

88

Thinnes curbed the car in front of an old red brick building, six stories, wrapped like a U around a trashy, weed-filled central courtyard. He fished his notebook from his inside pocket and flipped it open. "Mrs. Emilio Campos. Says she speaks English."

"These people never speak English," Crowne said, "even when they do. We ought to save this one for Viernes."

Thinnes shook his head. "We'll try. If we strike out, we'll give it to Viernes."

"I speak Spanish," Caleb said, "if that's any help."

Thinnes turned to Crowne. "See there? You gotta think horse. You'll get grass."

"Yeah. Then you'll get busted."

They got out of the car and went in. There was no security door, no elevator. Mrs. Campos lived on the third floor and answered the door with, *"No hablo inglés,"* to which Caleb responded, *"Hablo español."* A rapid conversation followed, completely in Spanish, during which Mrs. Campos did most of the talking, and Caleb interrupted, occasionally, with *"¿Quién?"* or *"¿cómo?"* Finally she shook her head and went back into her apartment. Caleb stared after her with a troubled expression.

"Well?" Crowne demanded.

"She's afraid if she says who shot him, they'll kill her or her family."

It was about what Thinnes expected, but Crowne got angry. "These damn people—"

"She's afraid to be the first," Caleb interrupted, scarcely concealing his annoyance. "If we can get someone else to identify him, she'll corroborate. She said at least a dozen other people saw the shooting."

Crowne shook his head.

Thinnes nodded. "Then if the doctor doesn't object . . . " He looked at Caleb, who shook his head. "Let's start knocking on doors."

They canvassed the entire building, questioning anyone who would open the door, with Crowne and Thinnes asking in English, Caleb translating. If the sighs and shrugs and heads shaking were anything to judge by, no one ever saw anything. Caleb spoke as much with his hands and shoulders and face as with words. Thinnes's hunch was confirmed—the doctor had depths to him not hinted at by his life-style or profession.

Their last interview was with a family on the fifth floor. Caleb spoke with the man of the household as Crowne, Thinnes, the man's family, and neighbors looked on. There was much gesturing on both sides, and a good deal of commentary from the onlookers. Suddenly the general debate was too much for the man.

"¡Ya basta! ¡Silencio!" he demanded. The spectators fell silent. The man turned to Caleb and said, "Lo siento, no puedo ayudarles." Caleb shrugged and nodded with apparent sympathy.

"Nadie vió nada," another man said.

"Váyanse, por favor," a woman added. "Vimos nada."

Three or four people nodded in agreement and stared at the detectives. Caleb turned to Thinnes. "They know, but they're afraid to speak out. They're pretty adamant."

"Okay. Let's get out of here."

A modest crowd had gathered by the time they reached the street. Neighbors called back and forth in Spanish as the three of them got in the car. "Well Ray," Thinnes was forced to concede, "looks like you're going to get your wish. We're definitely going to have to call in Viernes."

TWENTY-TWO

Clark and Ontario. McDonald's. Thinnes sat with Crowne and Caleb in the car with the motor running as Crowne dispensed "dinner" from a paper bag. He watched Caleb remove the bun from his Quarter Pounder as they talked and roll the meat up like a taco.

Crowne asked Caleb, "You still think Thinnes is right? Somebody killed Finley?"

Caleb swallowed and said, "Yes."

"You never been wrong?"

"Certainly. But in Finley's case, I doubt it."

"But he was crazy, wasn't he? Else why was he seeing you? A crazy's just as likely to kill himself as any other damn thing."

"By crazy, I assume you mean unpredictable, illogical, deviant from the norm."

"Yeah."

"He wasn't crazy." Caleb looked at Thinnes as he expanded on what he was telling Crowne. "Craziness isn't the only reason people see psychiatrists."

He held Thinnes's eyes a moment longer than the conversation warranted, and Thinnes felt a shock. The doctor had a disconcerting way of staring that gave you the feeling he knew what you were thinking. It made Thinnes think of cats and gave him the impression that Caleb was making a discreet, roundabout suggestion. To Thinnes.

"So he wasn't crazy," Thinnes said, to steer the subject back to Finley. "How can you be sure he didn't kill himself for some 'logical' reason? Why *do* people kill themselves?"

"There're several theories."

91

Crowne said, "Such as?"

"Common sense has it that suicide results from despair, an utter absence of hope, if you will."

Crowne nodded. Thinnes watched Caleb's body language.

"Then there's the anger-in, anger-out theory. That suicide is the result of deep-seated anger directed at one's self, homicide being the result of anger directed at others." He seemed to assess their reactions to this, then continued. "There's the evil spirits theory—possession by demons."

Crowne laughed. "So which theory is right?"

"I'd say it depends." They waited. "You have to remember that any theory is a metaphor, at best. A view of the world. To put it metaphorically, what you describe with your theory depends on what you see, and that depends on where you're standing."

"So everything's relative, and nobody can really explain anything," Thinnes said. "That's a cop-out." It seemed pretty weird to be discussing philosophy with a murder suspect in a McDonald's parking lot.

Caleb shook his head and paused, perhaps to get his words right. "If you live in a culture where mental illness is thought to be caused by demon possession, you're more likely to be cured by a ceremony to exorcise the demons than you are by psychotherapy." Thinnes nodded. "And if you believe that the proper medication will cure you, even a sugar pill will give you relief, unless you're a raving manic-depressive or a process schizophrenic."

"So you're saying modern medical science is voodoo?"

"Not at all. If someone's behavior improves when you administer a chemical in a double-blind situation, it's safe to assume the chemical is having a theraputic effect, and that his brain chemistry has been changed."

"Yeah. So the devil didn't make him do it," Crowne said.

Caleb shrugged. "We can't say that with certainty if we don't know what caused his impairment."

Thinnes said, "Either heredity or environment."

Caleb smiled. "You might just as well say karma. Why do some members of a family develop schizophrenia when others don't?"

"It seems to me we've gotten pretty far from why people kill themselves, Doctor," Thinnes said. "What do you think?"

"I think human beings are wonderfully adept at solving problems—even if we have to create problems to solve." He paused. "I see most suicides as a misplaced attempt to solve a problem, a normal coping mechanism run amok."

"Makes sense," Crowne said. "Okay, say Finley *was* murdered. What can you tell us about who might have done it?"

"A successful murderer's intention is to avoid detection, and the best way to avoid detection is to prevent anyone from knowing a murder's been committed, either by making the victim completely disappear, or by making it appear that the victim died by natural causes or his own hand. I'd say our murderer is quite intelligent, and particularly subtle or cowardly."

"You got any hunches about his motive?" Thinnes asked.

"Allan wasn't dishonest or malicious, but he had access to people's secrets."

"You think maybe he was blackmailing somebody?"

Caleb shook his head. "Someone might have *thought* he might, or just that he would go to the police about something."

"You one of those, ah . . . *liberal types,*" Crowne asked Caleb, "who thinks all criminals are either victims of society or had rotten parents?"

"There's evidence that a significant number of those we classify as having antisocial personality disorder had a father with the same problem or were abused or head-injured as children."

"So you think bad guys are all just sick?"

"I didn't say that." He paused. "Personally, I believe some 'bad guys' are just bad. Evil, to use an old- fashioned word."

"How do you tell the difference?" Thinnes asked.

"Sometimes you can't."

Caleb seemed to change the focus of his interest, as he spoke, to fix on something going on outside the car. Thinnes followed his gaze to two passers-by, a black man and the small black boy he was dragging along by the collar. The boy seemed to be in trouble, and the man's urgings to hurry were none too gentle. As he watched them, Caleb became as alert as a hunting cat. Thinnes asked, "What is it?"

"Unless I'm mistaken, that child's being abused."

Crowne stared openmouthed.

"Sure?" Thinnes asked Caleb.

"Enough to stick my neck out and say so."

"We don't have any probable," Crowne said.

Thinnes looked at Caleb. "Citizen's complaint?"

"In writing, if you like."

"Sounds like a probable to me," Thinnes said. He put the car in gear and pulled alongside the man and boy. As Crowne and Caleb got out of the car, the man took off running. Crowne was after him without a second's hesitation. Thinnes shoved the Mars light out the window and slapped it on the car roof as he yelled, "Doctor, stay with the kid!" He grabbed his radio transmitter and took off after Crowne in a frenzy of flashing blue light.

With Crowne half a car length behind, the suspect tore around the building and through the parking lot, dodging parked cars and McD's patrons. He charged across Ontario Street, disregarding the frantic pulse of homeward-bound suburbanites.

Thinnes attempted to follow in the car. After several blocks of heart-jarring near misses, with more police vehicles joining the Keystone Kops parade every minute, Crowne chased the suspect into an alley. Thinnes screeched into the narrow passage two car-lengths behind them with lights, horn, and siren blaring. Past the dumpsters and garbage drums, just beyond Crowne and the suspect, the headlights flattened on a brick wall. Thinnes tramped on the brake; the car fishtailed with a banshee shriek. The suspect spotted the dead end and stopped. Whirling around, he dragged a gun from his belt and aimed it at Crowne.

Thinnes slammed the accelerator and pointed the car at the gunman. The gunman shifted his aim toward Thinnes and fired wildly, missing even the car. Half a heartbeat from impact, Crowne jerked the suspect out of Thinnes's path, as Thinnes tried to put the brake pedal through the floor. The car stopped, hard, against the alley's dead-end brick wall. Crowne slammed the offender into the corner between the wall and the car's fender, forcing him to face into the reflected headlight beam, smashing his head and hands against the red stone. The reddish reflection off the brick made them both look devilish. Thinnes took a deep breath and very carefully and deliberately turned off the motor. He got out of the car, breathing as hard as Crowne, shaking visibly, as Crowne relieved the suspect of his gun. Thinnes kept the perp covered while Crowne frisked him and snapped the cuffs on. Crowne was just reciting Miranda as the reinforcements arrived.

TWENTY-THREE

The boy reminded Caleb of a feral kitten, curious but terrified. A small crowd surrounded them as they sat a few feet apart on the curb. It was obvious that the child couldn't decide if he was more scared of the onlookers or of Caleb, who patiently tried to discover his name. "Is there some reason you can't tell me your name?"

The boy nodded.

"What is it?"

"Can't talk to strangers."

"My name is Jack. Do you know any strangers named Jack?" The boy shook his head. "Then how about telling me your name?"

He shook his head again.

Caleb raised his eyebrows. "Could it be you don't *know* your name? Maybe you've forgotten it?"

This last was too much for the boy. "Did not! Name's Joey Williams."

Caleb nodded as if he'd known it all the time. "I'll bet you know your address, too," he said, and Joey nodded.

Cabrini-Green. The concrete and pink brick compound straddling Division Street between Sedgwick and Halsted. Chicago's most infamous projects.

Thinnes parked the unmarked car in front of the police roll call building, next to the beat officers' private cars. Up close. Where the roof-top snipers had a poorer shot at it. A blue and white pulled up next to the unmarked car, but its occupants stayed inside as Thinnes, Crowne, Caleb, and Joey got out. The few people around stared hostilely.

The Green wasn't a place you went into unarmed, especially in street clothes. "Fools rush in," as Crowne put it. They picked up two regular beat cops before they headed into the bowels. Ironically, Joey like Allen Finley, also lived on Cleveland.

They kept an eye on the roof tops as they walked—nineteen stories isn't far down as the stray bullet wanders. Even in the orange glow of the streetlights, the area looked like a war zone or a set from *The Terminator*. You didn't need to see the gang slogans or the bullet craters in the walls. It brought back memories of the time before Thimmes had made detective, when he'd needed the OT. Eight hours of nerve-jangling fear that left you Jello-kneed with relief once you were out of sniper range. But if you were honest, you had to admit the duty was exciting. The constant flow of adrenaline gave you a rush that made any other work dull by comparison.

Joey's building was typical of Cabrini-Green. The front entry was claustrophobic, piled with garbage, walls decorated with graffiti and gang slogans, the muttering of idle minds. Half the mailboxes were broken open. The elevators were out. Naturally.

Caleb wasn't naive enough to be surprised. Chicago residents knew about Cabrini, learned early not to even drive too close. Tourists were warned in the guide books. And he'd read the article in the *Tribune Magazine,* so he had some idea of what the cops were feeling: fear. He felt it himself. He was in Nam again, indentured again to an occupying army. No matter their good intentions, they weren't innocents. And they weren't welcomed by the natives. An absurd parallel, he told himself. Intellectually. But emotionally close enough.

He looked at Thinnes, Crowne, and the uniformed cops. They had the nervous intensity of soldiers on point. Nor did articles and folklore convey the stupefying reality of the place, or the bleak, gnawing anxiety it evoked, stress that eroded the mind and soul, then ate away at the body, nerves first, then heart and innards. Craziness was a defense here. Psychopathology was the norm—a hidden epidemic. Cabrini was a psychological black hole with a gravity that warped minds and distorted perceptions. If light couldn't escape, what hope had human beings?

* * *

They started to climb the stairs, stumbling over garbage and scattering night creatures, both the two and four-legged variety. The two beat cops were fit and didn't seem to be bothered by the climb. Crowne was winded by the second floor, Thinnes by the third. Joey lagged behind, more out of fear—as far as Thinnes could tell—than from exhaustion.

Caleb's stamina surprised Thinnes. When Joey began to fall back, Caleb hoisted the child up and carried him piggyback.

They had to watch their step on the fifth-floor landing, because someone had been using it for a shit house. Thinnes felt a wave of disgust that left him ready to puke. And there was shock, too, as he realized how disgust and rage seemed to be the only things he *could* feel any more. Stop it, Thinnes, he told himself. You're making yourself crazy. Still, he was surprised that after so many years as a cop, people could still disappoint him. It was the sort of sappy idealism that made rookie cops so smarmy. Why did he expect humans to behave differently from other animals? The fucking stupidity that left the elevators out, garbage and shit in the halls, and walls filthy with graffiti probably wasn't even intentional. An untrained dog is an untrained dog. The two-legged type that crapped in the stairwell was no different, no worse, than the four-legged kind that did it on the sidewalks.

The door on the eighth floor was missing its knob. They pushed it open and came out into a hall that smelled like garbage. Caleb, who was scarcely winded, let Joey down, and the boy ran past the elevator—propped open with a chair—and stopped in front of an open apartment door. A small fan in the doorway blew stale, hot air into the hall. Inside the apartment, three young black men were watching TV with a young woman. There was an empty pizza box on the table, along with pop and beer cans and an ashtray full of butts. The woman got off the couch and came to meet them.

"Joey, what you doin' up so late?"

Joey stared at her with open-eyed amazement. "Momma's *daid*."

"What kinda bullshit you talkin'?" She spotted Caleb and the detectives. "What you honkeys doin' here?"

This brought the other occupants of the apartment swarming into the hall. When they spotted the uniforms, they lapsed into sullen watchfulness. Like the inmates Thinnes had seen at Stateville when he'd gone to interview a murderer. Their hostility was as obvious as the stench in the hall. He flashed his star.

Caleb attempted to make peace. "We took Joey away from—"

"Joey, where's Momma?" the woman demanded, ignoring Caleb.

By way of answering, Joey walked down the hall, looking to be sure the others were following. Everyone did, the beat cops watchfully trailing the group. Joey stopped in front of an apartment three doors down and waited, eyeing the doorknob, until Thinnes and Caleb came up behind him. Then he very fearfully tried turning the knob. The door was locked.

Thinnes knocked. No one answered. He asked the woman, "Have you got a key?"

She gave him a look but turned toward a man at the edge of the group and said, "Leroy, han' me my bag."

Thinnes knocked again as Leroy went back to the first apartment. Still there was no answer. Leroy came back with the bag and tossed it to the woman. She fished out a key. No one spoke as she unlocked the door. Pushed it open. Felt inside for the light switch without going in.

As the the door opened, Joey reached up and grabbed Caleb's hand. The woman screamed.

The beat cops started pushing past the spectators. With Crowne, Thinnes stepped through the doorway, past the woman as she moaned, "Oh, Momma!" Caleb stayed put, holding Joey's hand. The residents crowded in for a look.

The room had been tossed and scrambled. The remains of Joey's mother lay on the floor in a pool of blood. She'd been beaten to death.

Thinnes felt a familiar, flat, hopeless feeling. Joey's sister buried her face in her hands and started sobbing, hugging herself, rocking herself. Crowne seemed shocked. Behind them, the residents were mesmerized. The beat cops stared indifferently. As he gripped Joey's hand, Caleb seemed to be hyperventilating, and Thinnes thanked God the boy was screened from the view by the bodies of the adults.

"Come away from here, Miss," Thinnes told Joey's sister. He

gently pushed her away from the door, into the crowd that was forming as people poured out of their apartments to investigate the scream. Neighbors took hold of her, offering cold comfort. Thinnes closed the apartment door and told them to disperse. The cops began to herd them away. The woman started back to the first apartment, then turned back. She gave Caleb a bleak look, took Joey's hand, and led him away.

"I'll call this in," Thinnes told Crowne, "you start getting statements." He looked at Caleb, who was sweating profusely, and whose pale face and rapid breathing betrayed his distress. He said, sharply, "Doctor, are you all right?" without troubling to hide his annoyance.

Breathing deeply, Caleb nodded and turned away. He pushed through the crowd to the elevator, removed the chair from the door, and leaned on it while he got himself together. Crowne started to help the cops disperse the crowd as Thinnes radioed for reinforcements.

TWENTY-FOUR

Some time later, Thinnes, Crowne, and Caleb pulled into the parking lot north of Area Six. Crowne got out. "You oughta save the rest of the paper for tomorrow," he told Thinnes.

"I'll sleep in tomorrow."

"Yeah." He gave them a perfunctory good-bye nod, closed the door, and went to his little red Fiero. Thinnes parked between two blue-and-whites. Crowne screeched out of the lot as Thinnes turned off the motor.

"Joey'll have to testify in court?" Caleb asked.

The question depressed Thinnes. "Probably not. The asshole'll plead guilty to a lesser charge and get a couple a years. He'll be out beating his next girlfriend before Joey drops out of school." He stared straight ahead. "How do you go home and make love to your wife after that?" He watched out of the corner of his eye as Caleb shook his head. "How do you *tell* your wife about something like that?"

Caleb continued to listen without comment.

"How do you even *sleep?*" He shrugged and looked at Caleb. "You can see why the bars around here are so full after hours."

The squad room was temporarily deserted when they entered. Thinnes went to get report forms, which he put next to his typewriter.

"Now you'll get to see the real police work." He glanced at the coffee maker. "Want some coffee?"

"Why not?"

When Thinnes got to the coffee maker, he noticed Karsch's door was slightly ajar. He walked over and pushed it open, and looked in without turning on the light. The room was empty. He pulled the door shut, and went back to plug in the coffee maker, which someone—Karsch probably—had left ready to go. Then he went back to his desk where Caleb was waiting and watching.

"You were pretty good with the kid tonight," he told Caleb. "I hate working with scared kids. I'm always afraid I'll make 'em worse."

"It's like making friends with a cat." Caleb looked deliberately at Thinnes. "Have you ever belonged to a cat, John?"

Thinnes put a report form in the typewriter and rolled it up to the first line. "No. Why?"

"You can't make friends with a cat by charging up and patting it on the head. You have to hold back and let it see you won't hurt it, let it prowl around in your territory and check out the amenities and the other residents. It's a process that takes time."

"So why bother? With a cat, I mean."

"Because when you've made friends with a cat, you've accomplished something."

TWENTY-FIVE

Caleb entered his apartment and stopped, puzzled. The living room looked orderly and normal, except that there were no cats in sight.

"Freud? Skinner?"

He waited, but they didn't appear. He turned on lights, the stereo. He began to be concerned. He started to search. He noticed a drawer in the coffee table ajar. He pulled it open, but couldn't determine if the contents had been disturbed. The oil painting listed just perceptibly—he straightened it. The hall-closet door was open half an inch, though nothing was missing from the closet.

He was aware of becoming hyper-alert, of breathing faster, of his accelerated heart rate. As the search progressed, he began to open doors rapidly, in case someone was hiding inside.

Finally he'd searched every room but the bedroom. He entered cautiously. Nothing seemed amiss. He opened the closet door, fast, relaxing when he found no intruder. He got down to look under the bed. Freud glared out at him. Caleb let his breath out slowly. He stood up and started to undress.

And then he was momentarily terrified as something leapt on him from the top closet shelf. His relief was immediate and profound as he realized he had found B. F. Skinner.

TWENTY-SIX

Somehow it seemed natural that Thinnes would end the day in Uptown, the section he thought of in his head as Little Saigon, where all the shop signs were in Vietnamese, all billboards were in Vietnamese, and all the people seemed to be Vietnamese. Déja vù. It was the part of the city where he felt—as he had in Saigon—that every corner had its hidden watcher, every alleyway its ambush. He stopped the car in front of a porno shop and got out to look.

Jack Daniels's broken body lay in state in the alley mouth, unmourned, beneath a single overhead reflecting dully off the paving bricks. The light developed a pattern underfoot, patched where hollows were leveled with asphalt, glittering with glass shards. On either side, windowless walls of dirty brick rose into darkness without interruption.

The alley dead-ended at the El tracks; he could see blue fire race along the third rail, though the passing train made no sound. A bus lurched to the curb and dropped off passengers without the usual air-brake hiss or studs-on-drums screeching. He could feel his back-hairs rising—no city is ever so totally silent. Was someone walking on his grave?

A blond-wigged young black woman, standing in a storefront doorway to his right, raised her eyebrows and puckered her lips, silently mocking and inviting him. The gaudy neon ADULT VIDEOS sign over her head gave her a ruddy look of good health, but Thinnes could see the yellow whites of her eyes, and the skin of her face seemed stretched too tight under her garish makeup. He showed her the photo of the missing woman, but she leered and shook her head. "Maybe we can work something' out, Sugah." She vanished as he wondered if he'd only imagined she'd spoken.

He heard a bottle drop in the alley, a window open, a car door slam, though nothing could be seen but the everpresent trash. He followed the sounds down the alley, attuned to scurryings and stirrings that weren't actual sounds as much as inklings that things were moving just beyond the edge of sight.

The alley seemed to go on forever. The woman lay at the far, dead end, under a single streetlight, that gave everything a bluish tint and made the edges seem sharper, until it had all gone beyond focused. She was surrounded by a little group of night creatures, crowding over her, peering down at her. In the distance they looked like so many enormous rats, gray and cringing. Thinnes felt more and more uneasy. As he got nearer, the rat people shrank to the size of dogs, then to house-cat size, and when he looked closer, he saw that they **were** rats, red-eyed and lousy. They stood their ground over the woman, over the corpse; the body had no face, only a shocking black emptiness in the strange half-light, where the rats had chewed her face away. He kicked at them, and they gnashed their teeth with sounds like the sharpening of knives. Their eyes glowed like red purgatory lights in a satanic church. He pulled his gun and fired, sending little spurts of flame streaking toward the gray bodies, which jerked and fell but kept swarming deathlessly just beyond the light. He saw—with a sort of helpless shock—that the corpse had Rhonda's hair and Rhonda's body. He felt a mild dismay and was surprised to feel so little.

Suddenly the rats scurried for cover. Thinnes could smell their fear—or maybe his own. He squinted, trying to pierce the darkness beyond the circle of light. Two large yellow eyes peered back. Darkness seemed to condense around the eyes, like an image developing on Polaroid, and a huge cat stepped majestically out of the shadows. It was black, and the eerie light gleamed off every hair and whisker. Powerful muscles bulged and rippled beneath its glossy coat, and its tail whipped back and forth spasmodically. Thinnes felt both terror and fascination. The hand holding his gun hung uselessly at his side.

The cat stopped in front of him and slapped him with a velvet paw, with claws retracted. It stood on hind legs and boxed his head with powerful blows. It began to toss him like a catnip mouse, throwing him skyward like a toy and joyfully shaking him when he fell to earth. The cat started screaming. . . .

"John, wake up!"

Thinnes's eyes stretched wide. Even in the near-dark, he could see fear in Rhonda's face where formerly he would have seen concern.

TWENTY-SEVEN

The assignment officer stopped in front of Thinnes, and Thinnes stopped typing. "We're getting a felony review on the Williams case," Thinnes told him. "And Ray's talking to the state's attorney about a search warrant for that traffic shooting last week. And we got a warrant issued for the Belmont rapist."

"An arrest is imminent?"

"As we speak."

"Good. You got time for a coupla follow-up interviews this morning?"

"Yeah, I guess."

Thinnes's phone started ringing just as Crowne walked up and dropped a pile of folders on the table. Crowne picked up the phone, listened, and said, "Thinnes, you got a visitor. Your wannabe cop's downstairs."

"Who?"

"Dr. Caleb. Said he wants to talk to you."

"Dr. Caleb?" the officer asked Thinnes.

"The citizen who put us onto the Williams thing," Thinnes said. The sergeant nodded. "Check with me when you're ready to go."

Crowne waited until he was out of earshot before he said, "You left out the good part—about Caleb being your prime suspect in the Finley case."

Thinnes shrugged, picking up the phone. "Finley killed himself, remember? The ME said so."

He had just hung up when Caleb arrived. The doctor said, "May I speak with you privately?"

Thinnes nodded and looked for an empty interview room. They

all seemed to be in use. He walked over to tap on Karsch's door. Caleb followed.

"Could I borrow your office?" Thinnes asked Karsch when he opened the door.

Karsch glanced at Caleb. "Surely," he said, and went back inside to get his coffee cup.

Thinnes stepped back to let Karsch pass and then ushered Caleb in, offering him one of the chairs at the end of the room opposite Karsch's desk. They both sat. Thinnes noticed Caleb gave the room a quick once over, fixing on the posters. For the first time, Thinnes noticed they were actually poster-size photos of downtown buildings, not the usual landmarks, just artistic shots of ordinary real estate, signed J.K.

Thinnes said, "What can I do for you, Doctor?"

"Someone was in my apartment while I was out last night."

"Not a burglar, or you'd have called the police." Caleb nodded. Thinnes said, "Go on."

"One or both of my cats always greets me at the door when I come in. Last night, it took me ten minutes to find them." He paused for a second. "They only behave that way when strangers have been in the apartment."

"That's all? Nothing out of place? Nothing broken?"

Caleb shook his head. "I didn't think anything of it last night. I thought perhaps they'd been fighting and were out of sorts."

"So what made you change your mind?"

"How confidential is your investigation?"

Thinnes looked at him speculatively. "Now we're finally getting to the point, aren't we?" Caleb squirmed, and Thinnes shrugged. "If I find out things that aren't pertinent to the case and aren't outright illegal, I keep 'em to myself. That what you mean?"

Caleb nodded, fishing a note from his pocket. "I'm afraid I got fingerprints all over it before I realized . . . " He handed it to Thinnes.

The note said, STOP POKING INTO FINLEY'S AFFAIRS OR YOUR PRIVATE LIFE WILL BECOME VERY PUBLIC.

Blackmail, Thinnes thought. There's a nice motive. He had a cop's contempt for the subject and didn't keep it from his voice as he said, "What's this about? Some little indiscretion with an under-age girl maybe?"

Caleb seemed amused. "Hardly that."

"Or maybe an affair with a client? Strictly theraputic, of course."

Caleb still wasn't offended. "My guess is that someone's about twenty years behind what's going on with the gay community."

A little shock of disappointment jolted Thinnes, and something settled in his gut region like two pounds of lunch meat or like the stone he'd swallowed when he discovered his first detective partner was on the take. You couldn't tell anymore—maybe that accounted for the hostility you felt in spite of yourself. It was too scary when you couldn't tell. As fast as the feeling gripped him, he quashed it.

Caleb met his gaze without apology or defiance, and Thinnes knew the doctor had anticipated and understood his reaction. Another shock stabbed through him as he realized how far out in front of him the shrink was on this. And on what else? He was not used to being outguessed.

He said, "So?"

"I believe there are only two ways to deal with a blackmailer," Caleb said. "And I'm not about to shoot him."

"So why are you telling me?"

"Because when our murderer finds he can't scare me off, he may try to make it appear that I killed Allan because *he* was blackmailing me."

"Unless you *did* kill Finley, and this little blackmail threat is a red herring."

"Why? Why would I kill him?"

"Maybe because he knew about you. It wouldn't help your practice to have it known you're queer."

"Really, Detective, this is the nineties. And I prefer to think of us as sexually left-handed—wired a little differently, but otherwise functionally human." He paused; Thinnes didn't comment.

"It's not a motive for murder these days," he continued. "And if I had killed him, I could think of better red herrings."

109

TWENTY-EIGHT

Caleb managed to put his interview with Thinnes out of mind by the time he arrived at Spaulding House. Things there were unsettled. Rafe had been out of sorts all day—because of Donald, Caleb surmised. Rafe was prepared to have Donald die but not to have him suspended interminably on machines that couldn't mend him. Donald's family wasn't ready to let go. Caleb had had to ask Rafe to leave the hospital to stop him from smashing the machines.

"Goin' to Lou's to get drunk, Jack," Rafe said. "Send someone to get me when it's time."

He meant when Donald was finally gone.

Caleb set to work loading the dishwasher with Paul, gently probing the fears that kept Paul from living out his life.

Brian stuck his head into the room. "Lady to see you, Jack." He made it sound like a smirk.

Caleb dried his hands and went to see whom he was talking about.

The scene in the front room could have been comedic. A woman stood in the center of the room watching Bill and Lenny scramble about, straining to make polite conversation and set her at ease while they unobtrusively straightened up. She seemed bewildered—as if she'd like to call time out but didn't know the vocabulary. Caleb's entrance was like a signal from the ref.

The woman was Donald's mother. She greeted Caleb with relief, and when he made introductions—Brian hadn't offered; Bill and Lenny were too flustered, too embarrassed by the condition of the living room to think of it—she solemnly offered her hand to each of them.

As if the appearance of a mother—anyone's—was a mandate to behave, Brian was suddenly attentive.

"I came to tell you, Dr. Caleb," she said, then, looking around, added, "to tell all of you: Donald died an hour ago. I can't say it's a blessing. It's a relief."

After the commonplace ritual of the handshake, the announcement had a silencing effect.

"You've been more a family to him, these past months, than his blood kin. You have a right to know."

What sort of mother was she? Caleb wondered. No Medea. No Mary of Nazareth either, though the *Pieta*—stone cold—might have been an apt comparison. She was so strangely formal. Someone who'd lived through so much, she hadn't an emotion left to show. Someone who'd reached across the chasm of estrangement too late, perhaps discovered that the rules she'd lived by never had applied—who thought up these outrageous precepts anyway?— and she was too old to easily learn new ones.

The younger men seemed too stunned by her presence and her announcement to act or speak or even register the content of her news.

Caleb asked, "Can we get you anything? Coffee? Or something stronger?"

She gave a small, sad smile. "No, thank you. I have a cab waiting. I just came by to tell you. And to see where he lived." She looked around the room and at each of their faces, then turned and went to the door before any of them could get there to open it for her. She said, "The wake will be Thursday." She didn't say goodbye.

It was Brian who said, "I'll go get Rafe."

TWENTY-NINE

Lincoln Park Zoo. A familiar local reporter was taping her newscast with her minicam crew in front of the old lion house when Thinnes arrived. "We're here at the Lincoln Park Zoo where the Friends of the Zoo are holding a gala benefit to help fund major capital improvements. . . ."

Thinnes merged with the crowd entering the building, which was packed with people dressed to the nines, drinking champagne and sampling the hors d'oeurves being passed around. Tables had been set for dinner. A small orchestra played, and a few couples were dancing. Among the guests, Thinnes could see Vincent Margolis bending the ear of an unhappy Marshall Close. He spotted Lieutenant Evanger in a huddle with some of the top brass, including the superintendent and a couple of the in-house shrinks, Karsch among them. In fact, everybody who was anyone in Chicago was probably there. Rumor had it that the mayor himself would put in an appearance later, at what was billed as a nonpartisan, nonpolitical event.

Dr. Caleb was sipping champagne, studying the snow leopards. As Thinnes watched, an attractive woman in her fifties went up and slipped a hand under his arm. Caleb was obviously startled, but pleased. Thinnes worked his way close enough to hear Caleb tell the woman, "As far as I can tell, cocktail parties attract the greatest assemblages of canines outside the city pound. And anyone who doesn't telegraph his every thought to them makes them very uncomfortable."

The woman laughed. "Your infamous cat-people, dog-people theory. You ought to write it up."

"I may." He seemed to sober and get to the real point. "I was

112

with the police Monday night, when they found a woman who'd been beaten to death."

"Ah."

"They got the man who killed her." Caleb seemed to squirm. "He killed her in front of her five-year-old son. I still can't understand . . . " He shook his head slowly, then seemed to dismiss the thought as he noticed Thinnes.

"Margaret, may I introduce John Thinnes? John, Dr. Margaret Linsey, a colleague."

"How do you do?" she said. "Jack and I were just discussing motivation."

Thinnes nodded and offered her his hand.

"You mean like Freud's theory that everything's motivated by sex?"

"Freud was close," Caleb said mildly.

Thinnes found the conversation suddenly fascinating.

"Power's the primary drive, not sex," Caleb added.

"Really?" Thinnes said.

"It's true. Look around." Caleb gestured with his glass. "All of them trying to get or consolidate or exercise power." He looked pointedly at Vincent Margolis. "Or deprive someone of it."

Suddenly, Anita Margolis appeared at Caleb's elbow, holding a glass of champagne. Her simple black floor-length dress showed off a stunning figure and diamonds—at her wrist and throat and earlobes. Her hair was piled up in glossy curls—she was incredibly beautiful, a woman for whom superlatives had been invented.

"You must be talking about Vincent," she said.

Caleb smiled at her and nodded. "Do you know Dr. Linsey?"

"Margaret. Please."

Anita offered Margaret her hand. "How do you do, Margaret?"

Caleb indicated Thinnes as they shook hands, and Thinnes could hear the gentle irony as he said, "And you know Mr. Thinnes?"

Anita smiled mischievously, offering Thinnes her hand. "We've met. John, isn't it?" Thinnes nodded and shook hands. "I wouldn't have thought this was your sort of party, John."

"I'm just here on business."

Caleb raised an eyebrow.

"Nothing concerning our mutual acquaintance," Thinnes told him. He said to Anita, "You were saying about Vincent?"

She laughed. "Power is Vincent's raison d'etre. I quote: 'I may be more powerful than God, because God is compelled to behave well.' "

Thinnes found himself exchanging glances with Caleb, who appeared amused.

"I rest my case," Caleb said.

Anita waited to be let in on the conversation and, when no one volunteered anything, said, "Is one of you gentlemen going to ask me to dance?"

"Would you like to dance?" Caleb asked her—to Thinnes's surprise. Caleb took her glass and put it with his own on the tray of a passing waiter, then led her to the dance floor. Thinnes watched with great interest.

As they danced, Anita asked Caleb, "Having a good time?"

"Mm-hm."

"But I'll bet you'd rather be dancing with Detective Thinnes."

Caleb smiled. "Not here."

Anita giggled, looking over his shoulder at Thinnes. "He *is* sexy, isn't he?"

"And straight as laser light."

"Light bends, doesn't it?"

"Only around black holes."

She put her face against his chest and said, sadly, "Life's so unfair sometimes." Caleb smiled and held her close. She looked at Thinnes again. "He looks confused."

"Because he still thinks 'homosexual' is synonymous with 'misogynous.' "

"You told him?"

"Mm-hm."

"I suppose he's married."

"Probably. Anyway, he's not your type either."

"Oh?"

"Too obsessive. They say he never gives up on a case."

"Sort of like you?"

THIRTY

It was quite late when Caleb drove the Jaguar into his deserted parking garage. His usual space was occupied, and he drove around looking for another, finally parking some distance from the door. As he walked toward the exit, his footsteps echoed like the sound track in a suspense film. He stopped to look around and listen.

He had almost reached the elevator, sighing with a relief that made him feel sheepish, when two men rose from behind a parked car and blocked his path. Their faces were distorted by the stockings pulled over their heads, their hands hidden by gloves. As Caleb looked sideways for an escape route, they advanced. He feinted and dodged, but there was no room to maneuver in the narrow lane between the parked cars. One of them lunged at his head, the other went for his legs, from behind, with the battering-ram efficiency of a pro tackle. Caleb found himself hitting the pavement, with a small stab of shock that he didn't feel pain.

One of the attackers straddled his back, wrenched his arm behind him and grabbed his hair, jerking his head back, while the other slapped a cloth over his nose and mouth and held it there. A sweet, familiar odor shot a warning through his brain, and he tried to hold his breath. He tried to get his knees under him, to lever the man off his back, but he was no match for two. His chest felt as if it was imploding. When the man holding his arm bounced his full weight on Caleb's spine, he couldn't avoid gasping through the cloth. How very unfair, was his last thought.

Caleb lay face down on his own couch, semicomatose. The single lamp on the end table cast a soft cone of light over the end of the

115

couch, onto the floor beneath it, and on the table itself, spotlighting one untouched line of white powder and the remains of another on the polished wood. The telephone on the other side of the lamp might as well have been in Indiana.

B. F. Skinner strolled into the room and stood on hind legs to rub his face against Caleb's. He jumped onto Caleb's back and sat there, watching the door to the hall. He started to growl. Suddenly a small black comet streaked across the intervening space as Freud leapt onto the other end of the couch. The growls heightened into screams. Freud jumped Skinner, and suddenly a loud fight was in progress on top of Caleb. Clawing and spitting, the cats fell to the floor.

The noise roused him to near wakefulness. He looked at the coffee table without comprehension, but alarm stirred on some deep level, and he groped for the phone. He managed to knock it to the floor before he passed out again. The cats screamed as the fight continued. Caleb's eyes opened and slowly focused on the phone. He reached for it and tried to punch in 911, struggling to remain conscious. He passed out after pressing the second *1*.

"Chicago Police Emergency," the officer answered, but he heard only the growls and screams of cats fighting.

"CHICAGO POLICE. OPEN UP!"

The door burst open, and a uniformed officer charged into the room with his gun drawn. He found Caleb lying comatose on the couch. The cats had disappeared. The officer sheathed his gun as he hurried toward Caleb.

Emergency lights flashed. As fire department paramedics carried Caleb from the building, police officers waved away curious residents and passers-by.

THIRTY-ONE

Ferris was building paper airplanes. Swann was typing. Karsch was making coffee. Crowne was lounging with his feet up on the table, reading the *Tribune*, when Thinnes came in. Ferris gave Thinnes a mocking standing ovation, which he took with scarcely concealed loathing. He looked at Crowne for the explanation.

"If you're gonna miss roll call, you're gonna be the last to know," Crowne told him. He sat up and put his feet down.

Thinnes waited.

"Seriously, you don't know?"

Thinnes sat down, shaking his head. Crowne tossed the Chicagoland section of the Trib onto the desk. The headline read PSYCHIATRIST OD'S. Thinnes read the story aloud.

" 'Prominent local psychiatrist Dr. James Caleb was rushed to Northwestern Memorial Hospital early Thursday morning by fire department paramedics responding to a call from Caleb's apartment. Police speculate that Dr. Caleb managed to dial 911 before collapsing from an overdose of cocaine, but they were unable to question Caleb, who was listed in serious but stable condition. A police spokesman said Caleb is being charged with illegal possession of a controlled substance. . . . ' "

"So you were right about Caleb," Crowne said. "Now all we need is a motive. Maybe this'll help. Finley did the books for Spaulding House, and guess who owns it."

"Margolis?"

"Dr. Caleb!"

"Cozy."

"Thinne-tuition strikes again!" Ferris interjected. "You do lottery numbers, Thinnes?" Thinnes ignored him. "I ran a credit check on this shrink of yours, Thinnes." He handed Thinnes the report and added, "six-figure salary, real estate, stocks, the whole wad."

Thinnes glanced over the paper, and felt vaguely resentful that assholes like Ferris could learn the intimate details of peoples lives so easily. He hid the resentment behind indifference. "You want a medal?"

Ferris started to get mad, pointing to the report. "You telling me that's not important?"

Thinnes shrugged. "There's no law against being rich." He turned to Crowne. "Where's the report on Caleb?"

Crowne gave him a what's-with-you? look, took it from the table in front of him, and dropped it in front of Thinnes. Then he went back to his newspaper.

The top form, filled out in longhand, was the beat cop's report of his response to a 911 call. The second form was typed and signed by Detective Oster, the report of a search of the premises made with a search warrant issued on the strength of the beat cop's report.

While Thinnes was reading, Ferris tried to bait Karsch, who was passing around the coffee he'd been making. "Hey, Karsch, don't you know that stuff causes cancer?"

"Karsch," Crowne said, "maybe you could trade offices with Ferris. You're never in yours anyway. We could put your desk right by the machine, and you could drink coffee till you float away. And we wouldn't have to put up with any more of his shit."

"Maybe both of you should come in my office for a little group therapy."

"Hey, get this guy," Ferris announced. "They upgrade him from consultant to resident irrelevant and he thinks he's one of the cops. Get used to it," he told Karsch. "When this little in-house-shrink experiment's over, they're gonna ship you back to Rent-a-Shrink or wherever they got you."

Crowne shook his head. "Don't worry, Karsch. Even though we

118

don't need a shrink, we'll probably keep you around to make coffee."

Thinnes had been only half listening to the exchange as he studied the reports. He put them down and picked up his phone. "Oster still here? Thinnes." He waited, then said, "Don't you have a home? I got a couple questions about this OD you investigated last night." He listened for a moment, then said "Yeah, okay," and hung up. "He said he's coming back up," Thinnes told Karsch, "cause we got better coffee than he gets at home."

The man who stepped through the doorway a few minutes later was about five eight and heavy. He wore a suit that made him look like an insurance salesman. Thinnes drummed on the tabletop with his fingers as Oster made a beeline for the coffee machine; he stopped when Oster sat down next to him with a cup.

"So what's the story on this OD?" Thinnes asked.

"No story." He pointed to the report in front of Thinnes. "That's all there is. Yuppie shrink ODs on coke. Happens all the time. The only surprising thing is he called 911. Use'ly they just pass out and pass on."

"Says here you found 'a line of a white, powdery substance—possibly cocaine'. . ."

"Very definitely cocaine. Very pure stuff. Somm'a bitch's real lucky to be alive, snortin' that stuff."

". . . And 'a Ziploc bag of a suspicious powder.' "

"One point two-nine grams, to be exact."

"You didn't find anything else?"

Oster shook his head. "That's not enough? Anyway drugs and guns is all we had a warrant for. No guns."

Thinnes looked at the report. "What's this dried plant material?"

"We thought it might be cannabis but it was just oregano and stuff."

"This is pretty fast work for the lab boys, wouldn't you say?"

"You complaining?"

"No, just wondering."

Oster shrugged.

Thinnes asked, "You talk to Caleb?"

Oster shook his head. "Doc said tomorrow. I got better things to do than wait for some cokehead to come round."

"But he's in custody?"

"Not until he's out of intensive care. But I sure got a warrant."

"Who tipped the papers?"

"Sure as hell wasn't me." Oster took another sip of his coffee. "That it?"

"Yeah, thanks."

Oster refilled his cup before he left, as Thinnes was reaching for his phone.

"I just wanted to thank you," Thinnes said, when he had the technician on the line, "for the fast work on this report."

"Waddaya mean?" the technician fairly screamed. "You guys made like it was a matter of losin' the war if you didn't get it yesterday!"

"Not me."

"Well," the technician said, more calmly, "somebody up there was sure hot to have it. Called in before the stuff even got here." He thought about it a minute. "The dick in charge of the case, probably. Mabley wasn't here, but he thinks it might've been Ferris."

Thinnes didn't think it was Ferris and wondered if he should try to trace the call. He said, "Thanks, Buddy. And thank Mabley, too."

THIRTY-TWO

The Fodor's guide describes the Billy Goat Tavern on East Hubbard as a favorite hangout for newspaper types, among others. It wasn't a favorite hangout of cops, whose feelings about reporters were summed up by the detective who said, "Reporters are like mystery writers—they never let facts get in the way of a good story."

Thinnes sat at the bar with his contact from the Trib. Harry was twice as old as he looked, red-haired and freckled. Some of his coworkers called him Jimmy Olsen, which he hated. He liked Thinnes because Thinnes always called him Harry. He was having a grilled cheese and a beer, Thinnes a soft drink and a tuna sandwich.

After the bartender wandered out of earshot, Harry said, "So you're not buying 'cause you love my baby blues. What's it this time?"

"I need to know who tipped you about the 'society shrink' OD."

"Yesterday?"

"Last night."

"I mean, you need to know yesterday?"

Thinnes laughed. "Anything else new?"

Harry caught the eye of the bartender, who gave him an inquiring look. "Use your phone?"

The bartender shrugged and put the phone on the bar. Harry dialed, said, "Thanks," to the bartender and "Dave?" into the phone. "Yeah, I know what time. Listen, I got a rush need-to-know." He nodded as if Dave could see. "Yeah. Who tipped you to that society shrink story?" He listened, then said, "Figures. Thanks, Dave." He put the receiver down. Thinnes didn't try to hurry him as he returned the phone to the bartender. Finally, Harry said, "A Mr. A. Nonymous—frequent contributor. That help?"

Thinnes patted him on the shoulder, putting enough to cover the tab on the bar with his other hand. "Every little bit. Thanks."

THIRTY-THREE

Northwestern Memorial Hospital's cafeteria. Part of the art of detecting is developing contacts. The hours spent waiting at the hospital for someone to sew up a suspect or to interview a victim—who is often reluctant to be victimized a second time by the necessity of answering police questions—are put to use cultivating the hospital staff. Commiserating. Swapping yarns. You can make points with the nurses by buying them coffee once in a while, sometimes just by listening when they have a second to stop and talk. Interns and residents, especially the men, are easy to make up to because their unrelenting schedules, their isolation from the outside world, and long hours with little sleep make them as open to suggestion as POWs. And it's easy to be sympathetic—they're fighting a hopeless war against the forces of death and destruction. Just like the cops. Their checkbooks are usually running on empty too. So buying one of them a decent meal can make you a friend for life and a receiver of all sorts of info.

Having eaten at the Billy Goat, Thinnes had only coffee while the resident had lunch.

"Tell me about this OD you got in last night, a Dr. Caleb."

"Very strange. Possible suicide." Thinnes waited for him to explain. "He had no withdrawal symptoms. And with the blood level of coke he had in him, he should be crawling the walls. But he isn't. He wasn't habituated."

"So he's not a user?"

"I'd say not. And with his background, he should have known what he was taking could kill him. It nearly did."

"He'll recover?"

"Looks like it."

"Any other drugs?"

"Not even alcohol."

"Needle tracks?"

"After the paramedics and the ER staff get through, who could tell?"

"Any chance he was set up?"

"That's your department."

THIRTY-FOUR

When Thinnes sneaked in past the nursing staff, Caleb lay in bed looking very hung over, with tubes in his nose and an IV in his arm. The doctor had a private room, but it was still a hospital room, and it brought Thinnes unpleasant memories.

"You feel up to telling me what happened?" he asked.

Caleb made a face; clearly, he didn't.

"You been advised of your rights?" Thinnes persisted. Caleb nodded. Thinnes indicated he should continue.

"Someone . . ." Caleb took two deep breaths. "No. Two people—I think—grabbed me in my parking garage. . . ." He took another breath. "And held something soaked in ether over my face . . . until I passed out. That's all I remember."

"How do you know it was ether?"

"How do you know a thirty-eight from a forty-five?"

Thinnes nodded. "You ever use cocaine before?"

"Once. I tried it, once, in Nam." He laughed without humor. "I tried everything in Nam."

Thinnes barely hid his surprise. "Since Nam?"

Caleb shook his head, then winced. "Too dangerous."

"You treat any cokeheads?"

"A few."

"Any with a reason to hate you?"

"Every patient hates his therapist at some time in his treatment. But I can't think of anyone in particular right now." He thought about it for a minute. "Does this line of questioning mean I'm off the hook?"

"Hardly," Thinnes said, dryly. Caleb waited for him to elaborate. "I can't think of a better way to remove yourself from the suspect list than by becoming a victim."

"That would be pretty stupid. Even if I'm not convicted of the drug charge, I could lose my license."

"You don't look very worried."

"I've made inquiries about you. They say you're a real Mountie."

"Is that some kind of faggot jargon?"

Caleb wasn't offended. He shook his head, wincing. "They say you always get your man. So why should I worry? *I* didn't kill Allan."

Thinnes nodded, not agreeing especially. "Never the less, Doctor, I advise you to get a good lawyer."

"I have."

"And if you're so convinced I can't hurt you, maybe you wouldn't mind giving me permission to poke around your apartment a bit?" He watched carefully for Caleb's reaction and was ever so slightly taken aback when Caleb seemed pleased.

"Be my guest."

THIRTY-FIVE

Thinnes let himself in and was mildly startled when the cats, waiting at the door for Caleb, scattered.

The living room was in the state of chaos left by the paramedics and evidence technicians. Thinnes went to the center of the room to look around. The bright assortment of colors and periods shouldn't have fit together but did. A painting caught his eye, and he walked over for a closer look. It was a portrait of a good-looking kid in his early twenties. Thinnes studied it a long time. The furniture was of several styles, all solid wood. Thinnes opened a drawer and took note of the dovetail construction. He turned over the edge of one of the oriental rugs to see if it looked machine made. It didn't. The books were all hardcovers, literature mostly, from Dostoyevski to Zola, with a heavy concentration of Americans—Faulkner, Hemingway, and Steinbeck, Cheever, Updike, and Bellow—and a whole shelf of mystery writers—Doyle, Chandler, Hammett, John D. MacDonald and Ross Macdonald— among them many from Chicago—Granger, Paretsky, Turow, Levitsky, Zubro, Bland, and D'Amato. Caleb also had a state-of-the-art sound system, records, and CDs—mostly classical, but with some good jazz and classic sixties, and a smattering of bluegrass, country, and exotic stuff. His liquor cabinet would have put most liquor stores to shame.

The kitchen was a gourmet's delight. As clean as Finley's, it resembled the accountant's in no other way, crowded as it was with the tools of the chef's trade. The refrigerator was stocked with healthy-ingredient-type stuff—tomatoes and alfalfa sprouts and fresh mushrooms—nothing precooked or prepackaged except the all-natural-no-preservatives tacos and a quart of Häagen-Dazs.

One of the cats ventured out, the orange one, and meowed by an empty food dish. Thinnes found what looked like a year's supply of gourmet and prescription cat food in little flat cans. He opened one of them and put it on the floor, stooping to pet the animal as it ate. The sound of the can opener brought a black cat out of hiding, which nearly started a fight. Thinnes opened another can and put it across the room from the first. He put water in the middle.

In the bedroom and bathroom he opened closets and drawers, registering only mild interest at what he found, though the silk sheets made him stop and wonder. The spare bedroom, which was obviously used as an office, had another wall of books, also hard-cover, mostly psychology and medical texts. Thinnes paged through Caleb's appointment calendar. There was no entry for the day of Finley's death. For the Saturday before Finley's death, he found the entry *Mexico*. There was an identical entry for each month of the year. Next to the calendar the kid in the living room portrait smiled from a framed photo that was signed: *Jack, My best always. Love, Chris.*

"Christopher Margolis, I presume." Thinnes said aloud.

He opened all the desk drawers, finding office supplies, utility bills, rent receipts. In one there was a plane ticket for Mexico City. He wrote the particulars in his notebook, and after a last look around he returned to the front door and let himself out.

THIRTY-SIX

The squad room was temporarily deserted when Thinnes got back. He decided to "table" the Finley case. He spread the police, autopsy, and lab reports, plus the photos and street files from the case, out in front of him, trying to find something he'd missed. He'd done the same thing every day, and he'd keep doing it until something jumped out at him.

Finley had been well off for a young man, but with a good salary and no dependents, that wasn't surprising. He'd owned his late-model car outright, paid cash for it. He'd invested a lot of his money in his wardrobe, bought the best and took good care of it. He had a few thousands in stocks, a diversified portfolio, according to his attorney. He'd had fifteen thousand in CDs and five thousand in a passbook account. All of it went to his sister, along with the fifty thousand in life insurance, less burial expenses—which wouldn't be much because Close had offered to pick up the tab. Why? Then again, why not?

What motive could anyone have had to kill him? Not passion. The murderer had displayed too much control for passion. Passion was messy. Passion was careless. According to one and all, Finley had never aroused passion in anyone. If he'd had a wife, she might have reason to kill him, but he didn't have a wife. Even his girlfriend wasn't that close. And he wasn't the sort to be messing with someone else's wife. So it had to be self-interest: Finley knew something or was in a position to find out something that somebody thought was threatening. What? Who?

Thinnes made a note to subpoena Finley's phone records. It was a slim chance—he could just as well have made a call from work or Margolis's office or a pay phone. Or not called anyone. Maybe the killer just thought he *might* go to the cops or to whoever with whatever. Jesus!

The only hope was that the asshole was capable of making stupid mistakes when he was scared. It was a stupid mistake to try to blackmail and kill Dr. Caleb. The killer must have been afraid that if they kept digging, they'd find the whatever. So the thing was to keep digging. And warn Dr. Caleb he'd better butt out.

And speaking of Caleb, he'd better find out about this Mexico thing. Wouldn't do to find out later he was a smuggler or something. He picked up the phone and dialed. "Special Agent James Avery, please." While he waited, he paged through his notebook.

Eventually someone came on the line and Thinnes said, "Avery? Thinnes." He let the name register, then asked, "You remember that favor you owe me?"

The U.S. Customs office at O'Hare Airport is located off the waiting area for the international terminal. Avery's was a typical upper-level government office, with a computer on the desk. James Avery, thirty-five, was a typical, upper-level public servant, GS-12. He was naturally tan and unnaturally blond, and he seemed very fit for a desk jockey. He was on the phone when Thinnes was shown in by his GS-6 secretary. Avery held out his hand for Thinnes to shake, then waved him to a chair. "Yeah. Sure," he told his caller. "You do that. And keep me posted." He hung up the phone. "So, what can I do for you today?" he asked Thinnes.

"Tell me about smugglers."

"You got a couple weeks?"

"You search everyone who comes through?"

Avery shook his head. "We go with hunches a lot. And some people just beg us to nail 'em. Sometimes nervousness or excitement gives 'em away, sometimes little incongruities in their story."

"You keep tabs on frequent flyers?"

"Sure. And people who pay cash for their tickets."

"What have you got on a Dr. James Caleb? That's C-A-L-E-B."

Avery typed the name into his computer, and after a few seconds it beeped. He swung the monitor around so Thinnes could read the entry. "This the guy?" Thinnes nodded. Avery picked up the phone. "Miss Henderson, is Schifflin here? Yeah, thanks," he said, and hung up. "Schifflin's an inspector," he told Thinnes. "He might remember this Caleb."

"You ever check on what people are taking out?"

"Only currency and electronics."

"What about drugs?"

"Just whether they're bringing 'em in. What they take out is someone else's problem."

There was a tap on the door, and Shifflin entered. He looked about eighty years old and walked with a shuffle, but he had very agile eyes. He studied Thinnes as they were introduced.

"Do you remember a Dr. James Caleb?" Thinnes asked him.

"Big fellow? Expensive suits? Goes to Mexico once a month?" Thinnes nodded, impressed. "What about him?"

"You ever search him?"

"Yep. First two times he came through. By the third time, we had him trained to turn his pockets out, so we don't bother anymore. S'waste of time to search everyone."

"You ever ask what he takes out?"

"Drug samples for some clinic he works at down there."

"Have you been checking recently to see if he's bringing drugs in?"

"Should we be?"

THIRTY-SEVEN

Twenty-sixth and California. Cook County Criminal Court. Fourth floor. Caleb stood in the holding room outside the court of Judge Leticia Wilson and listened for his name. Now that he'd been arrested, it was harder to be optimistic about his chance of being cleared, even if Finley's nemesis had slipped up. The frame-up was proof he was treading on someone's heels. Or at least making that someone uncomfortable. Caleb should have felt elated, but he felt only exceptionally tired. The after-effect of a cocaine OD, he told himself, exacerbated by heat and humidity and record ozone levels. Something that would pass.

A hand-lettered sign on the wall said:

> PROCESS TO BOND OUT.
> 1) ASK SHERIFF FOR PAPERS
> 2) GO TO DIVISION #5 AND PAY BOND
> 3) RETURN BOND SLIP TO THE SHERIFF
> 4) BE SEATED AND WAIT
> 5) BOND ROOM HOURS 9:00 AM TO 3:00 AM.

Through the open door to the courtroom, Caleb could hear the judge announce, "probable cause," and set an I-bond of two thousand dollars and a court date in six weeks time.

"Do you understand, Mr. Washington," she asked the defendant, "that a condition of your bond is that you attend every court date? If you fail to appear in court, you can, under Illinois law, be tried and found guilty in your absence. And you could be sentenced in your absence." Caleb couldn't hear the defendant's answer. Shortly Mr. Washington, who looked all of seventeen years old and was dressed in ragged jeans and untied athletic shoes, was escorted back to the holding room by a dark-uniformed sheriff's deputy who was courteous but totally detached. Caleb heard the clerk call, "James Caleb. Detective Oster." The deputy motioned for him to enter the courtroom.

The room was high-ceilinged and walled with travertine marble and had tall windows and genuine dark wood and bronze ornamentation. The floor was green and white linoleum, though a worn carpet covered the half occupied by the Court itself. There was a photocopied sign taped on the bench to the left of the judge's seat that said DO NOT APPROACH CLERK WHILE COURT IS IN SESSION. Above the message, the clerk sat in his brown uniform jacket and passed papers to the judge, who looked like somebody's grandmother, tiny and gray-haired, peering down through her little half-frame reading glasses. When she looked up, Caleb noticed, her eyes were as hard as Justice's, under the blindfold, and impartial as marble.

Harrison, Caleb's attorney, was waiting for him by a heavy wooden table in front of the judge. Another man in a blue business suit stood pawing through a tan metal tote-file on a similar table nearby. Caleb guessed he was the state's attorney, and the seven men seated in the pewlike jury benches were police officers; two wore the regular blue Chicago Police Department uniform, with handcuffs and service revolvers on their belts and name badges and stars on their shirtfronts. The other five, including the detective who'd arrested him, wore slacks and shirts and IDs. And inconspicuous guns. Four of them had ties. Their suit jackets were thrown or neatly folded on the pews nearby. A white-shirted police sergeant sat near the clerk. He seemed to be part of the court, as did a dark-uniformed sheriff's deputy. There were about two dozen people, primarily black people, sitting in the spectators' pews.

The room was hot. The air conditioning couldn't cope with all the radiating bodies, each with its envelope of self-generated steam. A fan set up near the bench served only to rearrange the heat; cops and attorneys, prosecutors and defendants suffered equally. The police had removed their coats and loosened their ties, but the state's attorney and Harrison and Caleb all wore theirs. Caleb wondered why they didn't strip them off in rebellion. Were they too stupefied by the heat to ponder the absurdity of the convention? Even the judge looked slightly wilted in her robe.

When Caleb got to the table, the clerk said, "Dr. Caleb is being charged with possession of a controlled substance." It sounded like something you read about in the paper. It probably wasn't serious enough to send him to prison forever and ever, but it was enough to get his license revoked.

Detective Oster stepped up next to the state's attorney. Except for the gun on his belt and his wary eyes, he looked like a shoe salesman. The judge asked, "Are you the arresting officer?" Oster nodded.

The clerk said, "Raise your right hand. Do you swear to tell the truth, the whole truth, and nothing but the truth, so help you God?"

"I do."

The state's attorney said, "Officer, would you please state your name, star number, and unit of assignment for the record?"

Oster complied. Caleb listened while the state's attorney led him through a recital of how he'd been called to Caleb's apartment to investigate a suspicious substance found when police and para-medics responded to a 911 call. A subsequent search of the apart-ment—with a duly issued warrant—had yielded an additional 1.29 grams of the substance, which the crime lab had since identified as cocaine. Harrison was allowed to ask Oster some questions, but the judge eventually said, "Finding of probable cause. Dr. Caleb, do you understand the charges against you?"

Harrison said, "He does, Your Honor."

"Bond set at fifty thousand dollars. Counselor, you'll advise your client of the seriousness of the charge and the consequences if he doesn't show up in court?"

"Yes, your Honor."

Caleb felt profound uninterest, as if someone else had just been charged. The proceeding was a formality; bail had already been arranged. Harrison was sure he'd get off, and Harrison got paid plenty to know these things. "You're lucky," he'd said. "They could have shipped you to Cermak, or sent uniform cops to put the cuffs on at your place of business, or trucked you down here in a squadrol."

And Caleb agreed. He'd been lucky. County jail was one of those places you read about, then put out of your mind as quickly as possible. One of the great unmanageables, like illiteracy or unemployment. Depressing. He had been lucky. He hadn't been raped. He hadn't been strip-searched, or put in with cellmates like the young toughs in the next pen who made no bones about what they'd like to do with a fat-cat honkey. It was bad enough that they'd cuffed him when they got to the jail. Bad enough to be fingerprinted and photographed and stuck in a holding cell with a drunk. Enough to make you go straight. Even though Detective Oster had been almost deferential.

He wondered about that. After all, as far as the police were concerned, he'd been caught red-handed. Red-handed? Red herring. Caleb hadn't seen Thinnes, but why should he? As far as the police were concerned, this wasn't a crime of violence. He wondered if Thinnes had spoken to Oster, if Thinnes believed him. Maybe they were just giving him more rope.

Then the sheriff's deputy said he could go, and Harrison said he'd meet him in the hall. As he walked out, Caleb looked over the faces of the spectators. How many were reporters? How many were seeking justice? How many the perversion of it?

He spotted Thinnes near the door. The detective must've come in during the hearing. He'd seated himself in the jury pew nearest the holding room door. Thinnes took a key from his pocket and held it up, then tossed it to Caleb, who caught it. It was his apartment key. Thinnes said nothing and his face gave no clue to what he was thinking.

Outside the courthouse the sun filtered through a chemical haze and lay in shimmering mirage pools far down California Avenue. As he and Harrison left the building, the heat hit Caleb like a sedative. Ozone and auto emissions irritated his eyelids like the Sandman's sand. *Nada,* he thought, paraphrasing Hemingway, Nothing. *Nada y nada y nada. Nothing was important.*

Harrison had found a parking space in front of the old ornate entrance of the courthouse, the one that for security reasons was no longer used. They walked toward the car in silence. The attorney unlocked the car, and Caleb, following his example, took his suit coat off and folded it neatly on the center of the seat back. Copycat, Caleb thought. Cats sleep twenty hours a day. Estivate. Curl up and sleep until fall. Let Thinnes take care of the murder, and Harrison the law.

Harrison paused and leaned on the roof of the car before getting in, rapping on it with a knuckle to get Caleb's attention. "This is just bail, Jack. You get so much as a parking ticket, and you'll be back in before you can say help."

Caleb stifled a yawn. *We hold these truths to be self evident . . . Back in. Back in. Back in.* He nodded, feeling as uncoordinated as a drunk. Got to get some sleep. He got in the car. As Harrison pulled out into traffic, Caleb glanced back at the building and saw that far above the average viewer's notice, flanking the statues on their Roman columns, was engraved VERITAS on the left, and on the right, JVSTICIA.

THIRTY-EIGHT

Hey, Mister. Wake up! We're here!"

Caleb snapped awake. He looked up at the funeral home, yawning, and handed the cabbie a twenty. "Keep the change."

The man looked at the bill, then scrambled to get out and open the door. It took a long time for his "Thank you, sir" to penetrate. Caleb's watch said 10:05, but it felt like 4:00 A.M. It was hot. Doubly hot outside the air-conditioned cab. Ninety degrees, at least.

Inside, the funeral home was fittingly chill. Caleb could see the image of Allan's face in his mind's eye more clearly than any trace of Donald in the remains before him. The corpse looked like some waxworks replica of Donald, although they had managed to make him appear at peace.

Caleb hadn't let himself love Donald, so the fact of his death brought him only the impersonal pain of an accident of nature. Acts of God didn't leave him with the feelings of—what? Dread? Anxiety? Depression?—that malice did. He couldn't think of AIDS as maliciously intended, not even the government foot-dragging.

"Ahem." Coming in so quietly, the man startled Caleb. Professional quiet. "Sorry to disturb you, sir, but I'm afraid . . . It's time . . ."

Time to close the case on Donald. Literally. Caleb nodded and stepped back to let the man get on with it.

They were short a pallbearer; one of Donald's cousins was late or had decided against coming. The funeral director ahemmed and er'ed until Caleb volunteered. The others seemed relieved that they could finally get it over with.

The family—Donald's mother, sister, and brothers—was waiting at the church, closed like sealed caskets to all but the most superficial expressions of sympathy. Having known Donald, Caleb felt he knew them and couldn't feel much empathy, only a professional interest. Donald had been dead to them so long that this present burial was like a reinterment, socially discomforting more than cause for deep anguish. Caleb thought again of Allan, who lay unclaimed in the morgue, whose family wouldn't be prepared, whose sister had no one left.

He found it impossible to stay awake during the service. Sitting, standing, and kneeling like an automaton, he dozed, dreaming disquieting dreams forgotten before waking. Each catnap ended with a start and the fear that his inattention had been noticed.

At the cemetery, the August heat pressed all feeling but discomfort from the mourners. Caleb fought the urge to stretch out on the grass. The service seemed like a charade or a rehearsal for the death of someone truly cherished.

Someone like Chris.

Caleb felt a wave of anxiety flooding through him. Death. Empty. Awful. Permanent.

He'd gone to the morgue that night, talked his way in. He'd made himself look. And realize. And believe.

The wake had been for Anita, who'd loved Chris too. And in a mundane, human way, for Margolis, who'd stared all night like a catatonic at the closed casket—Chris closed to him in death as in life.

The day of the funeral had been cool and cloudless and brilliant—spring green and crystal blue—with an intensity that hurt the eyes. A day of superlatives. The private funeral, ironically—family only.

Stop it! Caleb told himself. *Just stop!*

THIRTY-NINE

A lanky, sandy-haired teen was staring into the fish tank when Caleb came out of his office with a client. The boy looked vaguely familiar. Irene waited until Caleb closed the outer door behind the man, then said, "Dr. Caleb, this young man has been waiting to see you. He didn't have an appointment, but he says it's urgent."

On this cue, the boy came toward him and shoved his hand out. "Dr. Caleb, I'm Rob Thinnes."

Caleb shook the hand. "How do you do?" The boy favored his father to a degree that made Caleb feel they'd met before. Déjà vu. Caleb indicated his office door. "Shall we talk in my office?"

Rob seemed relieved. "Sure."

As they crossed the room, Caleb told Irene, "You can take off, Mrs. Sleighton. I'll lock up."

Rob waited nervously by the door until Caleb followed him in and pointed to a chair. "Sit down, Rob." He sat, and Caleb sat opposite. "What can I do for you?"

"My dad's seeing you, right?"

"What makes you think that?"

"I found your card on his dresser."

"One of my clients was murdered. Your father's working on the case."

"Damm it! My dad needs help. I thought . . . I hoped . . ."

"Why did you come to me?"

"My folks had a big fight today, and Ma walked out. She made me go with . . ." Caleb continued to look interested and to wait. "I mean, she told me to come, and he didn't tell me to stay . . ." Rob shrugged, then said, defensively, "What would you do?" He looked down at his hands, which promised great size one day.

"Probably what you did. How did you think I could help?"

"I don't know. I thought . . ." Rob looked up, imploring. "If you were treating my dad . . . I just thought you ought to know." He slouched back in his seat, unable to hide his disappointment.

"Have you told your father how you feel?"

"I tried, but adults never listen to kids, especially if it's something they don't want to hear. He just says, 'Don't worry about it.' "

"And?"

"He's got a gun—and every once in a while some cop goes wacko and shoots himself or something," he finished in a rush.

"You think he's suicidal?"

"I don't know. My mom said he's afraid to go to the police shrink. I tried calling—the phone's busy. I think he took it off the hook."

"Would you like me to drive over and see if he's okay?"

"Would you?"

FORTY

Thinnes's battered Chevy was in the drive. Caleb pulled the Jaguar in behind it and got out. He rang the doorbell. No one answered. No one answered his knock. He fished the key Rob had given him from his pocket and let himself in.

The entryway struck him as typically middle class, midwestern, middle American. Caleb closed the door quietly and called out, "Detective Thinnes? John?" He glanced up the stairs and peered into the family room, then walked through the living–dining room to the kitchen. The house had a deserted air. Caleb felt the discomfort appropriate for a man invading a comparative stranger's home under peculiar circumstances.

The kitchen was clean and empty. He noted the bright curtains, the carefully matched wallpaper, the cosseted houseplants, and the real, if aging, rose in the bud-vase on the table. He began to have serious doubts about his motives.

Coming uninvited into the heart of a stranger's family-place seems an invasion. What am I really doing here? What is it about Thinnes that is so engaging?

Through the open door on the far side of the room he could see utility sinks and, moving closer, a washer and dryer. The light in the utility room was off. He entered and felt for the light switch. Through the half open door of an adjoining lavatory, he could see a sink and, on the floor, the lower half of a man's body. Alarmed, he ran and pushed the door open and switched on the light. Thinnes was lying with his head near the toilet, in a pool of vomit. Caleb hurriedly felt for a carotid pulse and relaxed when he found one. He grabbed for a towel.

*   *   *

141

Later he came into the kitchen with his jacket and tie removed and his sleeves rolled. The phone was off the hook. Wiping his hands on a towel, he hung the phone up, then lifted the receiver and dialed. He checked the contents of the refrigerator as he waited, extracting a beer, and when the phone was answered, he said, "Hello. Rob Thinnes please. Thank you." While he waited, he sipped the beer, then opened the broom closet and extracted a mop. Rob came on the line.

"Rob? This is Dr. Caleb. He's okay. No, asleep." Caleb removed a pail and cleanser from a cabinet as he spoke, and began to fill the pail with water. "He had too much to drink, but he'll be okay."

FORTY-ONE

Thinnes felt gray. He came down the stairs dressed only in Levi's, very hung over. As he reached the bottom, he heard something out of the ordinary and was instantly alert. He quietly opened the closet door and reached his holstered .38 down from the top shelf. He took out the gun, silently laid the empty holster on the stairs, and entered the family room.

The room had a fireplace with a large console TV set next to it. The TV was flanked by comfortable chairs and had a couch opposite. A coffee table in front of the couch displayed magazines. There was a man sitting on the couch, back to the door, paging through the Thinnes family album. Shaking from both the hangover and rage at finding a stranger in his house, Thinnes stepped into the room and assumed a firing position. He aimed the gun at the back of the man's head, cocking it.

"Freeze!"

Caleb jerked around on the couch.

Thinnes was not sure who was more surprised. His shaking became worse as he lowered the gun, easing the hammer back in place. "What the hell are you doing here?"

Caleb let his breath out. "Your son asked me to look in."

"Why you?"

"He found my business card and drew the wrong conclusion."

Thinnes let the hand holding the gun drop to his side as he leaned against the doorjamb. "How long you been here?"

"Since last night. I'm afraid your reputation is hopelessly compromised."

"What the . . . ?" Thinnes felt his butt pucker and his skin crawl, and he knew the sudden fear and disgust nearly overwhelming him were as obvious to Caleb as Caleb's momentary contempt was to him. Then he realized he was being razzed and began to be angry.

"Don't worry," Caleb continued, "I didn't take any liberties." As Thinnes relaxed, he added dryly, "Far worse. I've been probing your psyche." He pointed to the album.

"You think you got me pegged?"

"No."

"You think you know why I got drunk?" Thinnes opened a small drawer in the coffee table and pulled out a pack of five-by-seven glossy photos. He looked at the top print, then tapped the pack against his thigh. "You study these while you were snoopin' around?"

"No . . ."

"My walking papers. Forged, but they'll do the job." He tossed the photos on the table. Caleb picked them up. They showed Thinnes and a woman, both naked, making love. Caleb glanced through them without comment. "My wife's divorcing me," Thinnes said. "After seventeen years." He shook his head. "Women!"

"Stop thinking like a fucking macho shithead prick and start thinking like a cop."

"Huh?" The clumsy obscenity made Thinnes laugh. He grabbed his head and, almost with a grin, said, "Fuck you."

Caleb grinned back suggestively. "Really?"

Thinnes laughed again, heartily this time, then groaned and held his head. "What's your point?"

"Why did your wife just happen to get those pictures now?"

"My guess is some bastard where she works has had his eye on her, and figured those . . ." he pointed to the pictures, ". . . would be all it would take for her to cut me loose." As Caleb thought about it, Thinnes added, "As to why now, Murphy's law. Whatever can fuck up *will*, at the worst possible time."

"Pfui! That kind of coincidence happens only in inept fiction." To Thinnes's discomfort, Caleb started to look over the photos carefully. "How reasonable is your wife?"

"Why?"

"I don't know much about photography, but I've got a friend in the business. If he could demonstrate how these were faked, would she buy it?"

"Probably."

"Good. I'll get in touch with him, and call you."

"What do you get out of all this?"

"I might need a traffic ticket fixed sometime."

"Don't count on it."

FORTY-TWO

Thinnes didn't feel much better that afternoon as he waited by the hydrant in front of Caleb's building. His dis-ease wasn't a result of the hangover that'd left him feeling leaden and strung out and battered; the two-pound weight in his gut was due mainly to the gradual awareness of the position he was in after yesterday's bender. The prime suspect in a murder investigation had spent the night in his house and was preparing to help him resolve a personal, domestic problem. Thinnes shuddered and considered calling the expedition off. But what the hell. Might as well buy the whole nine yards. If he took the photos to the cops and forensics couldn't prove they were fakes, his position in the department would be compromised anyway. And Ronnie would still walk. Ronnie was about the only thing in the universe he'd put his job on the line for. Even if the lab boys did prove the shots were faked, he'd never hear the end of it. This way, if Caleb's buddy struck out, he could still quietly plead no contest to the divorce and at least save face and his job.

Unless Caleb killed Finley. The doctor's eagerness to help might just be motivated by the desire to put Thinnes in his debt, so that he'd keep quiet about Caleb being a fag.

If he really was a fag. Thinnes thought back over the encounters he'd had with Caleb and tried unsuccessfully to think of a gesture or phrase, even a glance at a passing man that'd confirm the doctor's claim. He couldn't see a reason why Caleb would say he was gay if he wasn't, but forty could be one. That was the trouble with a case like this; by the time you figured it all out, all the hidden motives, you could be in deep shit. Up to your ass-hole.

He cursed the impulse that had made him even consider trusting Caleb. Better forget the whole idea and let Oster look into this. He started the engine and was about to pull away when the passenger door opened and Caleb slid into the seat.

Caleb said, "North Halsted Street."

After driving for a mile, Thinnes gave up trying to figure a way to phrase the question delicately. "Why?" he asked. "Even if you're on the level, why go out of your way to help someone who may be trying to pin a murder rap on you?"

"I didn't murder anyone."

"Protestations of innocence are so convincing."

"Maybe because there are no innocents. But Allan was honest and conscientious. I can't believe I'd be so inept as to miss it if he was blackmailing someone, or stealing, or suicidal."

"You got any new thoughts on the killer?"

"In the movies, it always turns out to be some homicidal sociopath—who just happens to be smarter than the cops. But real mentally ill people usually aren't capable of planning a grocery list. I'm not an expert on murderers, but I imagine real-life killers are motivated by mundane vices—greed or anger or fear of ruin."

Thinnes nodded.

"Someone who deliberately plans a murder and commits it in cold blood cuts himself off from the rest of us as radically as does the suicide. Dostoyevski wrote a whole classic novel about how the average man can't do it."

"So we're looking for a professional killer?"

"They don't usually try to make murder look like suicide, do they?"

"No. Word around is Finley killed himself."

"You and I know better." When Thinnes didn't answer, he added, "In answer to your original question, I want to help because I want you to succeed."

As he turned onto Halsted, Thinnes said, "Even if this works, she'll probably dump me."

"She's found someone else?"

"Naw. Oh, hell. I don't know. I don't think so. But she's suddenly got this career. . . ."

Caleb nodded. "You know, you can't hold on to a cat—they hate it—but if you let go and just sit tight, most of them will eventually climb into your lap."

"What's your point? What's that got to do with anything?"

"Some women are a lot like cats."

"*You'd* know a lot about women."

"It's my job. And I may have a more objective viewpoint."

Thinnes conceded the point grudgingly. "It sounds like the old sixties bullshit—'if you love something, let it go.' "

"How do you think these things get to be clichés?"

"You telling me I ought to just give up and kiss her off?"

"No. But you could try thinking of her not just as your wife, but as an adult human with needs and aspirations that may differ from yours. How do you get along with Crowne?"

"Just fine. Don't change the subject."

"I'm not. Do you assume you know what he wants or what's bugging him?"

"I ask."

"And you ask your wife?"

"Yeah, sure. She just jumps down my throat."

"*How* do you ask?"

"Oh, for chrissake!"

Caleb smiled as if he'd made his point. "It seems to me that your problem with your wife is a bit like Allan's death—not quite what it seems. You might try applying your professional skills to your personal problems."

"You trying to make me feel uncomfortable?"

"I'm trying to make you think, which for most people is synonymous with being uncomfortable."

Thinnes didn't have to think about that.

FORTY-THREE

Jeremy's was one of those little specialty studio-shops set up in rehabbed houses on Halsted south of Diversey. The sign was microscopic; and you wouldn't notice it if you weren't looking for it. The shop was the sort of place where you could have pictures framed; browse through framed prints by the next Ansel Adams; find how-to books or photographic trivia; or stock up on camera supplies with instructions or tips or history thrown in at no extra charge. According to Caleb, Jeremy didn't have to advertise; word of mouth brought in all the business he could handle.

When Thinnes and Caleb arrived, a young man stood behind the counter next to the cash register studying a college text. He greeted Caleb and waved them to a doorway at the rear of the shop. They found their path blocked by a white pit bull—stained gray with what was probably printers' ink—that was stretched out in the doorway on sheets of *The Reader*. Caleb said, "Jeb, move," but he didn't. He didn't even open an eye as they stepped over him. Thinnes imagined they didn't have trouble with shoplifters.

The studio itself was a loftlike space created by gutting the old house's interior. Residential rooms off a balcony above were reached by a wrought iron spiral stairs. The work area below was divided, by movable walls, into spaces for photographing, matting, and framing. The door labeled DARK ROOM had a naked light bulb above it and a sign next to the doorknob that said DO NOT OPEN DOOR WHILE LIGHT IS ON.

A rail thin man in his early twenties was cutting a mat at a table with his back to the entrance. He was wearing only a pair of carpenter's overalls. His hair was the color of Rhonda's, dingy blond; it came past his shoulders and was tied back in a ponytail.

He didn't look up to see who'd come in. "Be with you in a minute."

Caleb walked up and put an arm around him, startling him, but when he saw who it was, he relaxed and gave Caleb a hug and a kiss. Thinnes was startled to be reminded so graphically that Caleb was gay. He felt himself blush. Caleb pretended not to notice. He pointed at Thinnes, then at the skinny man.

"John. My friend, Jeremy."

Jeremy eyed Thinnes speculatively as they shook hands. When Caleb elbowed him in the chest and shoved the compromising photos at him, he barely glanced at them. The subject matter obviously held no interest, and beyond the obligatory smirk, he had no particular interest in having fun at the expense of a stranger. "I see," he said.

Caleb tapped the hand holding the photos. "No, you don't. John didn't pose for those. They could be faked?"

"Anything could be faked. Except a hard-on."

Caleb laughed; Thinnes squirmed. Jeremy looked at the photos again, this time carefully. He nodded. "A piece of cake."

"Educate us."

"You start with your base photo . . ." He looked at the photos again, then crossed the room to take a loose-leaf notebook from a shelf. He paged through it until he found what he wanted and showed it to Caleb. "Picture number one."

Caleb showed it to Thinnes—two curvaceous females in bikinis, standing arm in arm on a beach. The photo had an index number on the side. Jeremy put the book away and got the negative with its corresponding index number from a file cabinet. He put the negative in his pocket, picked up a businesslike Nikon, and pointed it at Caleb. "I'll also need a couple of mug shots." He shot Caleb, then shot Thinnes before he could protest. Then he advanced the film and took it from the camera. As he went toward the darkroom he said, "Make yourselves at home." The light above the darkroom door went on as he closed it.

Thinnes prowled around impatiently while they waited; Caleb studied the picture Jeremy'd been matting.

After about twenty minutes, Jeremy called through the darkroom door, "Jack, be a love and get me a wine cooler, will you? And something for John and yourself."

"Surely," Caleb called back and he went off up the spiral stairs.

A framed photo on the wall caught Thinnes's eye, and he took it down for a closer look. It showed Caleb with a young man resembling Jeremy—an older brother maybe—and a third man. All three were in combat fatigues, arms around one another's necks, laughing. He was still studying the picture when Jeremy came out of the darkroom.

Jeremy eyed the object of Thinnes's interest. "You can't let Jack's wimpy exterior fool you. He left Nam with a couple medals and a fist full of citations."

"Somehow I can't picture him carrying a gun."

At that moment Caleb returned with wine coolers and a beer. "I didn't. I carried a stretcher."

Jeremy gave him a wry smile. "Touchy!"

Caleb handed the beer to Thinnes and one of the coolers to Jeremy, asking, "How's it going?"

Jeremy said, "That reminds me . . ." and dodged back into the darkroom. He came out minutes later with a dripping wet eight-by-ten print. "Here you are, gents."

The print showed the two curvaceous females depicted earlier, now sporting Caleb's and Thinnes's heads. Neither Caleb nor Thinnes could resist laughing.

"I ought to charge you double time for Sunday work."

"I thought you artistes charge by the print," Caleb said.

"That's right. If this is to be a limited edition, it could cost . . ." He noticed Thinnes's face and stopped.

The banter was getting on his nerves.

Jeremy shrugged. "Forget it."

"You done anything like this for anyone else lately?" Thinnes asked.

"Not since high school," Jeremy said defensively.

Caleb put an arm around his neck, and said, "Loosen up." He relaxed and Thinnes eased up. "Someone's trying to come between John and his missus. Naturally, he's a little sore."

"Naturally." Jeremy didn't try to hide the sarcasm.

"And he's anxious to know whom he should thank for those charming candid shots."

Jeremy nodded in a way that echoed *naturally*. "Well, the only one I can think of takes a dim view of that kind of recommendation."

Caleb raised an eyebrow; Jeremy shrugged. "They say he carries a very popular line of kiddie porn. He runs a sleazy joint on Broadway. Name's Berringer . . ."

FORTY-FOUR

Thinnes," the desk sergeant said, "see Keys." Keys was District Nineteen's acting community relations officer while the regular guy was on vacation. Thinnes made a left down the corridor leading to the district offices. The CR office was on the right. The room was too small for the three desks crammed into it. Keys was sitting at one of them. The relieved look on his face when Thinnes came through the door must've given the woman sitting across the desk from him a cue. She stood and faced him.

"Detective Thinnes?"

Caucasian, five two, 110 pounds, blue eyes, strawberry blond. Shell-shocked. Her face was puffy and lined. Thinnes had seen the face before.

"Ms. Finley."

He decided he'd be the bad guy. Since he wasn't dealing with a career criminal or a likely suspect, he'd only have to be moderately officious. Crowne, who was closer in age, could offer her coffee and sympathy.

"See if you can locate Ray Crowne for me, would you?" Thinnes asked Keys. "We'll use one of your interview rooms." He meant one of the district's rooms, which were less stark than those upstairs in Area Six. "Miss Finley, if you'll come with me . . ."

He waited for her to precede him into the hall, then passed her. He led her across the District Nineteen lobby, into the corridor leading to the lockup. He waved her into one of the interview rooms opening on the corridor. It was small; the table and chairs took up most of the space. She edged around the table and turned to face him. Thinnes closed the door.

Soften her up first. "I'm sorry about your brother, Miss Finley."

She sucked her lower lip and nodded, as if unable to answer. Fighting tears.

Thinnes was unmoved. He'd learned to ignore women's tears. They seemed to be something all women used—like they used makeup or bras. Some cried as easily and thoughtlessly as they talked. One of the things Thinnes loved about Rhonda was that she never used tears against him.

He mentally reviewed the data NYPD had faxed him. She was twenty-seven and made a hundred grand a year as a commodities broker. Very sharp woman. Nothing, in fact, like the sniffling wreck before him. So you watch. You wait for the actress to blow her lines. If she doesn't, maybe she's not acting. Maybe she's just very good.

"Can you give me any reason your brother would kill himself, Miss Finnley?"

"He wouldn't! He couldn't have!"

"He was found shot to death in his apartment with the door locked from the inside. Nothing was out of place. Nothing was missing. He doesn't seem to have had any enemies. We gotta go with the evidence."

"Someone must have killed him and locked the door on the way out."

"Who?"

"I don't know."

"And why?"

"That's what you're supposed to find out. You're the detective."

That didn't sound like a murderer talking. If she'd had him killed, she might be delighted to have the cops write it off as suicide. It wasn't likely she was planning on a big insurance payoff; she made more in six months than Finley's policy would pay. She'd hardly risk ruin for that. Thinnes decided to get the rest of the formalities over with and go back to work. He wished Crowne would show. "When was the last time you saw him?" he asked.

"At Christmas."

"Talk to him since then?"

"Just before I left for vacation. And he was *fine*."

There was a knock on the door. Thinnes excused himself and went out.

Crowne said, "What's up."

"Finley's sister's here." Thinnes thumbed in her direction. "I've let her jump to the conclusion that I think he killed himself. Why don't I leave the two of you alone and you can tell her you think he didn't. See what happens."

"You're nuts, Thinnes."

Thinnes waited.

"Okay. Whatever you say."

They went into the room and Thinnes introduced Crowne.

Crowne said, "I'm really sorry about your brother, Miss Finley."

Thinnes thought she looked like she was tired of hearing it. He said, "Excuse me a minute," and went out.

He stuck his head in Karsch's office and said, "Karsch, Finley's sister's here."

"Finley?"

"The murder victim the ME wrote off as a suicide."

"Ah."

"Do you think you could talk to her or something?"

"Of course, if she wants me to. But I don't think it's a good idea to mention murder without proof."

Thinnes laughed humorlessly. "Maybe murder's not the greatest way to go, but if it was my brother, I'd damn sure rather know he didn't kill himself, even if the cops never get the guy. Besides, what's the difference what she thinks if it makes her happy?"

"Just that if you can't come up with a killer, she may make the department her scapegoat. In which case you'll look pretty foolish."

Thinnes shook his head. "You've been spending too much time with Evanger—you're getting to sound just like him. Anyway, I'll take the chance."

"Tell her I'd be happy to speak with her. But don't pressure her."

"Yeah. Thanks."

Thinnes went back downstairs to the interview room and closed the door behind him before he said, "Miss Finley, we have a counselor here, a psychologist. If you feel like talking."

She took a deep breath and said, "I'd rather just get on with the arrangements."

Crowne said, "Is there anything we can do to help?" She shook her head. "Do you have any questions?"

"Will I have to identify him?"

"No, his landlord did that. You'll have to make arrangements for the—for his remains." Crowne couldn't seem to bring himself to say *body*.

"You *will* have to talk to the medical examiner," Thinnes said.

Crowne added, "Your brother's employer, Mr. Close, offered to help out, so maybe you'd like to see him first."

"Do you have a car?" Thinnes asked.

"No. I took a cab from the airport."

"Detective Crowne will drive you wherever you have to go."

"Thank you." She looked at Crowne when she said it.

FORTY-FIVE

Thinnes spent most of the rest of the day working on other cases, carefully not thinking about his domestic affairs. He was putting the finishing touches on the last report when the desk sergeant phoned upstairs, "Woman to see you, Thinnes. On her way up." Thirty seconds later, Bettina Calder came through the door. The WR&C office manager spotted Thinnes and stalked over to his table. A woman with a mission. Or an axe to grind.

Thinnes stood and said mildly, "Miss Calder."

They sat down and she started in the middle. "I was on my way home—I had to stop at the Newberry Library, so I thought I'd save you coming to the office. I may have found something."

He wondered why she hadn't phoned.

"It's probably nothing, but you said to let you know if anything unusual turned up." Her grammar and pronunciation were carefully perfect. A sign she was insecure?

"Well?"

"A few days before Allan died, he and Miss Baynes traded jobs without telling me."

She didn't emphasize the "without telling me," but Thinnes knew that was the point. Crowne was defensive that way when dealing with someone like Margolis, who didn't take Crowne's authority seriously. He wondered if Calder's preoccupation with authority had anything to do with the fact that she was black and Alicia Baynes was white. He said, "Could you explain that?"

"I can't. I mean, I can't explain why they did it. I wouldn't have known, except Allan signed the report Alicia was supposed to turn in. She signed his name on his report. She admitted that."

"That commonly done?"

157

"It's highly irregular, possibly illegal."

"You told Mr. Close?"

"Of course. He said to forget it. He said he would take care of it. I noticed the discrepancy when I was doing my billing. We are about a week behind because of Allan's death or I would have noticed it sooner. Allan's name, not Alicia's, was on the statement." Thinnes nodded, encouraging her to go on. "Alicia said Allan asked her to trade, and she signed his name because it was his job. She said he wouldn't say *why* he wanted her to trade. It was not like Allan, and I told her so."

"What'd she say to that?"

"That shooting himself wasn't like Allan either."

"It's possible she's right."

She snorted. "And it's possible I'll win the lottery."

"I'll have a talk with her. Will she be in tomorrow?"

"No. She sweet-talked Mr. Close into giving her the rest of the week off. To recover from Allan's death."

"I see." He did see. Plainly, there was no love lost between the two women. "Well, maybe I can get her at home."

"If not, she might be at the service Mr. Close has arranged for Wednesday evening. Allan's sister came to the office this morning, and Mr. Close helped her arrange a memorial service for him."

She gave him the address and the time, and Thinnes walked her out to her car, mainly because he wanted to get a look at it and save contacting the DMV for her licence plate number. Probably irrelevant, but you never know.

He decided to give Alicia Baynes a call before he left for the day. If she was in, he might be able to stop on his way home. There was no answer. He was just leaving the building when the desk sergeant called him back.

"Thinnes, a *Ms.* Margolis on the line."

FORTY-SIX

Thinnes parked in the no-parking zone in front of the glass doors. He put his four-ways on and flipped the OFFICIAL POLICE BUSINESS sign onto the dash. When he tapped on the glass, Anita Margolis opened the door and held it for him, and then locked it behind him.

"That was quick," she said as they walked toward the back. "It can't have been twenty minutes since I called."

She'd called because he'd mentioned he'd like to see one of the bohemian's paintings before she turned it over to Margolis. "Have you ever inspected one carefully?" he asked.

"Well, no. Customs is supposed to check the crates for contraband and make sure what's on the bill of lading is what's in the crate. And they come with certificates of authenticity. The paintings themselves are too awful to study closely."

In the office, Anita pointed to a table bearing a shallow wooden crate, about four feet square, covered with labels and bearing a U.S. Customs stamp. "There it is. I haven't called him yet to let him know it's arrived."

"Mind if we open it?"

"Be my guest." She dug a pry-bar out of the clutter beneath the table.

Thinnes took it and started in on the crate, then stopped. "Who was Christopher Margolis?"

She appeared startled by the abrupt change of subject but answered steadily, "Technically my stepson. Vincent's only child."

"How did he die?"

"In a car accident."

She took up the pry-bar and attacked the crate. Thinnes waited for her to elaborate. "It was such a waste," she said, sadly. "He was a wild boy—typical poor little rich kid whose father was willing to spend anything on him but time. So eventually he got into drugs, and trouble . . ." She kept working as she spoke. Thinnes helped without distracting her. "Then he met Jack Caleb. Jack gave him a chance to kick the drugs and find something to do with his life. Instead of being grateful, Vincent resented it."

"You said helping suicidal people is Jack's specialty. Was Chris suicidal?"

"No. I was."

Thinnes was surprised.

She smiled sadly. "Eight and a half years ago, I had a mastectomy and went to pieces. Suicidal depression—the depths. After I OD'd on pills, Jack was called in to consult. He's one of the few shrinks with the guts to treat suicides." She shrugged. "Anyway, my doctor wanted to try electroconvulsive therapy. Jack was against it—it can cause memory loss—and he fought for me. When I made a second attempt, instead of caving in to Vincent and his appearances-first shrink, Jack pointed out that I'd had to get enormously less depressed just to make the attempt. With Jack's help, I recovered. I even got strong enough to leave Vincent."

Thinnes smiled, almost in spite of himself. He felt again an attraction to her that was almost as strong as what he felt for Ronnie. He curbed the urge immediately. He was wise enough to know that the opposite of love isn't hate but indifference. He knew Ronnie didn't hate him, but she was growing daily more indifferent. An affair would be one more item for the account she kept in her head. She wouldn't throw it in his face in an argument—she wouldn't even argue—but the weight of it would add to the heavy silence between them and the long list of what couldn't be explained.

He remembered his original line of questioning. "Tell me about the accident."

She sighed. "Chris and Vincent had a terrific row, and Vincent told Chris that if he wouldn't carry on the Margolis family tradition—by which he meant his little financial empire—he never wanted to see him again. Chris drove away mad and wrapped his car around a tree. None of us has quite recovered." To hide the tears filling her eyes, she got very busy pulling the painting out of the crate.

"Pardon me, but were you lovers?"

"Chris and I? No, just friends. Kindred spirits—we had Vincent in common. And if he'd lived, Chris would have been one of our best contemporary painters." She took the final wrapping off the Bohemian's painting to reveal a hideous impasto done on wood. She shuddered. *"Et voila."*

He grinned. "Would you mind looking it over carefully to see if there's anything peculiar about it—apart from the painter's taste?"

She shrugged and examined the picture, which was on wood.

He tapped the back. "Is it unusual for a painting to be on wood like this?"

"Not when the paint's applied with a trowel." She looked closer at one corner. "Here's something strange." She pointed. "It looks like he put shrink wrap *under* the paint."

"Why?"

"No reason I know of." She got a letter opener from her desk and pried a large chunk of paint off one edge, exposing a very different painting beneath the wrap.

Thinnes was fascinated. "Very ingenious."

"The bastard!"

"What is it?"

"I don't know, but I'll bet it's stolen." She rummaged through her desk until she found a typed list. "Here it is. The number to call if you see one of these stolen works."

"Maybe you'd better let me take over from here."

She nodded and handed him the list, and stepped away from the phone. Thinnes picked it up and dialed.

Two hours later, it was Anita Margolis who dialed. Across the room, her phone call was being recorded. Thinnes and Detective Oster, a customs agent, and a man from the FBI were in the room listening in.

"Mr. Margolis, please. *Ms.* Marglis calling. . . . Vincent? Your latest atrocity has arrived. It looks as if it's been damaged, although I admit, it's hard to tell. Shall I send it back?" She frowned at Margolis's answer. "I'll be here for another half hour."

Later Thinnes watched her watch Vincent Margolis as he and an assistant loaded the crated painting into the back of a van. They got in and drove off. Thinnes pulled the unmarked car into traffic after them.

FORTY-SEVEN

Uptown again. Thinnes parked next to a hydrant on Broadway and kept the motor running as he slouched down to watch Oster in his rearview mirror. Oster was inside the XXX-Adult-Movies-Latest-Videos store, standing with his back to the glass storefront with its perpetually closed burglar gates, thumbing through a lurid magazine. He was waiting for someone. He seemed nervous.

The man who entered the shop from the back was tall and dark-skinned, and fat, with a Miami Vice shave and a short, shiny ponytail. Berringer. He shoved a brown paper package into Oster's hands. Oster slipped Berringer a wad of bills and scurried out of the store, getting away as fast as a happily married suburbanite would. In the unmarked car, Thinnes followed Oster around the corner. When he was sure Oster hadn't been tailed, he curbed the car and Oster climbed in.

He was ecstatic as he held up the package. "With any luck, this is all we'll need to get the warrant."

"Let's do this right," Thinnes said. "Let's see if Berringer has a warehouse where he stores the stuff. And maybe we can get a blueprint so we know the layout before we go in."

When they were almost back to HQ, Oster said, "Look on the bright side, Thinnes. "It could'a been worse if Evanger got those pictures instead of your wife."

"I'd rather he had. Ronnie was looking for an excuse to bail out. The worst Evanger can do is fire me. And he wouldn't do that."

"Hey, with any luck you can squeeze a confession out of this creep. Then you send her flowers; take her someplace nice to eat; you tell her you're sorry, that you'll get help."

"You talking a shrink here?"

"Marriage counselor. Women love 'em. They think the minute you agree to see one all their problems are solved."

Thinnes looked at Oster, then back at the road. "Sounds to me like the voice of experience."

"Don't knock it." Oster was quiet a minute, watching Belmont. "Something I never told anyone before." Thinnes could hear a warning in his voice. "Eight years ago my wife was fixin' to call it quits. Don't blame her; I was pretty fucked up. Evanger—he was a sergeant then—sent me to see Karsch. He's pretty good. And discreet. The way I see it is, you talk to a marriage counselor or a divorce lawyer."

"And spill my guts?"

"It's not so bad. Guy gets you talking by asking a few questions, then acts as a ref, calls time out when things get too heavy. And it's usually cheaper than the alternative."

"But Karsch?"

"You could do worse. I don't know if he still does it, but if not, I bet he could recommend someone good."

FORTY-EIGHT

Marina City. Chicago's signature. Twin towers on the river. Thinnes thought it was symbolic that they looked as if they'd been picked clean. He strolled up to the telephone company truck that was doubling as a surveillance van north of the east tower and got in the passenger's seat next to the FBI agent. She put down the newspaper.

Thinnes asked, "How's it going?"

"Same old same old."

"Have you identified the painting yet?"

"Sure. Stolen a year ago from a museum in Italy, insured value one point seven million dollars." Thinnes whistled. "Some of these thieves sit on a thing like this for years, but this one's almost cold because it's not famous. If Margolis was a dealer, I'd expect flyers to be circulating, in a figurative sense. But we checked around, and there's not a whisper in the wind that this piece is available. We're probably wasting our time."

"So?"

"So we got a tap on the phone. We'll give Margolis another day or two, then we'll get a warrant to see what he's got in his private collection."

Thinnes would've liked to arrest Margolis immediately, before he had time to dispose of the painting. But The G had to make a federal case out of it. They never seemed to do any thing small.

Like in the Graylord investigation. It took them three years, thousands of man-hours, and who knows how many millions of dollars to put a couple of rummy judges away. Thank God they

165

weren't getting in on the Berringer case, at least not initially. Later, if any interstate mailing lists turned up, the Feds could have a field day. All Thinnes wanted was to get the dirty-snapshot fiasco over with. To get Ronnie back.

FORTY-NINE

Viernes and Swann were on the phone and Crowne was typing when Thinnes came into the squad room that afternoon and dropped his paperwork on the table near the coffee maker. Karsch came out of his office. Thinnes dialed a number and, as he waited for someone to answer, Karsch poured himself coffee.

"How about finishing this so I can make another pot?"

Thinnes held up a finger and said, "Bob Fell, please," into the phone, he told Karsch "Okay."

Fell came on. Thinnes concentrated on the call, ignoring Karsch, who was setting up the pot again, and Crowne, who'd stopped typing to listen.

"Bob, John Thinnes. How are you?" He listened for a moment, then laughed. As he did, Evanger strolled in with his coffee cup and stood next to the coffee maker, waiting for it to finish running. He and Crowne, Swann, Karsch, and Viernes eavesdropped as Thinnes said, "Of course. Listen, Bob, I need to find out about one of your alums. Guy named Caleb. C-A-L-E-B, James Arthur. Don't know the dates, but he's supposed to have picked up some medals in Nam." Thinnes listened and said, "I appreciate it. I haven't any hot suspects; this one may be lukewarm. Depends on what you dig up. Thanks." He put down the phone and looked at the others. "Don't you people have anything to do?"

A few minutes later, Thinnes got up and knocked on Karsch's door. When Karsch called, "Come in," Thinnes said, "Got a minute?"

"Sure." Karsch waved Thinnes into a chair as he closed the door. The phone rang before Thinnes could begin. Karsch answered, listened, hung up. He said, "Excuse me a moment," and went out, closing the door.

Thinnes spent the two minutes he was gone looking at his poster-size photos. When Karsch returned, Thinnes asked, "You take these?"

"As a matter of fact, yes."

"Not bad."

Karsch acknowledged the compliment with a smile. "What can I do for you, Detective?"

Detective, not Detective Thinnes. Not just Thinnes. It occurred to Thinnes that Karsch had hit the perfect balance between formal and familiar. Thinnes hadn't planned what he'd say. No one was fooled by that old friend-of-mine-has-a-problem routine anymore.

"One of the guys told me . . ."

Karsch raised an eyebrow and waited.

You have the right to remain silent, Thinnes thought. *Out with it, Thinnes.* "Anything anyone tells you is privileged," he said.

"That's correct."

Anything you say can and will be held against you. Is this what it feels like to be on the receiving end in the interview room? Karsch won't tell, so who'll know? he told himself.

Karsch'll know. But if he's sworn to secrecy?

"You guys talk to each other about your cases?"

"Only hypothetically." Karsch smiled. "With the names changed to protect the guilty." He waited.

When you knew you had someone off balance, Thinnes thought, all you had to do was wait. He wanted to ask "Are you gay?" but that wasn't something you asked someone you were supposed to know. Damn Caleb! What difference would it make if Karsch were gay? Well, what would a faggot know about wife troubles? It'd be like asking a priest.

"I need the name of a marriage counselor."

If Karsch was surprised, he hid it. "Certainly. In fact, I'll give you several, because it's best if you choose someone you feel comfortable with. Sometimes you have to shop around." Karsch pulled a folder from a desk drawer and copied names and phone numbers onto a sheet of paper. He handed it to Thinnes. "Call them and tell them what your needs are. If you feel comfortable talking on the phone, make an appointment."

Thinnes didn't feel comfortable talking about it with Karsch. It was too much like talking with one of the dicks. And it was not something you talked about at work. But he had to talk to someone or he'd lose Rhonda.

Did they have refresher courses in how to talk to your wife? If he learned to be romantic, would she give him another chance? *Could* he learn?

Thinnes folded the paper and put it in his pocket. He'd let Rhonda choose. He said, "Thanks."

Karsch nodded and said, "Good luck."

Having got that over with, he went back to the squad room. Karsch followed him out, heading for the coffee machine.

The phone rang at Thinnes's place just as he reached for his own coffee. "Thinnes," he said into it, and paused. "Just a second." He grabbed a pen and note pad. "Okay, shoot. Twelve eighty-seven West Argyle, got it. You got the warrant? Have somebody look it over. We don't want to lose this over bad paper. Okay. See you then." He put down the phone and tore the sheet off the notepad.

"We've located Berringer's warehouse and we're gonna hit it tomorrow night. Anybody want to join the party?"

FIFTY

Thinnes got to the funeral home early so he could read the cards on the flowers. Murderers sometimes eased their consciences by sending flowers or condolences. You didn't need to be a shrink to figure that out. Sometimes you could judge the guilt by the size of the tab.

About thirty chairs had been set up in rows facing the front of the room, where the body would've been laid out at a wake. Finley wasn't there; the flowers were arranged around a framed eight-by-ten photo of him. When Thinnes asked, the funeral director hemmed and hawed but finally admitted Finley's remains were being cremated so that the sister could take them back to New York with her at the end of the week.

There was an ostentatious wreath from Margolis Enterprises and an expensive but tasteful arrangement from the Margolis Gallery. Same from North Michigan Avenue Associates. WR&C edged them all out, though. Its arrangement was smallest but made of things Thinnes'd never seen before. And orchids. It figured to be very pricey.

Dr. Caleb was the first to arrive, a little before seven. Thinnes stood quietly in a corner near the door and watched him do just what he himself had done—read the cards on all the flowers. Only he didn't take notes. When he turned to go back to the anteroom, he spotted Thinnes.

"Good evening, Detective Thinnes." Caleb's manner gave no hint of reference to their last meeting.

Thinnes nodded. "Doctor."

"Is this an official visit?"

"I'm not on the clock."

"But still curious?"

Thinnes smiled.

Caleb didn't ask for clarification. He said, "Then I'll see you later," and walked away.

Thinnes could hear that others had arrived, and before long Marshall Close escorted Adriana Finley into the room. Like Caleb and Thinnes, they went and read the cards on the flowers. Close looked the room over as if he'd paid for it. He noticed Thinnes immediately and nodded almost imperceptibly. If he was curious, he hid it well. He stood there with Adriana Finley, greeting the people starting to straggle in, making the introductions.

Thinnes thought the turnout was predictable. Almost everyone they'd interviewed at WR&C showed up, including Alicia Baynes. Finley's super was there with a few neighbors—they'd been notified, according to one tenant, by a handwritten notice left by the mailboxes—also Joseph Remora, Finley's attorney. Remora looked like the type of lawyer who represents hustlers and whores and wears loud suits to make his clients feel more comfortable. The guy'd sounded like a Harvard grad over the phone, sharp and professional. He'd probably discovered what good money there was in defending working girls and traffic violaters if you weren't too hung up on image. Thinnes's estimation of Finley rose, the kid'd been able to overlook the window dressing and go for talent.

He slipped out to the anteroom to check the names in the guest book. Only one was unfamiliar; the funeral director identified the older woman as a professional mourner. The only surprising arrival was Anita Margolis. She was dressed in navy blue and made the other women in the room look like cleaning ladies. Dr. Caleb took her by the arm and led her in to make introductions.

After expressing their condolences, most of the guests sat on the folding chairs and looked around at the room. Alicia Baynes, in black, sat as far as possible from Bettina Calder. It made Thinnes think of what he'd overheard Caleb tell Margaret Linsey at the zoo; they were like two big cats, hair on end, all but hissing. The looks they acknowledged each other with could have caused frostbite. Caleb and Anita Margolis sat together but didn't speak to each other. Didn't seem to need to. Thinnes found himself wondering if the doctor didn't swing both ways.

At exactly seven thirty, a man in a Roman collar entered to convene the service with a prayer. Thinnes watched the audience. Adriana sat clenching her jaw through the eulogy. Marshall Close and Dr. Caleb and Anita seemed to be paying careful attention. Alicia Baynes fought tears. Half the others appeared to be day-dreaming or falling asleep. When he was finished, the speaker invited the mourners to add their thoughts. Close got up and made Finley sound like Einstein or Abraham Lincoln. Several of Finley's coworkers talked about him. They all seemed uncomfortable, and Thinnes wondered if Close hadn't put them up to it. Then Adriana thanked all her brother's friends for coming, and the priest finished the program by leading the Lord's Prayer. He paused on his way out to express his condolences to the "family." People began to drift away as soon as he left.

Adriana walked up to Thinnes. She'd pulled herself together since their last meeting, and hostility replaced the tears. She said, "I understand why you couldn't tell me Allan was murdered." She made it sound as if she was sarcastically forgiving him for an oversight.

He wasn't particularly offended. Cops seldom see people at their best. Her anger was more believable than the dumb grief he'd seen Monday. This woman could be the financial barracuda NYPD had reported. He wondered about the change.

"What did Dr. Caleb tell you?"

"Just that you're playing the cat until you find out which mouse is really a rat."

Thinnes gave a noncommittal "Huh" and excused himself.

Playing the cat. The perfect analogy. To carry it a little further, sometimes you had to bat something off the shelf to see who'd jump. He looked around for Close.

"Detective Thinnes," Close said by way of a greeting. Thinnes nodded. "Does your presence here indicate dissatisfaction with the coroner's verdict?"

"Medical examiner," Thinnes corrected him. "Just a few loose ends to tie up. It's none of my business, Mr. Close, but I'm curious; you ever have any professional jealousy or personal clashes among your staff?"

"I suppose you have a good reason for asking?"

"It's more a lack of a good reason why Finley would kill himself. The medical examiner doesn't have to concern himself with motive, just cause and manner of death. But we like to come up with a reason. It makes a case a lot tidier."

Close thought about it. "You're suggesting Allan had difficulties with one of my staff that might have led to his suicide?"

Delicately put. "Failure, either professional or personal, can be a motive."

Close seemed satisfied with that. "As I told you, he was professionally very successful. I don't inquire into my employees personal business, in fact I encourage them to keep it to themselves. And to answer your question, my staff are adults. And professionals."

The implication was that they wouldn't be staff long otherwise. But there was nothing to suggest they wouldn't be terminated in the commonly accepted manner.

"Anything else?" If Close knew about Baynes and Calder, he wasn't letting on.

Thinnes caught up with Caleb in the anteroom. Anita Margolis had gone. Thinnes said, "Doctor, I thought I warned you about alerting my suspects."

"You and I have different goals, John. It's the nature of our jobs. In any case, you can't really suspect Adriana?"

"Everyone's a suspect until I have the killer."

Caleb smiled.

Thinnes said, "Monday she was coming apart, today she's ready to take *me* apart. Can you explain the change?"

"When I told her Allan didn't kill himself, I think it was an affirmation for her."

"Hunh?"

"She knew him well enough to believe he'd never commit suicide, but when the police—the experts in these matters—insisted, she began to doubt herself. Also, there's a great deal of rage engendered by the death of a loved one, and it's often directed at the perceived agent—disease, fate, God. When the agent is the victim himself, the survivor isn't usually able to add to the guilt he already feels for failing to prevent the death by being angry with the deceased. Even though the deceased may deserve it. So in cases of suicide, survivors often convert their anger into inconsolable grief or psychosomatic disorders. I'd say Adriana's redirected her anger away from herself and towards Allan's killer. And perhaps towards you for letting her believe the worst."

It made sense. But then almost everything Caleb said did. He was so damn reasonable, there wasn't much you could argue with him about. Sort of made you want to hate his guts. Or pin a murder rap on him. You're still pissed because you didn't guess he's gay, Thinnes told himself. Didn't have a clue.

Alicia Baynes was the last to leave. When she noticed Thinnes watching her, she turned to him and said, "It's so *unfair!*" Thinnes nodded. "He was so nice. Sort of compulsive about neatness, but at least he had a sense of humor about it."

"Why did you trade assignments with him?"

"She *told* you."

Thinnes nodded.

"Because he asked me to. He was the senior accountant. I mean, there were rumors Close was going to take him on as a partner. Why wouldn't I trade if he asked?"

It was understandable she'd be defensive, but there was something more. She was lying. Thinnes said, "I'll need you to come down to my office and sign a statement about it."

She was subtly alarmed. "Tonight?"

Might as well let her think it over. Maybe talk with her attorney. Maybe she'd decide to tell the truth. "Tomorrow or the next day'll be soon enough."

FIFTY-ONE

Berringer's warehouse was an old building, well-constructed but dilapidated, off an alley in the Uptown area. Next to a door with the street number stenciled on it was a garage-type overhead door. The raiding party—Thinnes, Crowne, Swann, Oster, Ferris, and half a dozen others—wearing jackets marked POLICE surrounded the building, coordinating their activities by hand radio. They had a wrecking truck with a huge front bumper standing by; a fire truck waited in the next block.

On a signal from the ranking officer, Oster went to the door, followed closely by the truck. The driver angled it so that a corner of the bumper was just in front of the door. Oster knocked softly and said, "Police! Search warrant. Open up!" just loud enough to be heard by the truck driver or anyone standing with his ear to the other side of the door. Naturally, nothing happened. Oster stepped aside and signaled. With a roar of the engine and a grind of gears, the truck smashed the door open, then backed away. Oster gave the signal and everyone swarmed in.

Inside, fires were being set. Choking smoke billowed out of cartons hastily slashed open and sloshed with gasoline. Bright tongues of flame licked the dark interior. As the police invaded, several men scrambled to escape. One turned on the police with a gun, saw how badly he was outnumbered, and threw down his weapon. The other suspects threw their arms over their heads, screaming, "Don't shoot!"

Oster called to the firemen on his hand radio and activated the overhead door, and fire fighters moved in to put the fires out.

Thinnes, Crowne, and Ferris skirted the main conflict, and Thinnes directed them with hand signals to surround a door marked OFFICE while he covered it. Ferris and Crowne moved to either side of the door. Crowne held up one finger, then two. On three, Ferris kicked the door with the ball of his foot. The lock flew apart. Ferris and Crowne burst into the room.

It was was deserted, containing only a metal desk, a chair, and a pile of empty cartons.

Thinnes ran to the next closed door and kicked it open as Crowne and Ferris continued down the hall.

The john was filthy. A sludge of grime covered the sink. The mirror was clouded by flyspecks, the toilet yellow with poor attempts to aim. Berringer was flushing something down as Thinnes smashed through the door with gun drawn. He flew into the room and slammed Berringer against the wall, holding the .38 to Berringer's head as he reached into the toilet for a large cellophane package lodged in the hole. He tugged and it came free with a splash and a gurgle. Thinnes dropped it in the sink.

"Nice try, Berringer. Grab the wall and spread 'em."

Berringer turned to fight, but faced with a .38, he shrugged and complied. Thinnes kept him covered while he patted him down for weapons. He found a .32.

"O for three, Berringer. Not your lucky day."

"I got a permit."

Thinnes prodded the soggy package in the sink. White powder. Cocaine. Bingo!

"For the junk?"

Berringer didn't answer. Thinnes cuffed him and holstered his own gun. Peering cautiously around the doorframe to see if it was safe to go out, he said, "You're under arrest," and pushed Berringer into the hall. He pocketed the .32 and picked up the sopping package. "You have the right to remain silent. . . ."

Mop-up activities were in progress as Thinnes walked Berringer out to the squadrol. When he came back, Oster was happily directing an invading army of dicks and evidence technicians. Police photographers were recording the scene before the property people moved in to grab the unopened and with luck undamaged cases of kiddie porn and slasher flicks and S&M stuff rescued from the fires. Cartons of unburned invoices and office files promised to keep the state's attorney's people busy for years. Everyone was gloating like toy salesmen at Christmastime.

Thinnes took a private tour before the area commander did his dog and pony show for the press. Different parts of the building had been devoted to different aspects of skin-flick production. Much of the space had housed storage and packaging operations, but there were impressive darkrooms and editing rooms, and a desktop computer set up for the graphics. The highlight of the tour was a set with a silk-sheeted bed surrounded by lighting, sound, and camera equipment.

Ferris spotted Thinnes and pointed it out. "Place look familiar, Thinnes?"

"Go ahead, laugh, Ferris. I got the collar."

FIFTY-TWO

The interview room at headquarters was small and plain, with hard chairs, an electric wall clock, and a view-through mirror. The simplicity was intended to eliminate distractions. Nothing was supposed to sidetrack suspects from the questions asked them. Oster had been staring at Berringer without saying a word for some time.

Berringer sat drenched with sweat, cuffed by one hand to the wall. "Look," he said, "I'm not talkin' until my lawyer gets here." When Oster shrugged, he wavered. "What kind of deal could I get?"

" 'Pends what you got. You know we'll do the best we can if you're helpful."

"You're not gonna believe it, but I don't know."

"Yeah, sure."

"I don't!"

"You got enough coke to buzz half the North Shore and you expect me to believe you don't know where you got it?"

"I swear it! I'll take a lie test!"

Oster let his disgust show plainly as he rose to leave.

"Wait! Hear me out!"

To Thinnes, watching the show through the one-way glass with Ferris, Viernes, Crowne, and Karsch, Berringer seemed as desperate as a man could be whose tale is hard to swallow and whose future depends on selling it.

"Ray, just for kicks, call the lab and ask them to compare the chromatograph of Berringer's coke with the one from the stuff they found in Caleb's apartment."

Crowne shrugged but went. Thinnes stuck his head into the room. "Oster?"

"Just hang loose," Oster told Berringer. He went out with Thinnes.

"Let him cool his heels for a minute," Thinnes told him. "I got a hunch I'd like to check out. Might give us more leverage."

The conference room was like the interview room, but without the mirror. Berringer had been conferring with his lawyer. He looked grim. The lawyer looked smug. "I've advised my client not to say anymore."

Oster ignored the lawyer and spoke directly to Berringer. "The one we're most interested in is the guy who gave you the coke."

"We're looking to get him on murder one," Thinnes added. "You want to buy into that?"

Alarmed, the lawyer looked at Berringer. "You didn't tell me—"

"He never said anything about murder!" Berringer blurted out. "I mean, the shrink didn't die."

Oster was surprised. Thinnes nodded.

"Don't say another word!" the attorney demanded.

"That was your good luck, Berringer," Thinnes said, "but as it happens, it wasn't the first murder attempt."

"The plan wasn't to kill him!"

"Berringer, I cannot defend you if you won't take my advice!"

This finally got through. "Yeah," Berringer said. He told Thinnes, "I'm not sayin' anymore."

Thinnes shrugged. "Go ahead," he told the attorney. "Advise him." He walked out of the room. Oster followed, angrily. "Thinnes, what is this?"

"Murder, Oster. You got him cold on the porn charge and possession with intent to sell. Look, I don't see that we got anything to lose here. He's not going to talk about those, even without the legal advice. But he might want to talk himself out of a murder rap. If the state's attorney'll go along—"

"If, if, if. If you can even prove you got a murder. I talked to the ME's office last week. They filed a termination report on Finley—as a suicide."

"And I talked to narcotics. They want the supplier. So do I—for Finley's murder!" He paused to run his fingers through his hair. "You gotta trust me on this."

Oster thought about it a minute. "All right. Let me talk to narcotics and the state's attorney and get back to you."

"Here's the deal," Thinnes told Berringer and his lawyer. "The state's attorney's office is willing to reduce the drug charge to simple possession if you help us nail your supplier. You may also clear yourself of any collusion in this murder we're investigating, and on the attempted murder charge we're preparing."

Berringer looked at his attorney, who nodded. "I don't know who the guy is." He looked from Thinnes to Oster. "Wait! Listen! The guy's been blackmailing me for years, to keep him quiet about my operation." Berringer looked at Thinnes. "Well, he never asked too much. It was like paying protection, and it was cheaper than moving the operation, which wouldn'ta got him off my back until the statute of limitations expired. So I paid." He looked at his attorney, who was silent and disapproving. "Every once in a while, he'd let me off the hook for a payment if I did some custom photo work for him."

Thinnes handed him one of the pornographic photos of himself. "Like this?"

Berringer glanced at it. "Yeah." He looked again and realized who it featured. He turned white. "Jesus! You gonna press?"

"That depends on how cooperative you are."

"Look, I'm sorry. I never knew who the guys were, or what he did with the pictures. I'd just get these phone calls with instructions—short calls, so I could never have 'em traced."

"So what were the instructions this time?" Oster asked.

"He said he wanted some pictures of a married guy in bed with a broad. "Said 'leave nothing to the imagination.' " Berringer looked nervously at Thinnes.

"Where'd you get the pictures of me, Berringer?"

Berringer shrugged. "The SOB told me where you lived and I staked it out. Standard surveillance stuff. I'm surprised you gotta ask."

Thinnes scowled. "A rusty white Econoline with a December tag?"

"Yeah. How . . . ?"

"You jacked it up and took a wheel off so no one would wonder why it was there so long."

"Yeah, and some broad asked you directions when you were leavin', so I got a couple a good angles." Berringer seemed pleased with his own cleverness. Neither Thinnes nor Oster was impressed.

"Tell us about Dr. Caleb," Oster said.

"He didn't say to kill him!" They waited. "Guy said the shrink was a heavy user, into him for big bucks. Said he wouldn't pay up. So he said we should ruin 'im—you know, set him up for felony possession. Guy in his position, that would put him outta business."

Thinnes asked, "How was he supposed to get busted in the privacy of his own apartment?"

"I don't know! I didn't think about it too much. I guess I thought it would go down something like it did. I didn't give the shrink enough to kill him. I swear! Just enough to keep him real happy till the cops arrived."

"It didn't occur to you that he might not be a user?"

"Are you kiddin'? He drives a Jag. All these rich assholes . . . If I'd had any idea I was being set up—I mean, why else would I do it? I don't know this Caleb." He looked earnestly at Oster. "And if I could finger this leech . . . Five years, he's been bleedin' me!"

Oster just waited.

"I should have followed instructions. I was supposed to leave all the coke with the shrink—make him look like a dealer—but I thought what the hell, who'd know?"

FIFTY-THREE

According to her license, Alicia Baynes was twenty-six. Right now she could have passed for forty. The dark roots showed in her blond hair; her makeup didn't hide the lines and dark circles around her eyes. Thinnes guessed she hadn't slept since the memorial service. Classic example, he'd bet, of a guilty conscience. Not necessarily guilty of murder but at least guilty of lying. She looked like she was about to cry again. She clasped her hands together on the table in front of her and looked all around the little District Nineteen interview room—everywhere but up at Thinnes, who was standing across the table from her.

He leaned back against the wall. He wanted to slap her and tell her to shape up. Instead he said, "You don't get on very well with Miss Calder."

"Not very." Thinnes waited. "She's one of those people who's *never* wrong. It's always me."

"How'd she get on with Finley?"

Baynes smiled wryly. "When Allan first came, she was always trying to get something on him. Only he was such a perfectionist, she couldn't. Then when Close started to take a liking to Allan, she started sucking up to him. She thinks we're all too stupid to notice. It's insulting."

"So why do you put up with it?"

"I don't know. When I first started, she was real nice—until she found out I was good. Then she started finding fault with everything I did."

Thinnes wondered how much of the friction was due to race, how much to plain old insecurity.

"She do the same with Finley?"

Baynes gave him a wry smile, almost forgetting she was about to cry. "He was a man. Besides, there was no way she could compete with Allan. He had an M.B.A. from Northwestern. She used to try and act like they were equals, though. She just can't stand not to be better than everyone else."

Thinnes had met people like that. If one was your supervisor, the best you could do was keep a low profile and cover your ass. Baynes sounded truthful. And from what he'd seen of Calder, she probably was just insecure enough to resent competition, especially from subordinates.

Enough to kill Finley? He doubted it. That type didn't have the nerve. The arrogance, maybe, but not the guts.

There was a tap on the door. Thinnes answered it, and Crowne entered with three plastic cups of coffee. He set them on the table in front of Thinnes and offered one to Baynes, sitting down opposite her. Sipping his coffee, he pulled out his notebook and pen and waited, looking expectantly at Baynes.

"I'd like you to give Detective Crowne your statement—about this job trade with Finley," Thinnes said. "Then we'll get it typed up and you can sign it and be on your way."

She squirmed. "Why? What has it to do with Allan's death, and why do I have to sign anything about it?"

"We don't know that it has anything to do with Finley's death, but it might. His showing up instead of you might be the reason someone killed him. As to why we want a statement from you . . ." Thinnes shrugged. "People forget things over time. Sometimes they lie. Sometimes they embroider. If we have a sworn statement, we've got the story on record. If you forget it all, we still have the story. If you lied, chances are you'll forget the story you told us and we'll catch you." He paused to let that sink in. "And there's no statute of limitations on murder. It might be years before we take this case to court. We want to be sure we don't lose any details."

Baynes nodded, then repeated what she'd told Thinnes at the wake—as he thought of the memorial service—that Allan had asked her to trade jobs. Finley hadn't said why. She'd signed his name to the job she'd done, the one he was supposed to do; he'd signed his own name to her job, because he'd done it, and presumably it would never occur to him to cover anything up. That was all there was to it.

Thinnes was quite sure she was lying. He said, "That's it?" and when she nodded, "Then if you'll wait a few minutes longer, we'll get this typed up for you to sign and you can go." He nudged Crowne with his knee, and Crowne stood up. "Excuse us a minute," Thinnes said.

When they were out in the hall, Crowne said, "Lying through her teeth."

"I'm counting on her having a change of heart when it comes to actually signing. Once she sees it down in black and white."

While Crowne typed the statement out Thinnes made a few calls for another case they were working on. They let Baynes wait almost half an hour. When Thinnes opened the door to the interview room, she jumped six inches in her chair, even though she was facing the door.

"Sorry to keep you waiting," Thinnes said as he put the statement on the table. "If you'll just read this over and sign it, we'll be done." Crowne closed the door.

She read it. And reread it. She picked up the pen Thinnes put in front of her and started to sign, then put it down. Staring at the paper, she told them, "I lied."

Thinnes said, "Are you ready to tell us what really happened?"

She glanced up at him. Appraising his anger, Thinnes guessed. Then she took a deep breath and plunged in.

"Allan didn't ask me to trade jobs. I asked him." She waited for them to ask why; they didn't. "I thought there was something wrong with the accounts I'd been doing, but I didn't know what. I thought there might be money laundering going on. I just wasn't . . . I wasn't experienced enough to prove it from the records they gave me. I couldn't make any accusations against the company without proof. And I couldn't say anything to Bettina— she'd have gotten me fired. So I asked Allan to go for me. I knew he'd be able to tell—he was sort of a genius that way. He loved that sort of challenge. I never dreamed there'd be any danger—I mean, nobody kills accountants!"

That sounded more like it. "Why didn't you tell us this in the first place?" Thinnes asked.

"I was afraid whoever killed Allan would come after me. And I was afraid Ms. Calder would fire me. I thought if I just put the reports through, they might be filed away. You know how sometimes people don't really look at things, routine things?"

He knew. "So to save your own skin, you were willing to let someone get away with murdering your boyfriend."

"I didn't think . . . I was just afraid."

Thinnes could feel Crowne's contempt for her, and he tried to hide his own. "You willing to swear to this new version? You're not going to change your story again?"

"No. I mean, yes, I'll swear to it. And I won't change it again." She seemed relieved. She probably was. Confession and all that.

"All right. We'll need the name of the company. And you'll have to wait while we type up another statement."

"And," Crowne added, "we'd like to have you tell your suspicions to one of our detectives who specializes in money laundering."

Thinnes managed to keep from gloating, but he couldn't hide his excitement. Or his disappointment that the company Baynes named wasn't Margolis Enterprises. Still, if they nailed Finley's killer and maybe put the skids under some money laundering operation, it would be well worth their time.

Crowne managed to rain on his parade. "Thinnes, when was the last time we got the goods on a mob operation? And it's got to be the organization—drug gangs are a whole lot messier."

FIFTY-FOUR

They hadn't shuffled out from under the paper work on the Berringer case, so the office was busy. Crowne was reading with his feet up on the table; Viernes was typing; Swann was talking to Karsch outside the door of the latter's office. Thinnes studied Finley's checkbook as if reading it again would force some new clue to appear like invisible writing held over a flame. The plastic bag it came from, with its identifying evidence number, lay on the desk, along with a copy of *Generally Accepted Accounting Practices.* The latest edition of the CPA's bible had been in the UPS package Finley's landlord had signed for; Thinnes'd checked on that too. Finley'd bought it by phone from Kroch's and Brentano's with his credit card. No mystery there. Just keeping current.

The phone rang and Viernes answered it. "Thinnes," he said. "Some guy from the VA for you. Name's Fell. Line six." He hung up when Thinnes answered. Viernes spotted Karsch going into his office. "Hey, Karsch. Got a minute?" Karsch nodded and ushered him in.

By the time Thinnes hung up, he was excited. He was about to tell Crowne about it when the phone rang again. Swann answered. "Thinnes."

Thinnes picked it up and listened for a while. "Twenty minutes," he said. He hung up and turned to Crowne. "They got a warrant and they're about to pick up Margolis. Wanna come?"

Crowne put his feet down and sat up. "I'd pay admission." He grinned like a kid. "Everything happens at once, doesn't it?" As they walked toward the stairs, he asked, "What did the VA come up with?"

"Seems our Dr. Caleb was a conscientious objector during the

war," Thinnes said. "Served as a medic. Cited "for unusual brav-
ery and ingenuity in rescuing the wounded.""

"So that makes him smart enough to kill Finley but damned
unlikely."

Thinnes looked back into the room. Swann was on the phone
again, and Viernes was coming out of Karsch's office.

"There's more," Thinnes told Crowne as they went out the
door. "He got a Silver Star for taking out an enemy sniper who'd
picked off two dozen men. Just charged the guy and blew him
away."

"A pacifist?"

"Claimed he went temporarily berserk."

FIFTY-FIVE

Margolis lived in the east tower of Marina City. Thinnes and Crowne joined Regg, an FBI agent who *looked* like a government operative, from his Secret Service haircut to his generous-in-the-armpits three-piece suit. Regg flashed his badge at the white-shirted security guard who let them in through a door that was like the laddered, stainless steel burglar doors found in bank vaults and prisons. That writer the reporters were always quoting was right, Thinnes reflected, about the very rich: they were as much a different breed as the very poor. It was hard not to be a snob about them. They were such slaves to their possessions and to the images they had of themselves. Thinnes had seen them do some very weird things to maintain appearances.

They didn't speak on the ride up. When they got off the elevator, an FBI agent dressed as a laborer—with utility belt, tools, and ladder—was standing between the elevator door and Margolis's apartment, watching the door. Thinnes reached in and pulled the stop button. Regg asked the agent, "He in there?"

The agent nodded. "He just had a pizza delivery." He laughed. "Guy must be delivering something more. Been in there five minutes."

Margolis's apartment door started to open, and the agent scrambled up the ladder and busied himself changing the tube in the overhead light fixture. Thinnes, Crowne, and Regg dodged back into the elevator as the delivery man came out with a large pizza box. He called out, "Hold the elevator!"

Thinnes pretended to pull the stop button. The pizza man hurried to get in, and Thinnes pushed the stop and hit the button for the lobby. As the elevator descended, the three officers stared at the man, who showed unmistakable signs of nervousness. "The guy didn't want it," he said. "Said it was cold."

"Just so your trip won't be a loss," Regg said, taking out his wallet, "how about selling it to me?" He began to extract money.

The pizza man shook his head. "Against company policy."

"How about letting me have a look?"

The man shook his head again and glanced nervously at Thinnes and Crowne. Crowne was pulling on gloves.

Regg flashed his ID. "Please?"

The man looked very unhappy but didn't protest as Crowne took the carton and opened it. Inside lay the stolen painting without its heavy coating of applied paint. The man blanched. "The guy told me he didn't want his wife's divorce lawyer to get hold of it." He looked from Thinnes to Crowne to Regg. "He gave me a hundred bucks to deliver it. Look. I'll show you." He dragged out his wallet and pulled a hundred-dollar bill from it, offering it to Regg, who shook his head and pointed to Crowne.

The man gave Crowne the bill. Crowne looked it over. "It's a hundred, all right," he said, and dropped it on top of the painting in the carton. The elevator stopped.

Regg asked the pizza man, "Would you be willing to sign a statement to that effect and testify in court?"

"Yeah, sure."

The doors opened. Thinnes showed his badge to people waiting to get on. "Use another elevator."

Regg told Crowne, "Give him a receipt."

The pizza man swallowed his outrage. Regg signaled through the security grids to a business-suited man with a newspaper—another agent—and a sharp-looking woman with a briefcase, who were waiting in the lobby. The guard let them pass. As they came to the elevator, Regg pointed to the pizza carton and asked the woman, "This what we're lookin' for?"

She looked inside. "I'll have to test it, but that looks like it." Her accent sounded Italian.

"We have to dust it for prints first." Regg said to the agent in the suit, "Why don't you take care of that? And take this gentleman in"—he indicated the pizza man—"and get his statement."

The agent nodded. "Oh, and we'll need another warrant, immediately, to search for stolen artwork. He pointed to the pizza man again. "He'll give you the address."

"Yeah." The agent took a folded plastic bag from between the pages of his newspaper and shook it out, holding it while Crowne put the pizza carton inside. Then he took the carton and jerked his head at the pizza man, and they started away.

Regg looked at the woman. "Let's get on with it."

When Margolis opened the door looking smug, Thinnes, Crowne, Regg, and the woman were standing outside.

"Vincent Margolis?" Regg asked. Margolis nodded. Regg took a folded paper out of his inside jacket pocket. "We have a warrant to search this apartment." He handed it to Margolis and stepped forward, forcing Margolis to step back into the room.

Margolis stared at the warrant. Thinnes and the others went past him and started looking around. It was a very North Shore apartment, with its crystal and chrome, "in" colors, original art, and excellent reproductions. Everything about it said money.

Crowne made a beeline for the nearest painting. "How about this one?"

The woman shook her head. "That's a reproduction."

"Who are you?" Margolis demanded. He sounded subtly alarmed.

"Dr. Julietta Maserati," Regg answered for her. "From the Department of Antiquities, Rome."

Margolis didn't have a response to that. Thinnes waited with him while Crowne, Regg, and Dr. Maserati traipsed through the apartment, examining every piece of art. Margolis appeared bored and annoyed by the whole procedure. When Crowne and the expert finally seemed to be giving up, Margolis began to relax, but he tensed as they neared the bathroom door.

Thinnes said, "Ray, check the bathroom."

Margolis froze.

Crowne went in the bathroom and came out with a tiny painting. He asked the woman, dubiously, "How about this?"

She took the picture and got very excited as she pored over it. Thinnes never took his eyes off Margolis.

Maserati looked at Regg. "This is almost certainly on the list."

Regg said, "Mr. Margolis, you're under arrest for possession of stolen art. You have the right to remain silent—"

"I want to call my attorney!"

"All in due time."

FIFTY-SIX

They used the same interview room they'd used to question Berringer. Thinnes and Crowne watched from outside with Evanger as Oster, Regg, and an agent from customs questioned Margolis. Margolis's attorney was blocking admirably.

Evanger was resigned. "We might as well cut him loose."

"Mind if we go a few rounds with him first?" Thinnes asked.

"Why not?" The lieutenant called the three interrogators out.

Crowne headed for the coffee maker. Thinnes went in. He nodded at the attorney.

"Counselor. I'm Thinnes, Violent Crimes. I'm investigating a homicide."

The attorney was obviously caught off guard. "Are you planning to charge my client?"

Margolis said nothing.

"At the present time, we're just trying to gather facts."

"My client doesn't have to—"

"Incriminate himself," Thinnes said, sharply. "But if he isn't guilty, he'd be wise to cooperate with our investigation. Isn't that so?"

The attorney pouted. "Yes."

Ignoring him, Thinnes said, "Sit down, Margolis."

Margolis sat on one side of the room; Thinnes sat across from him. The attorney stayed where he was, his arms folded and his disapproval obvious. Hostility seemed to condense in the air between them.

Crowne came in with four coffees in a cardboard tray. He handed one to Thinnes and offered one to the attorney. Obviously disgusted by the delay the coffee signaled, the attorney looked at the clock and shook his head. Crowne handed a cup to Margolis, who took it as if it was his due, and put the extra coffee on the floor, against the wall. "If you know anything, you might as well tell Thinnes," he told Margolis. "We call him 'Pit Bull' cause he never lets go." He pulled a chair over and sat down. Tipping back against the wall, he took out his notebook and pen.

Thinnes said, "Now, then. Mr. Margolis—may I call you Vincent?" Margolis didn't answer, except to scowl. "Vincent. Perhaps you can tell me what you know about Allan Finley?"

"Nothing." Thinnes waited. Margolis finally felt compelled to add, "I don't remember ever meeting the man, so I can't imagine why anyone would want to kill him."

Thinnes waited until he was sure Margolis wouldn't say any more.

"How long have you employed Wilson, Reynolds and Close?"

"Five years."

"You've never had any complaints about their accuracy?"

That got a rise. "Should I have?"

"I don't know. I'm with homicide, not bunko." Margolis relaxed. "The first time you ever heard of Finley was when I asked you about him?"

Margolis sighed. "I read about him in the paper the morning after he was found dead. I remember noticing the story because it involved my accounting agency. But I distinctly remember it said he killed himself. Why are you saying he was murdered?"

"I'm asking. Where were you the night he died?"

"What time?—"

He was interrupted as an officer stuck his head in the room and said, "Phone for you, Thinnes." Thinnes left and went to watch from outside through the one-way glass as Crowne took over his chair.

"Listen, Margolis," he said, "Thinnes's got his reputation on the line here. He's not gonna give up till you give him something."

"I don't have anything to give him!"

Crowne shook his head. "Just some little face-saving tidbit."

"Honest to God, I never met Finley."

"Well, what about this other thing? The smuggling?"

"My ex-wife set me up! *She* imported the stuff! It came from her gallery! I had no idea the paintings were stolen!"

"Okay, okay. Take it easy. Why don't you tell Thinnes that? Get his mind off Finley. He's kinda nuts about Finley—spoils his record."

The attorney stepped over and struck the back of the chair next to Margolis with his fingertips. "Vincent, these men are pulling the oldest con in the book! That one"—he indicated the door through which Thinnes just left—"plays the heavy, and this one"—he pointed to Crowne—"pretends to be your good friend. I'd advise you to keep quiet!"

Crowne stood and pretended to be furious. "Counselor, I'd advise *you* to confine your advice to matters of law."

At that point Thinnes went back in. Crowne vacated his seat and Thinnes sat down, staring at Margolis. "Was Finley blackmailing you?"

Margolis just missed hiding his surprise.

"Is that why you had him killed?"

"No!"

"No, he wasn't blackmailing you, or no, you didn't have him killed?"

The attorney said, "I protest!" He moved away from the wall, Crowne casually stepped between him and Margolis, anticipating the man's attempt to go around by coincidentally sidestepping in the same direction as the lawyer, then reversing himself in the old shall-we-dance? maneuver. While this was going on, Thinnes continued grilling Margolis.

"You *were* being blackmailed?"

Margolis didn't answer, but it was obvious that he was.

"Who was blackmailing you?"

"I don't know! No one!"

"Why was Finley killed?!"

"I don't know!" Margolis was unconvincing.

The attorney finally disengaged himself from Crowne. "That's all!" He told Thinnes. "Vincent, don't say another word. Thinnes, you have no right to browbeat—"

"Just one more question," Thinnes said, mildly. He turned back to Margolis and asked softly, "Who was *Christopher* Margolis?"

Margolis, already on the ropes, turned white. He seemed almost terrified. "How did you know?" He looked at Crowne, who shrugged.

The attorney looked totally bewildered as Margolis put his elbows on his knees and covered his face with his hands.

"You want to tell me about it?" Thinnes asked Margolis gently. *It's funny*, he thought. I can think like a man like Margolis, but to save my life, I can't imagine what it feels like to be him.

Thinnes wondered how his own son felt about him. The obvious hero-worship of Rob's childhood had long since disappeared, but Thinnes liked to think that the boy at least was not ashamed of him. What could Margolis's son think—what could he have thought, he corrected himself—of his old man?

Margolis said, "I killed him." He didn't look up.

Crowne was dumbfounded. "Finley?"

The attorney snapped, "Vincent, shut up!"

Margolis was oblivious to the attorney. He looked at Thinnes. "I told him if he wouldn't change his life-style, I'd disown him. I said I never wanted to see him again." He looked away. "I didn't. The next time . . ." Margolis covered his face to hide his sobs. The others were shocked; the attorney livid as well. Margolis finished without looking up, ". . . was at the morgue."

Thinnes asked, even more gently, "Your son?"

Margolis nodded. The attorney made an I-give-up gesture.

"He was gay and someone threatened to make it public?"

"Worse!" The attorney started to say something, but Crowne nudged him to get his attention and put a finger over his lips; the delay let Margolis decide to go on. "He threatened to make it public that—that *my son* was turning tricks for a living. It would have sabotaged the biggest deal of my life."

"It was true? He was hustling?"

Thinnes's question broke through Margolis's anguish. "Yes!" he shouted, suddenly outraged. "I've spilled my guts—happy?" he practically spat at Thinnes.

Thinnes didn't seem to notice the anger. He kept at it like a cat after a bird. "Who was blackmailing you?"

"I don't know!" Thinnes's lack of emotional response seemed to calm Margolis. "It started before Chris died. A phone call, a man. Said he'd—said everyone would find out my son was whoring for queers if I didn't pay. So I paid. After Chris died, I thought it would end. But it didn't. By then, it wasn't money, it was real estate deals. He'd call and give me instructions."

"You never thought of going to the police?"

"By that time, I was in over my head." He looked at his attorney. "I want to talk to my lawyer before I say more." Thinnes nodded. "Believe me, if I could identify the . . ." He shook his head. "I would."

"Your son was an artist, wasn't he?"

"A fiction invented by my ex-wife and her lover."

"Who?"

"Dr. James Caleb. He turned my wife against me. He convinced my son he was an artist with no head for business. Caleb denied it, of course. He said his lawyers would crucify me if I said anything in public that I couldn't prove. But I *know*."

"How did your son die?"

"In a car accident."

In the hall outside the interrogation room, Crowne asked, "How did you know he was being blackmailed?"

"I didn't, but he seems to be telling the truth about Finley, so the whole thing hinges on whether we can believe Dr. Caleb. If he's honest, our killer is also a blackmailer. And it stands to reason that if Margolis is involved at all, he's as likely to be a victim as anyone else with something to hide."

Crowne nodded. *"If* you can believe Caleb."

"Caleb's the one who brought up blackmail in the first place. If he's not on the level, he could be our killer. I think it's time I lean on him a bit." He looked at his watch. "You want to go pick him up?"

"What're you gonna be doing?"

"Looking up Christopher Margolis's death certificate and the report on the investigation."

"All right, but I'm off at five and I've got a date. You can take Caleb home . . . or whatever."

FIFTY-SEVEN

Translated into English, the death certificate listed the cause of death as blood loss due to severe, multiple injuries sustained in a car crash. The manner of death was accidental. The only surprise was that Swann had conducted the death investigation. He hadn't had anything to add to the patrol officer's report.

The desk sergeant told Thinnes that Swann had the day off, so Thinnes hunted him down by phone.

"You got the wrong number buddy," Swann's voice told him. "Ain't no cops live here."

"Mind if I come over and see?"

"Hell, yes. What's so damn important it can't wait till tomorrow, Thinnes?"

"You did the death investigation on a Christopher Margolis a few years back."

"If you say so."

"This is important."

"This is *po*lice business. An' I'm off duty. I ain't crazy, like you. When I'm off, I am *off*."

"Please." When Swann didn't answer immediately, Thinnes added, "I'm gettin' near to the end on this one."

"I don't remember the name." There was a resigned shrug in Swann's voice. Thinnes read him some of the particulars. "When was that?" Swann asked.

"Five years ago."

"Five years ago! How d'you expect . . . ? Oh, yeah. I *do* remember. Kid killed in a car crash. Musta been goin' ninety."

"Any possibility of foul play?"

"No way."

"You sure?"

"Damn straight. Kid's old man came screamin' into Area Six that queers killed his kid. Guy had money and clout, so you can be sure we went over that car with a fine-tooth comb."

"And?"

"And what we found is just what's in that report. Only good the old man's accusations did was to make damn sure everybody connected with the case'd remember his name, and everybody in the district'd talk about it. The dumb fuck."

It wasn't unusual for bereaved parents to say outlandish things. Usually no one paid much attention. Thinnes waited for the punch line.

"Commotion jogged the memory of one of the guys in vice. Seems the kid was suckin' somebody's cock in Grant Park, right in front of God'n a coupl'a shocked old maids, who insisted on callin' the cops. Kid was a juvenile at the time, so his old man got him off an' got the whole thing hushed up. But of course, he couldn't get the vice cop's memory expunged."

"Guy still around?"

"Retired last year. Grove or Groove, something like that. Ask Evanger. He was around then."

Thinnes wasn't ready to ask Evanger. Yet. He said, "Thanks, Swann," and hung up.

A helpful clerk in the personnel department came up with the name of the vice cop. Grove. Thinnes found him in the phone book. As luck would have it, he was home, but he wasn't anxious to discuss old cases. At least, not the Margolis case.

"Yeah, I remember the kid," he told Thinnes after he'd called Area Six back to be sure Thinnes was on the level. "Basically a good kid. Had an asshole for an old man. I was real sorry to hear he bought it; I'd heard he'd cleaned up his act."

"What was his act? You arrested him once."

"Him'n his buddy. Wasn't my idea. These two old biddies insisted. I'da just rousted 'em."

"What'd you charge them with?"

"Public indecency, just in case something leaked."

"Like what?"

"Like who the kid was with."

"Well?"

"Sorry. That was a long time ago. And the kid's death was his own damn fault."

"Bottom line?"

"I gave my word only a grand jury'd get it outta me."

"That high up, huh?" Grove didn't answer. "Will you at least tell me who you gave your word to?"

"The patrol supervisor." Thinnes waited. "A Sergeant Evanger."

Evanger was talking with Karsch when Thinnes stuck his head in the lieutenant's office. He told Thinnes to come in.

Thinnes asked Karsch, "The lieutenant tell you about Margolis's confession?"

Karsch nodded. "Don't be too hard on him. Survivor guilt can drive people to do and say some very irrational things."

"You think he could've killed Finley?"

"I'm not convinced Finley didn't kill himself."

Karsch couldn't back down from his original diagnosis of suicide, Thinnes decided. Couldn't admit he could be wrong.

"Given the right provocation," Karsch said, "anyone can kill. But why would Margolis kill Finley?"

"Maybe he thought he was gay. Margolis doesn't like gays." Thinnes turned to Evanger. "Does he, Lieutenant?" Evanger didn't say anything. Thinnes turned back to Karsch, who looked like he was torn between leaving to avoid a messy scene and staying to hear the latest dirt. "You see, this wasn't Margolis's first performance. Last time he was here, he claimed his son was murdered by gays." Thinnes looked at Evanger. "Did you tell Karsch that, Lieutenant? You didn't tell me."

"I don't see that it's relevant."

"But I'm supposed to be the judge of that," Thinnes said softly. "I'm the detective in charge of this case."

"You don't have a case, Thinnes. You have no proof Finley's death wasn't suicide."

"I'll get the proof." Thinnes let his tone imply *with or without your help.*

"And while you're out poking into five-year-old accidents and thirteen-year-old misdemeanors, who's working up the current cases? Do you know how many homicides we've had this year? If we clear two a day, we won't solve 'em all."

"This one sticks in my craw."

"They *all* stick in *my* craw. Why get worked up over the ones you can't solve?"

"Sooner or later, I'll solve it. There's something about murder— even the otherwise intelligent perpetrator gets nervous and screws up. All you have to do is keep poking around. They get this urge to cover their tracks—even if they're already covered—and they fuck themselves up."

Evanger and Karsch exchanged glances that told Thinnes they'd already discussed him and the Finley case.

"Whoever Finley's killer is," Thinnes told them, as if he thought they might be convinced, "has pretty good sources. He knew I wasn't buying Finley's death was suicide. And he tried to scare off and then set up the only other person who didn't believe Finley killed himself. He knew we weren't buying Dr. Caleb as a dealer, so then he moved immediately to set me up, to get me off his trail."

"It seems to me," Evanger said, "that wasn't so bright."

It was actually stupid to try and set up a cop. Thinnes didn't have to say so. "He couldn't have known I'd get on to Berringer—I almost didn't."

Thinnes wondered how the killer knew where to send Berringer to get the pictures of him. Not the phone book; he had an unpublished number. ". . . Or that Margolis'd get caught smuggling and spill the beans about the blackmail."

"But you haven't got any proof that whoever set you up had anything to do with Finley. You've put a lot of men away, Thinnes. Every one of them has a good reason to get you."

"*And* plant coke on Dr. Caleb?" Thinnes shook his head. "Who did the Margolis kid get arrested with?"

Evanger shook his head. "He has nothing to do with this, and I'm not dragging him into it."

"That big, hunh? Must be a captain or an alderman by now." Evanger's look said he'd heard enough. Thinnes turned to Karsch. "Say for the sake of argument, Doctor, that Finley *was* murdered. What light can you shed on his killer?"

200

"You're asking me to analyze someone I've never met?"

"A profile. The feds do it all the time."

Karsch shrugged. "People react differently to having killed someone. Some are devastated and have to confess and be punished or absolved. Others, when they realize God isn't going to strike them dead, begin to see it as no big thing. They may be tempted to kill again because they've gotten away with it. I'd say that if you really had a murder here, you'd be dealing with the latter type of killer. He's not going to get caught."

FIFTY-EIGHT

Caleb looked speculatively at his reflection in the one-way glass while he waited. To most of those watching him from the outside, he might have just been checking his hair, but Thinnes knew he was aware he was being watched. Thinnes decided Caleb would wait a long time before he'd complain about the wait, because he knew its purpose was to unnerve him.

Thinnes joined him. "Afternoon, Dr. Caleb." Caleb nodded cautiously. "We're investigating Vincent Margolis, and we'd appreciate hearing what you can tell us about him. You know him well?"

"That depends on what you mean by *know* him."

"What do you think I mean?"

"I have no idea."

"You're not close friends?"

"He blames me for his wife's leaving him."

Thinnes nodded empathetically.

"I believed he was more concerned with appearances than with his wife's mental health, and I said so. That didn't endear me to him, especially after Anita asked for a divorce."

"Could Margolis have killed Finley?"

"I take it he hasn't an alibi, or you wouldn't be asking." When Thinnes didn't answer, Caleb shrugged and said, "I doubt it. He might kill in anger, but if he decided in advance he wanted someone dead, I suspect he'd probably hire someone to do it. His arrogance is camouflage for profound insecurity."

"You know, Doctor, you're real good at getting into people's heads."

"Call me Jack."

Thinnes ignored the attempt to keep it friendly. "What can you tell me about Christopher Margolis?"

Caleb look at the mirror again and then at Thinnes. "Can we speak privately?"

Thinnes looked around the room as if pointing out that it was empty. Caleb seemed annoyed. Thinnes waited.

Caleb finally said, "I see no reason to discuss Christopher Margolis. He's been dead five years. He could hardly be involved."

Thinnes shrugged as if it didn't matter anyway. "You go to Mexico quite often. What do you do there?"

The question obviously was not unexpected. Caleb answered matter-of-factly, "I work as a volunteer at a clinic."

"Is that a front to smuggle drugs?"

Caleb was subtly thrown off balance; Thinnes pressed his advantage. "You bringing back cocaine?"

"No."

"What is it you have to hide?" Thinnes asked more aggressively.

"I know how this works, John: you try to make me angry so I'll lose control and say something imprudent."

"So you never lose control?" Caleb shook his head. "What about Nam?"

Caleb was momentarily, subtly startled, but quickly relaxed. "Of course you'd have looked up my record." He shrugged. "So you already know about Nam. It's what my attorney might call irrelevant and immaterial."

Thinnes moved closer to almost whisper, "It proves you *can* kill."

"Not in cold blood." Caleb looked at Thinnes and said very evenly and calmly, "You can question me all night, but we both know it's a game. The real issue is whether you can believe that I killed Allan Finley, that I could coldly and deliberately put a gun to his head and blow his brains out—after I spent three years of my life trying to help him straighten out." He seemed almost disappointed that Thinnes could believe him capable of such an act.

"It's something I can't believe of anyone—until I have the evidence."

Caleb seemed to find this satisfactory, if equivocal. "Well then, until you have the evidence, don't."

An uncomfortable silence ensued. Thinnes could think of nothing penetrating to ask. Caleb seemed to be playing some shrink's waiting game. Finally the doctor said, "I'd like to leave. I have clients to see."

Thinnes shrugged and went to the door.

As he rose, Caleb said, "Tell me something, Detective. If anyone else had been assigned to investigate Finley's death, would it have been written off as a suicide?"

"It may be yet. Why?"

"Who's the one person who knows enough about both of us to screw us both?"

"Not Ray Crowne. Why would he?"

"Would he have access to cocaine?"

"Are you kidding? The only place you'll find more drugs than a cop shop is a pharmaceutical warehouse."

"Does he know about me?"

"I didn't."

"Would he know how to circumvent my security system?"

Thinnes shrugged. "You learn all sorts of skills in this line of work. But why? He hasn't got a motive."

"*Someone* has a motive. We just don't know yet what it is. Where was Ray the night my apartment was broken into?"

"With us," Thinnes said defensively.

"While you were filling out your report?"

Thinnes shook his head, not buying it. As he waved Caleb out the door, he could hear the Levolor blind drop over the one-way glass outside. The group—Evanger, Viernes, Ferris, and Karsch—tried to act casual. Thinnes said, "Dr. Caleb, if you'll wait downstairs, I'll give you a lift back to your office."

Caleb, who'd been looking the others over, nodded and walked off without comment.

Thinnes glared at Evanger. "Well?"

"What'd you say to him?" Thinnes knew he meant when he'd lowered his voice.

"Something he didn't want us to hear," Viernes said.

"You seem to be pulling your punches today, Thinnes," Karsch said.

"Maybe the rumors about him stressing out are true," Ferris

told Karsch. "When he didn't have a shred of proof against Caleb, he was sure he was guilty; now there's some evidence he's involved, he's going out of his way to clear the guy."

"It might make *some* sense," Evanger said, dryly, "to take the word of a respected psychiatrist over some blackmailer caught red-handed."

"My money's on the shrink here," Ferris said. "I think Thinnes finally met his match. What do you think, Karsch?"

"Dr. Caleb is very good," Karsch said, "but whether he can shake Thinnes off . . ." He shrugged.

"You will have a report for me in the morning," Evanger told Thinnes.

Thinnes turned and walked away.

FIFTY-NINE

They got in Thinnes's car, and he burned rubber out of the lot and ran the yellow at Western. His mood paralleled the rubber marks he left on the pavement. Crowne hadn't the brains or the ambition! Damn Caleb! And damn Evanger!

He took Clybourn and drove like the damn-it-all mood he was in, cutting in and out without signals, riding the brakes, tearing up to lights. Caleb didn't comment, even when they approached Cabrini with its DMZ of empty lawns.

God damn Caleb! He'd been a fool to trust him. A shrink. A professional mind fucker! Thinnes stole a sideways look at him, slouched against the door like the Cheshire cat, smiling inside. And there probably wasn't a dick at Area Six that didn't know by now that Thinnes had soft-pedaled the interrogation. Why? Was he afraid Caleb would let something slip about the favors he'd done Thinnes? He'd never let a suspect get close before, much less mess with his mind.

Caleb broke the silence. "Are you afraid you were wrong about me, or just afraid of me?"

"That's cryptic."

"The average straight male knows absolutely nothing about homosexuality and doesn't want to know because he might learn something uncomfortable about himself." His near-smile dared Thinnes to challenge him.

That was only part of it. Fags *had* to be different—and you didn't want to know if they weren't. But the worst of it was, you couldn't always tell. He hadn't known about Caleb. Hadn't even suspected!

"What's to know? You telling me you don't like boys?"

206

"I'd be a damn liar, wouldn't I?"

"What about your professional ethics, Doctor?"

"You've met a lot of teenaged hookers in your line, haven't you?"

"What's your point?" Thinnes could tell Caleb knew he'd met far too many.

"You ever screw any of them?"

The analogy was unnerving. Thinnes felt his reaction showing. He said, "No," very quietly.

"Then why do you assume . . . ?"

Thinnes didn't answer. Caleb persisted. "Were you ever tempted?"

"Yeah," Thinnes admitted, grudgingly.

"My experience exactly."

"You were screwing a patient's stepson. How does that jibe with your professional code of ethics?"

"About as well as life ever fits the rules. Chris and I had already been living together two years when I was asked to consult on Anita. I agreed to see her before I learned her name—just on the basis of her history." He paused. "We don't always have the luxury of choosing between good and evil—most often it's evil or worse. If I'd refused to treat Anita, she'd almost certainly have been subjected to Draconian procedures just to satisfy her husband's egoism."

"You didn't worry about a malpractice suit?"

Caleb's wry smile was almost a grimace. "Margolis would have had to admit publicly that his son was gay. It was easier for him to convince himself that he didn't know who Chris was living with, and that Anita left him for another man."

"What is it you *want?*" Thinnes asked.

Caleb smiled as if the question was naive. "What most people want, I expect." Thinnes waited. "Love and work."

"You found 'em?"

"The work."

"You're pretty damn candid."

"I should think a detective would be used to confessions."

"What do you want from *me?*"

"I want you to catch Allan's killer."

Caleb's conviction was quietly chilling. But there was more. There had to be.

"And?"

"What else could there be?"

There was a long, uncomfortable silence before Thinnes said, softly, "Tell me about Christopher Margolis. Was he a client?"

"Of course not."

Thinnes nodded. He'd expected as much. "How old was he?"

"Seventeen. When I met him he was hustling in a bar. A dark bar. I didn't think about his age until I got him out of there and into the light.

"And?"

"I fed him and told him to come back when he grew up."

"According to Anita, you helped him get started as an artist."

Caleb shrugged. "He gave me a line—he wanted to go to art school, but his old man wouldn't pay. It was a logical variation of the standard hustle. You've seen my place. It wouldn't take a genius to guess my interest is in art. But there's often a grain of truth in such fictions, so I told him that if he and his portfolio could get accepted at an accredited art school, I'd see to it that he didn't have to worry about the tuition—a challenge he accepted, I'm happy to say."

"So when did you start sleeping with him?"

Caleb looked annoyed. "Years later."

Thinnes waited to see if silence would compel Caleb to elaborate.

"If it comes back to you, it's yours."

"What's that?"

"More of your sixties cliché. Chris eventually repaid me with six paintings, independently valued at ten percent above what I paid out for his expenses. He never *had* to sleep with me."

"He lived with you?"

"After he'd made it and could've had anyone he wanted." Caleb gave Thinnes a look that was a challenge. "Do you want all the intimate details?"

Thinnes flinched. "How about just the punch line?"

"I loved him. More than anyone or anything on earth." He

208

looked very deliberately at Thinnes. "Can you understand that?"

Thinnes was concentrating on traffic, which lowered his usual defenses. Without thinking, he said, "That's how I feel about my wife." He slammed his fist on the steering wheel. "Why did I tell you that?"

Caleb smiled gently. "Because you're lonely and combat-fatigued, and you've become too estranged from your wife to tell her. And because on some level you'd just about decided I mean you no harm."

"I *had,* until I saw that picture of you at Jeremy's and looked up your war record." He stole a glance at Caleb, who was looking straight ahead."

"I lost control."

Thinnes laughed humorlessly. "Nobody's ever really in control. It's an illusion."

"Did you ever kill a man?"

"No, thank God."

The conversation seemed to choke to death on that. Caleb stared out at Division Street. Thinnes concentrated on traffic. The silence was uncomfortable. Eventually Thinnes felt compelled to fill it.

"In the academy, they teach you to draw your weapon only to save life and shoot only if it's absolutely necessary. But you're taught to shoot to kill if you do fire."

"In any case, it's supposed to be a considered decision."

"If you stop to debate the ethics, you're dead."

Caleb didn't say anything.

"Oh, I get it. You think because you didn't stop and calmly decide that the asshole who was taking out your buddies deserved to be killed, it somehow makes killing him wrong?" He shot a glance at Caleb. "Or are you one of those killing-is-never-justified fanatics?"

Caleb thought before answering. "I hadn't thought of it that way. I've been too obsessed with losing control."

"Like I said, nobody's ever really in control except maybe someone like Finley's killer." Caleb shuddered. Thinnes added, "The best we can hope for is to contain our little explosions. Or divert 'em." He paused to deal with traffic. "Speaking of losing control, Margolis broke down and confessed to killing his son. His lawyer's claiming we browbeat him into it and it's nonsense."

"In a sense, he did kill him, but not literally. He goaded him into a white rage and let him drive away mad. Chris drove too fast and lost control of his car." Caleb seemed to be trying to get control of some strong feeling. "I believe Margolis has paid with remorse every day since."

Thinnes pretended not to notice the pause. He said, "Survivor guilt?"

Caleb nodded.

When you get a second opinion and it agrees with the first, it's probably right.

"Do you know who might be blackmailing Margolis?"

"Anyone who knew Chris was gay."

Thinnes nodded. "And about you and him?"

Caleb shook his head. "We were discreet. But Chris was arrested once—caught with his pants down, so to speak. Margolis got him off and eventually had the arrest record expunged, but who knows who saw it first?"

SIXTY

Forest Avenue, Wilmette. Fifty foot elms and maples overarched and shaded the brick street where Thinnes had left his Chevy. He wondered what had become of "cooler near the lake" as he stood on his in-laws' imposing porch and waited for someone to answer the door. His shirt was cotton and short-sleeved, but it was damp, and he fanned himself with the manila envelope and the papers he'd brought. The house seemed smaller than the first time he'd stood here, but it was no less impressive—a three-story, pale gray stucco with white trim and tall windows. He was about to lift the brass knocker again when Rhonda's mother opened the door.

Louise Coates was five five, blond and gray eyed, what Thinnes's mother would have called genteel.

"Hello, Louise. How've you been?"

Anger, or something like it, made frown lines in her flawless makeup. "She won't see you."

He'd never known Louise to be rude, not even when, as a rookie cop, he'd had the nerve to ask to marry Rhonda. He said, "She has to."

Something like fear replaced the anger, and Thinnes remembered what Caleb had told him about Rob's assessment of his, Thinnes's, mental state. He pulled the hem of his shirt up above his beltline so Louise could see that he wasn't carrying. "No gun," he said. He let the shirt drop.

"She doesn't want to see you," Louise repeated, and closed the door.

Thinnes gripped the photo envelope between his teeth and rolled the papers into a cylinder, which he slid into his hip pocket. He banged the brass door knocker for five minutes.

Louise finally opened the door the width of the security chain. "Go away," she told him, "or I'll call the police."

For a domestic dispute involving a Chicago cop? Wilmette's finest would love that. But he knew she wouldn't call. She couldn't stand any kind of scene. He said, "Go ahead."

She started to close the door again, but Thinnes put his right arm against it, above his head, and leaned on the arm.

"Tell Ronnie if she'll just hear me out I'll go away forever. If she still wants me to. Just five minutes—that's all." He backed away from the door and let her close it.

Fifteen minutes later, Rhonda stepped out on the porch looking as dragged out and miserable as Thinnes felt. She pulled the door shut behind her, then leaned against it. She let her "show me" expression speak for her.

Thinnes slipped Jeremy's "morphodite" photograph out of the envelope. "Those pictures of me were faked," he said. "Just like this one." He handed her the photo and watched the sullen anger in her face fade to puzzlement as she studied it.

The puzzlement changed to incredulity.

Thinnes took the paper roll from his pocket and peeled off the copy of Berringer's confession. "Somebody figured to get my mind off a case I'm working by making trouble for me at home."

Rhonda glanced at him suspiciously, but took the paper. He stepped back and worked the remaining papers—a copy of the report on the raid; statements by some of Berringer's associates; and the names Karsch had given him—into a tighter roll. He had to keep his hands busy. Keep them off her.

When she finished reading the first report, he handed her another, then another—as fast as she could read them—until all he had left was the paper with the references.

He held it out and she took it. She read it, turned it over. "What's this?"

"Marriage counselors." When she didn't respond to that, he added, "Give me another chance, Ronnie—I'll go to counseling with you. One of those, or anybody you say."

He studied her face. She was clamping her lower lip between her teeth, trying not to cry. At least she cared enough for that. Finally she handed the reports back, keeping the picture and the reference

212

list. "I'll think about it." She couldn't resist smiling as she added, "Who's your cute friend?"

Thinnes and Rhonda arrived home in Rhonda's car. Thinnes parked in the driveway behind his own car and turned the engine off before he turned to Rhonda and let out an exaggerated sigh of relief.

"Does this mean you'll have to work late next Thursday night?"

"I said I'd go. I won't promise to like it."

They sat in silence for a minute.

He said, "Remember when we used to sit like this outside your folks' house?"

She smiled. He grabbed her and kissed her with mock ferocity. After token resistance, she responded eagerly, and they kissed long enough to leave both of them breathless.

"Let's continue this conversation inside," he said, grinning.

She nodded. While she gathered up her things, he hurried around to open her door—a gesture sufficiently uncharacteristic to surprise her.

Rob was sitting on the stairs when they come in. He studied their faces hopefully while Thinnes took off his gun and put it on the top shelf of the closet. "Everything go all right?" Rob asked. Anxiety pitched his voice higher.

"She's a marriage counselor," Thinnes said, dryly, "not a miracle worker." He reached up to ruffle his hair. "Bedtime."

"Rob, your father and I love each other. We'll work it out."

Rob hardly seemed comforted. He started up the stairs, then paused. "I almost forgot," he said, looking down at Thinnes. "You're supposed to call the station ASAP."

Thinnes put the phone very deliberately in its cradle and went grimly to the foot of the stairs. "Rhonda!" He got his gun from the closet.

"What is it, John?"

"I've got to go. They just found Ray Crowne's car in the lake."

A crowd had gathered and was lit by the floodlights of TV mini-cam trucks. Uniformed officers were trying to keep the curious at

213

bay as Thinnes made his way through. Strobe flashes of red, yellow, and blue light from emergency vehicles and police cars gave the scene a surrealistic quality. A giant tow truck backed up to the water. Its cable disappeared beneath the surface. Diver's followed it under, making little roiling whirlpools.

Moments later, accompanied by shouts from emergency workers and an awed murmur from the crowd, Crowne's red sports car was hauled out of the water. Thinnes grabbed a flashlight from someone and shined it on the driver's window. He could see Crowne's drowned face clearly. He tried frantically to open the door, but it was locked.

A fireman put a hand on Thinnes's shoulder. He spoke gently. "There's no rush. He's been in there over an hour." A police officer took Thinnes's arm, and Thinnes let himself be led away as the firemen started to pry the door open. He looked back to see it pop open. Crowne swam earthward in a flood of water, like something aborted. They put his body on a stretcher and covered it with a tarp.

SIXTY-ONE

Swann got the case. Another death investigation. Another death that didn't sit right, even though everyone knew Crowne drove like a maniac.

Two "accidents"—if you counted the mysterious failure of his own brakes—in two weeks. Thinnes didn't buy it. Someone had arranged both incidents. Someone who knew Thinnes's car. Someone from Area Six. What was the connection with Finley?

Swann's first act had been to have Thinnes gently but firmly evicted from the crime scene.

"He said he had a date tonight," Thinnes insisted as Swann pushed him under the police barricade tape.

"What was her name?"

"I don't know. He played the field."

"He carry an address book with him?"

"No."

"Yeah, okay, Thinnes, we'll get to it. Meantime, why don't you go home?"

He didn't though. After the squadrol left with Crowne, while the tow truck driver got the Fiero ready to roll, the cops dispersed the crowd. Thinnes watched from behind the barricade tape as Swann did a careful preliminary search of the car, including a quick flashlight inspection of the undercarriage. Swann catalogued his findings out loud for Thinnes's benefit. The windshield was smashed where Crowne's head had hit. There was an empty half pint on the floor.

Swann put gloves on and pulled a .45 out from under the front seat—Crowne's backup piece. It hadn't done him any good. The rest of the contents were unremarkable: maps, registration, insurance card, and tire gauge in the glove box; a raincoat and a folding dash shade Crowne never used on the back seat; jumper cables, flares, jack and spare, boxes of ammo in the trunk. A pair of boots. And a soaked collection of the gravel and lint and bits of paper, hair, and miscellaneous dirt that settles on the floors and in the trunks of cars. Maybe the lab could sort some of it out.

Swann walked over and said, "I'm ridin' with it to the pound. You can give me a lift back if you like, 'n tell me what you know."

Thinnes nodded. Swann couldn't compromise his case by offering more.

Thinnes had watched autopsies before, but this, in its way, was a first. The room was cold. The medical examiner, a pathologist, began by putting on gloves and turning on the microphone that hung over the autopsy table. He had his assistant take photos while he studied Crowne's clothing before removing it. He handed the sodden notebook, from Crowne's jacket pocket, to Swann and covered the mike with his gloved palm before saying, "Be sure that's logged in before you walk off with it."

Swann said, "Yeah," quietly. He already had Crowne's gun and wallet and keys.

The notebook was folded back to Caleb's address. Significant? Or just an indication that Caleb had been the last subject Crowne had contact with? Swann put the book on one of the stainless steel countertops.

The ME carefully undressed the corpse. It gradually penetrated the dull misery Thinnes was feeling that the pathologist wasn't anxious for an audience. But who in his right mind would be, working with two dicks—who had a stake in the case—looking over your shoulder? The man described the color and condition as he took each item off, mentioning the brand name, before he handed it to his assistant.

"I have before me the body of a well-developed, well-nourished white male, who appears to be the stated twenty-nine years of age. . . ."

Thinnes had never seen Crowne naked before. He felt like a peeper. Couldn't look. Couldn't look away.

The ME was saying, ". . . Evidence of a blow to the face—

216

specifically, the forehead." He went on to describe the bloody wound in medical terms. He searched carefully, turning the body over, combing through the hair for other distinguishing marks or evidence of violence, describing every scrape and pimple to the microphone. In detail. His assistant took more pictures than a first-time parent. Thinnes thought it was odd there were no bruises from the steering wheel on Crowne's chest. The ME didn't comment, just described what was there in nauseating detail. Until Thinnes wanted to shout *get on with it!* He had plenty of time to sort through his feelings. Too much. Not enough feelings. He began to realize how little he'd understood what made Crowne tick. He wondered if Crowne himself had had much sense of who he was or what he could've been. The quick and the dead. Crowne hadn't been quick enough. Now he was dead. DOA.

Damn this addictive job! As with all addictions, Thinnes felt he was needing greater and greater fixes to stave off withdrawal. Why did it have to be Crowne who O.D.'d?

The ME began the exploration of Crowne's head injury. Thinnes felt his teeth grinding as the pathologist cut through scalp and bone. Brain surgery. Even Swann looked pale.

"Massive subdural hemorrhage of the frontal lobes due to blunt trauma. Lacerations . . . that's odd. There's no contrecoup."

"What?"

"There's none of the secondary damage you'd expect to find, due to rebound of the brain after the initial impact."

"In English, Doc," Swann said.

"In cases where a moving head strikes a hard stationary object, such as a windshield or a steering wheel, the front of the brain strikes the inside of the skull on impact and is damaged. The brain subsequently bounces—rebounds—off the skull and strikes the rear of the skull, sustaining secondary damage in the back. There's hardly any here. It's suspicious but inconclusive, especially since he'd been drinking so heavily."

"He didn't drink." Thinnes meant not more than a beer or two. Crowne had used to snort with disgust when someone bragged how he'd tied one on last night. Thinnes had never seen him hung over.

The pathologist stopped what he was doing to turn and look daggers at Thinnes. "Maybe the aroma in here is deisel fuel."

"He's right, Thinnes," Swann said. "You can smell it. So butt out or get out."

Thinnes turned around and left. He felt like puking but he knew he wouldn't. Crowne didn't drink. He always used his seat belt. He always said it would save him if his driving ever caught up with him. Thinnes walked up and down the hall until he felt in control again, then he went back in.

The ME had opened up Crowne's body with a Y-shaped incision that ran across his breasts diagonally from shoulder to midline, and down the midline to his pubic area. Retractors held rib-cage and abdominal cavity open for examination.

After what seemed an hour later, the ME said suddenly, "Here's something. Fluid in the lungs that has the smell and appearance of hard liquor. Get a sample of this," he told his assistant.

In the lungs. Thinnes didn't say I told you so, but Swann said, "Shut up, Thinnes."

The ME began to reexamine Crowne's throat.

Thinnes and Swann left the room when the ME began to close up. They went over the cases Crowne had been working on while they waited for the pathologist to finish. He gave them his report orally while he changed his gown and gloves because he had another urgent case waiting to be autopsied.

"This is unofficial, because we don't have the tox reports yet, but I'd say the cause of death was drowning—in alcohol. It's a close call, though, because the head injury undoubtedly rendered him unconscious—which is how some person or persons unknown managed to pour the booze into him—and it might have killed him without the alcohol. My guess is that the alcohol was introduced with a hard plastic or metal tube. Probably tried to get it into his stomach and it went down the wrong pipe. He no doubt would have drowned in the lake if the alcohol hadn't done the job." He looked from Swann to Thinnes. "The manner of death is unquestionably homicide."

SIXTY-TWO

Irene Sleighton opened the bills with a letter opener and a vengeance, and when Caleb had escorted his client across the outer office to the door, she held up one of the envelopes. She had a funny expression on her face.

"Doctor, this came in this morning's mail."

It was unopened, addressed to North Michigan Avenue Associates in Allan Finley's hand, with his return address. Caleb considered what to do for a moment, then borrowed the letter opener. He slit the envelope and dumped the contents onto Irene's desk without touching anything. He used the opener to turn the items over so he could see them. There were: the return portion of Finley's monthly statement; a check for the amount; and a small slip of paper with two long numbers and the word *Chartreuse* written on it.

"Mrs. Sleighton, do you have a tweezers I could borrow for a moment?"

Irene was surprised, but she dug a tweezers from her purse.

"Thank you."

He used the tweezers to lift the check, statement, and cryptic note over to the copy machine, where he made copies. Then, still using the tweezers, he returned the items to the envelope, which he also copied. He returned the tweezers, folded the copies, and put them in his pocket, then he got a business envelope and letterhead from Irene and took them in his office.

Caleb put the papers on his desk and picked up the phone.

"Detective Thinnes, please . . . Is he on duty today? . . . If I send something to him by messenger, could you be sure he gets it? . . . Thank you."

219

He wrote a note on the letterhead and put it in the business envelope with Finley's mailing. Then he sealed the business envelope and wrote *Detective John Thinnes, Area Six Headquarters, Western at Belmont* on the outside.

It took longer for his second call to be answered. He said, "Hello, Joe. What's your schedule like this afternoon? I have a little job that's right up your alley. My last appointment's at three. How about your place at four thirty?" Joe was agreeable, though he had a dinner engagement and he wanted to know how long it would take.

"That depends on how quickly you can figure this out."

Caleb hung up the phone and took the envelope to the outer office, where Irene was typing statements. "I'd like you to send this out immediately, Mrs. Sleighton. Be sure to ask the messenger for his ID, and get a receipt."

"Certainly, Doctor."

"I haven't anyone coming in until one; I'll be back before then."

"Have a nice lunch."

The medical examiner's seals had been removed, and Allan Finley's door was open. When Caleb knocked, Adriana Finley came to the doorway. She'd been crying.

"Dr. Caleb."

"The super sent me up. He said you were packing Allan's things."

"Just his personal things. I told the super to get rid of the rest. I can't deal with it." She turned away from the door without inviting him in, but she left it open and didn't object when he followed her inside. The bloody mess had been hastily cleaned, but the apartment was otherwise as the police left it. She went to the couch and sat down. Covering her face with one hand, she sobbed. "Why Allan? Oh, God!"

Caleb said, very gently, "Would you like me to help?"

She stopped crying and swallowed. "Please."

"Would you happen to have mailed a bill Allan left lying around the apartment?"

She sniffed and shook her head. "Bills. The super did. He

found them when he came in to clean up, and he asked me if I minded. They had to be paid and, well, it's clearly what Allan intended."

He nodded. "What needs to be done?"

SIXTY-THREE

8:45 A.M. No one was sitting around reading the paper. Those from the night watch who hadn't gone home had joined the day shift hitting the streets. Swann was closeted with the area commander. Ferris and Viernes were phoning purposefully. Everyone else moved through the squad room with urgency.

Except Thinnes. He sat reviewing his own private demons. It'd been less than two years since Frank Flynn had been shot trying to settle a fight after a traffic accident in the neighborhood he'd moved to for safety. Ray's death had the same sickening irony.

Evanger and Karsch came in together. Karsch said, "Excuse me, Lieutenant." He went over and put a hand on Thinnes's shoulder. "Thinnes, what is it?"

"Ray was murdered."

That meant it could be Caleb. Caleb could have set Crowne up for Finley's murder, then arranged a convenient "accident" to make the question moot. Or it was narrowed down to the cops who were present when Caleb suggested it was Crowne—Evanger, Viernes, Ferris. Karsch. But Karsch was always present. Evanger! Evanger'd known about the Margolis kid.

Karsch said, "Good Lord! Are you sure?"

Evanger said, "What?"

Thinnes didn't look at them. "I just came from the autopsy. Ray was dead before his car hit the water. He died from alcohol in his lungs after he was hit on the head. There were no other drugs in his system. No water in his lungs." He looked at Evanger. "Someone killed him, then smashed his windshield from the inside and pushed his car into the lake." He sat with his hands in his lap, staring at the tabletop. Suddenly, he raised his fists and slammed them down on the table.

"God *damn* him!"

Everyone in the room looked at Thinnes except Evanger. Evanger looked at Karsch.

Karsch said, "Let's talk about it in private." He put a hand under Thinnes's elbow and steered him toward his office, pausing to get water from the cooler in a paper cup.

Evanger called after them, "I'll get the ball rolling on this." As he passed Ferris and Viernes, he told them, "Come with me."

Karsch closed his door. "Sit down, Thinnes." He took a prescription vial from his top desk drawer and shook two tablets from it into Thinnes's palm.

"What's this?"

"Valium. Take them." Thinnes complied. "Now finish the water." He emptied the cup. "Good. Now tell me."

"We must've been getting too close. That's why he had to set Ray up as Finley's killer—yesterday in the interview room—then kill him."

"Who did?"

"It has to be Caleb!"

"Maybe you'd better explain."

"He asked who knew enough about both him and me to make trouble for both of us. And then he tried to make it look like Crowne's reckless driving finally got him. He knew about that— saw Crowne drive outta the lot the night the Williams woman was killed, saw the car he drove. Crowne wouldn't be expecting a physical attack from a shrink."

Even as he said it, Thinnes wondered if he had it right. What about the failure of his own brakes? Would Caleb know how to tamper with brakes? How would he do the fix without being seen? No. *It had to be somebody from here.* Viernes or Ferris or Evanger.

And Karsch reported to Evanger!

"I think I'd better get back to work," Thinnes said.

Karsch escorted him out of the office. Going to the table where he'd left his files, Thinnes had his feelings under control. As expected, Karsch went to Evanger's door, knocked, and went in.

Thinnes had returned to his work place more out of habit than for any other reason. An envelope addressed to him lay on top of the typewriter. From Caleb. He took out the envelope from Finley and Caleb's note: *John, This came in this morning's mail. I indulged my curiosity by opening it, but I was careful not to get fingerprints on the contents. Jack Caleb P.S. The writing on the odd slip isn't Allan's.*

Thinnes found Finley's statement, check, and cryptic note in the envelope and looked them over, handling them by their edges and not getting fingerprints on them. When you'd been doing things long enough, part of your brain just kept on doing them, no matter how fucked up you were, no matter how distracted.

Why had Finley put the paper in the envelope with Dr. Caleb's bill? Could he have figured it all out so quickly? Maybe he was going to talk it over with Caleb before he went to the cops. He had an appointment the next day. He might've put the paper with the bill so he wouldn't forget it. Maybe if they found the killer he'd shed some light on that. Maybe they'd never know.

He picked up the phone. He kept his voice too low for others around him to hear. "We got a print man in the building? I got something urgent." He hung up as Karsch came out of Evanger's office.

Karsch walked over to Thinnes's place. "Evanger wants to see you." He stood over Thinnes as the detective slid Caleb's note and Finley's papers back in the mailer.

Thinnes said, "I'm going."

As he went into Evanger's office, taking the envelope with him, he wondered how much Evanger knew about bleeding brakes.

"Sit down, John." Evanger said, and pointed to a chair.

"John, huh? Why don't you just get to the point?"

"All right. Take it easy. I assume you've told Swann everything you can think of that might help him." Thinnes nodded. "Then I want you to take the rest of the day off."

"What did Karsch tell you?"

"Nothing I didn't know already. You've been under stress, you're overdue for a vacation, and this is the second partner you've lost in two years. You also didn't get any sleep last night."

Thinnes expressed his exasperation by looking all around Evanger without looking at him. He didn't answer.

"An order, Thinnes. Turn in your car keys and your radio and go home. Come back Monday. I've got twenty dicks working on this, good people. If they come up with anything, I'll call you. Meanwhile, go home."

In one of the District Nineteen rooms, Thinnes yawned as he watched the evidence technician brush black powder all over Finley's check, statement, and note. He shouldn't have taken that Valium.

The tech finally shrugged. "Sorry, Thinnes. No luck."

"Thanks, anyway." He looked around the room as if for an answer. He felt tired. "Maybe you could do me a favor?"

The technician looked expectant.

"I'd like to make copies of these, then maybe you could log 'em in as evidence in the Finley case and drop them off at the lab. Ask them to see what they can find out about them."

"Sure."

Thinnes gave him the case report number. "And don't tell anyone we've got 'em. Not even Evanger."

The parking lot was deserted when Thinnes came out of the building, preoccupied and depressed, slowed by the tranquilizer. He opened his car door and was about to get in when something on the ground near the corner of the building caught his eye. He walked toward the object. A wallet. He bent to pick it up. For an instant, he saw something loom over him; he didn't have time to see what. Something hard and heavy struck the back of his head. He heard a thunking sound. Like a melon hit by a hammer. He felt the sandpaper surface of the concrete strike his face as he dropped.

In the scenario Thinnes reconstructed later, someone wearing a white shirt and gloves picked up the wallet, then searched him, taking his keys. Handcuffs. Gun. Someone dragged Thinnes to his car; opened the trunk; and lifted him inside. Someone taped his mouth and eyes. Someone took his jacket; cuffed his hands behind his back. Someone put the jacket on.

Thinnes vaguely remembered that the trunk slammed shut. The

back of the car dipped slightly. The door slammed. The engine started.

He supposed that the someone put the sun visor down to hide his face as he left the parking lot, and waved to other officers as Thinnes would have.

SIXTY-FOUR

Joe was a mathematics professor at Northwestern University who dabbled in hacking, tax law, and investing. His office was the playpen of a genius. On one wall equations covered a blackboard. Shelves of esoteric books filled another wall, geometric posters and quotes from Albert Einstein adorned a third. Sophisticated stereo and computer systems; a kinetic sculpture; and a disorderly desk occupied the space between. Joe's toys. Joe greeted Caleb warmly before demanding, "What's this 'matter of utmost urgency'?"

Caleb handed him the photocopy of Allan Finley's note. "What do you make of this?"

It took only a glance. "My guess is the numbers are tax index numbers. This other thing's probably a password." In answer to Caleb's look, he said, "I'd say this sheet belongs to a guy with extensive real estate holdings—maybe some in trusts. Probably files 'em by tax number."

"But writing it down defeats the purpose."

"It might be someone else's password, or the guy might have just had it changed and wrote it down to refer to. Lot of people don't know enough about their own systems to change the password themselves." Caleb nodded. Joe laughed. "It doesn't do you a lot of good to have the password if you don't know whose it is."

"I have an idea about that. Do you have a directory?"

Joe handed him the phone book, and Caleb looked up Margolis Enterprises. "Don't companies that have more than one phone number usually get them in sequence?"

"Yeah, if they can."

"Okay, here's the main number." Caleb pointed to the directory. Joe nodded and typed several things, including a consecutive number, into his computer. When that didn't work, he tried two more numbers. The second elicited the response USER NAME on the monitor. He typed MARGOLIS, and the computer responded with a beep and ENTER PASSWORD. Joe typed CHARTREUSE. The computer responded INVALID PASSWORD.

"Either it's the wrong computer or they changed the password."

"I'm fairly certain it's the right computer."

"Okay. What's this guy like?"

"Nouveau riche. Arrogant. He collects contemporary art and real estate."

Joe nodded and for the next five minutes tried other words, getting more beeps and INVALID PASSWORDS. Finally the computer responded, WELCOME TO MARGOLIS ENTERPRISES MASTER FILE.

Joe grinned. "Bingo!"

"How did you do that?"

"You don't want to know. Now, what would you like to see?"

"Something that would identify these numbers."

Joe conjured up a menu and studied it. "That would probably be real estate."

He typed another instruction, and the printer attached to his computer began printing furiously. Caleb was startled.

"I'm dumping it into my printer," Joe explained, "so we can log off. The longer we're on line, the better chance we have of getting caught."

The computer screen displayed the menu again, and he logged off, then studied the printout. Finally he said, "Here're your numbers." He whistled as he pointed to the addresses printed next to them, then to the owners of record, which were listed as trusts. "Do you know what we have here?"

"If those parcels are worth what I think, a motive for murder."

Joe went to his desk and dug out several legal-size sheets. He pointed to one of the numbers on the printout. "This one's quietly working its way through a zoning hearing right now. And I mean *quietly*. If it gets the requested changes, the agent's commission alone will be in the six-figure range. Who is this Margolis, anyway?"

"The goose who lays golden eggs."

Joe's puzzlement was apparent. "The name sounds familiar. He's in real estate?"

"Someone's been blackmailing him. When his accountant got hold of this . . ." Caleb waved the photocopy in the air, ". . . that *someone* murdered him, nearly killed me, and tried to push the police detective on the case off the deep end . . . The accountant was a client of mine. He must've slipped this in the envelope with my check to hide it from the murderer."

"Well, don't keep me in suspense. Who done it?"

"I don't know. Yet."

SIXTY-FIVE

Caleb stalked across the outer office past Miss Ellis, who grabbed her phone, and into Margolis's inner office. He made no attempt to conceal how close he was to losing his temper as he crossed the room, and there was a carefully implied threat as he leaned his large frame over the desk, into Margolis's personal space. He slapped the cryptic photocopy down in front of Margolis.

"Who knew you lost this?"

Margolis was too flabbergasted to equivocate. "How did you get that?"

"Allan had it. And he wasn't a thief or a spy, so he must've come by it innocently. Who did you tell about it?"

"No one."

"By trying to protect yourself on this real estate swindle, you're helping to cover up a murder!" Caleb could feel himself losing control, and he forced himself to breathe slowly and deeply.

His behavior had the effect of terrifying Margolis. "If my name is linked with that property, it'll destroy the deal and maybe attract enough attention to start an investigation. I'll be ruined!" Caleb waited, letting Margolis see he was unimpressed. "I swear I don't know who it is!"

"Who did you tell about losing the paper?"

"The man who's been blackmailing me. Over the phone. When he called to get those numbers and I couldn't tell him because I'd lost the paper and I couldn't remember the numbers!"

Margolis's fear shocked Caleb out of his rage. He eased up, nodding. "All the police would have to do would be to see who else has profited from your deals the last twelve or thirteen years. It has been about thirteen years since Chris was arrested, hasn't it?"

Margolis seemed to harden at the mention of Chris. "Don't you think I haven't thought of that? I couldn't get anywhere, not even with the best detectives money can buy."

"Ah, but the police have resources private detectives don't. And *they* don't have to cover their own trails."

Margolis's silence was assent.

Caleb continued, "You told this blackmailer about the paper and that Allan had been working on your books."

"I just told him it was someone from WR and C. I didn't tell him his name—I didn't even know . . ."

SIXTY-SIX

There were too damn many things Margolis didn't know, Caleb reflected as he leaned on the polished granite top of the District Nineteen front desk, waiting for the desk sergeant to get off the phone. The sergeant told him Thinnes was off for the weekend.

"But you can talk to one of the other detectives if you like."

He liked. Until he was halfway up to the Area Six squad room and he remembered that Finley's murderer knew a great deal about him. And about Thinnes. And Finley's death was all that the two of them had in common. You had to be careful, when you were poking into things, not to get your tail caught in the door. Speaking to one of the other detectives was beginning to seem like a dangerous idea, but he was past the point of no return.

A dozen people were at work in the room. It gave Caleb the impression of a cat shelter with its variety of individuals withdrawn in their police-officer reserve. One of the men stretched, and Caleb was aware of the handgun under his coat like a well developed muscle as the coat pulled away from his chest. And like cats detectives were neither pitiless nor cruel as they waited, remorselessly, for movement from their prey, their hunter's instincts merely an expression of their nature. He imagined dog people would find these men and women discomfiting. And which was the man-eater?

He went to the desk sergeant and asked if Thinnes was around. The man shook his head and shrugged.

"You'd better talk to Lieutenant Evanger," he said, pointing to Evanger's office.

"Thank you." As soon as he turned his back, Caleb could hear the sergeant pushing the buttons on his phone. The ordinarily innocuous sound made his hair stand up.

He knocked on Evanger's door. The lieutenant invited him in and offered him a seat. "Thinnes won't be in until Monday," he said. "Is there something I can help you with?"

He remembered seeing Evanger at the zoo, shaking hands with the politicians. And in Chicago, that meant with people in business and real estate. Finley would have opened the door to a cop as readily as to a friend.

Caleb didn't sit. "It's something of a personal nature. I think I'd better wait and speak to Thinnes."

Evanger shrugged and said, "Suit yourself. He'll be on night watch Monday." He escorted Caleb to the door.

As Evanger saw him out of the office, Caleb noted that Swann, Ferris, Viernes, and Karsch were all watching with catlike curiosity.

Downstairs, he turned the visitor's ID in and found a pay phone. Thinnes's line was busy. Caleb decided another house call was in order.

SIXTY-SEVEN

The front door was unlocked though, Caleb knew, the house was empty. He rang the bell anyway. And knocked. And waited a decent interval before entering. He called out, "Thinnes? John?" from time to time as he looked around.

He finished his tour of the house in the kitchen. The room was clean, orderly, and empty. There was a blank notepad like those he'd just seen in the Area Six squad room on the counter. A Post-it stuck to the refrigerator read *Dad, Gone to the game with Greg. Home late. Love, Rob. P.S. Mom's working late.*

The phone was off the hook; the receiver dangling on its cord. He hung it up.

He picked up the notepad, not really looking at it as he tried to decide what to do next. Then he realized that an imprint of the previous message had been left on the top sheet by the ball-point used to write the message. With the retractable pencil he carried in his inner jacket pocket, he covered the paper with a film of lead. The message appeared—an address: *1287 W. Argyle*—in Thinnes's hand.

SIXTY-EIGHT

The office contained a chair, a metal desk and metal pail, a car battery, and assorted debris in cartons. And Thinnes, half conscious, occupying the chair with his arms lashed to its arms and his ankles loosely tethered to its legs. Adhesive tape covered the lower half of his face, which was scraped and bruised. Apart from the tape, he was completely naked.

They'd flushed the rogue tiger, he thought, but how had he ended up as bait? He felt very, very tired.

Water trickled onto his head, rousing him. He heard a familiar voice say, "Wake up, Thinnes. You wouldn't want to miss the denouement." He knew instantly then who had killed Finley. Who would shortly kill him.

The how wasn't difficult to guess. A phone call to Wilson, Reynolds and Close: *This is Margolis Enterprises. The young man who was in earlier—I forget his name* . . . Even if someone remembered the call, they'd be honest—and convincing—in their denials. They *wouldn't* know who'd called. But as it happened, no one remembered. And Finley was in the book. All he'd needed was Finley's name. Finley would've cooperated with the cops. With someone identifying himself as a cop. He'd have opened the door . . . The how was easy enough to figure. That left the why.

Caleb had said it: power. Money was power. Absolutely corrupting. He must've been bleeding Margolis and the other victims he'd had Berringer set up with his privileged information for plenty. But it was probably more than money. There was probably a lot of pleasure pushing rich assholes like Margolis around and fooling the cops. As to why he thought he could get away with it,

Karsch had laid it all out: once some people realize God isn't going to strike them dead, they begin to see murder—or any other atrocity—as no big thing. But it was just speculation about the why. The tape prevented him from asking.

SIXTY-NINE

Thinnes's Chevy was parked in the deep shadows of the alley that ran behind the businesses on Broadway and the low warehouse at 1287 West Argyle. Caleb parked his car behind the Chevy and set the alarm.

The new hasp on the door had been pried loose; it hung from the doorframe by one screw. The police seal had been broken. The door was slightly ajar. Another clue in a bizarre scavenger hunt. Another invitation. A challenge.

Caleb accepted.

He pushed the door open. Listening carefully for sounds of life, he prowled quietly through an interior lit only by burglar lights. There were advantages to being a cat, small, inconspicuous, and able to see in the dark. A bar of light glowed from under the first of two doors in a dimly lit hall. He paused in front of it to listen, turned the doorknob, and pushed. The door opened silently. Caleb entered the room and froze. He had found Thinnes.

He felt a chill of dismay, then a hot flood of outrage. If he had been a cat, every hair would have stood upright. He started toward Thinnes before the invisible dimensions of the trap materialized in his mind's eye. Fear of the malignity who'd engineered Thinnes's predicament whirled him around. Too late. He froze again.

Jeffrey Karsch was pointing a revolver at him. Caleb didn't know much about handguns, but he was sure the one Karsch held was no .22. Too big. Too ugly. It would leave a hole far beyond his capacity to make repairs. He willed all of his muscles still.

Karsch said, "Good evening, Dr. Caleb. I'm glad you found my invitation. I was beginning to think I'd have to phone. Did you bring a gun?"

Caleb shook his head.

"You won't mind if I check? Keep your hands where I can see them." Caleb held his hands carefully away from his sides, "Now, walk over to the chair and put your hands on Thinnes's shoulders."

Caleb wasn't able to tell from Thinnes's face what he was feeling, but the detective shook as Caleb grasped his bare shoulders. Cold or anger, Caleb decided. Not fear. Rage. Caleb looked purposefully at the wall above his head. He could feel the detective's eyes boring into his fly. He could feel the blood rising in his own face as he blushed.

"Spread your feet apart more," Karsch continued. He rammed the gun against Caleb's right kidney as he patted down Caleb's left side, then he reversed the procedure, groping around Caleb's belt line and pawing at his socks. "That you're here is a tribute to your intelligence. Too bad." He took a step back. "At ease."

Caleb took a deep breath as he let go of Thinnes, and stepped quickly backward. There was a loud, startling click as Karsch cocked the gun.

"Don't make any more fast moves!"

Caleb let his breath out slowly and heard Thinnes do the same.

Karsch said, "Right now, you're wondering if you can somehow manage to jump me. Don't try it." He waved the gun at Thinnes. "He might be able to do it—that's why he's tied up. But you couldn't, Doctor. You're not sufficiently violent. Or suicidal."

Caleb didn't reply. Karsch went on. "I won't insult you by telling you fairy tales, but whether you die by a gut shot or a bullet through the head is entirely up to you. Take off your coat."

Caleb removed his suit coat with exaggerated care and draped it over Thinnes's naked lap. He thought Thinnes looked grateful. Karsch laughed. Caleb half turned, so that Karsch could see what he was doing, and very deliberately reached for the tape on Thinnes's face.

Karsch said, "Be my guest. Then grab your head."

Caleb put his palm on Thinnes's forehead and pulled the tape off quickly as Thinnes braced himself. Thinnes made no sound, though the tape tore abraded skin from his face and started it bleeding. His attention was fixed like a cat's. Caleb dropped the tape and laced his fingers together, resting his hands on his head.

Karsch eased the hammer back into place but kept the gun pointed at Caleb.

"I need to know from Thinnes what he did with the papers you sent him today." Karsch spoke as if Thinnes was absent or unconscious.

Or already dead, Caleb thought. And I'll be next.

"Go fuck yourself," Thinnes said.

"I didn't expect you to cooperate," Karsch told him. He looked at Caleb. "You're going to have to help me persuade him."

"And if I won't?"

Karsch went over to where the car battery and bucket sat on the floor and tapped the latter with his toe. "Then you'll have to watch me do it."

He kept the gun pointed at Caleb while he tipped the contents of one of the cartons on the floor. There was a pair of latex gloves, a jumper cable, and a car wash mop with a metal shaft. Karsch dropped the mop into the pail; water splashed out onto the floor. He gestured with the gun to indicate that Caleb should move toward the door, and when he obeyed, Karsch picked the pail up and sloshed water onto Thinnes. He slammed the pail down on the desk. Water splashed out. He put the battery on a dry corner of the desktop, keeping the gun pointed at Caleb even as he used his gun hand to lift the battery.

"It's crude and painful, but effective. ECT without the anesthetic. I got the idea from a movie."

Caleb looked at Thinnes and shuddered.

The detective showed no sign of fear—though he surely understood Karsch's intent—or of the anger that must be nearly overwhelming him; he was as alert as a cat poised over a mousehole with every nerve cell focused. He said, "ECT?"

"Electroconvulsive therapy," Caleb said. "A remedy for depression from the stone age of psychiatry. Without muscle relaxants, it can break bones."

Switching the gun to his left hand and using his teeth, Karsch pulled a latex glove onto his right hand and used it to connect the black jaws of the cable to the negative pole of the battery and the edge of the desktop. After connecting the positive pole to the mop with the red jaws of the jumper cable, he dabbed at the desktop. The short he created sizzled ominously. "Of course, you could choose to help me, Doctor."

Thinnes said, "No!" To Caleb he said, "Jack, he killed Finley on the outside chance he'd've doped out what that paper meant. And he's gonna kill us next."

Caleb remembered seeing an epileptic's seizure once. The man's convulsed muscles had torn his tendons loose from the bones. And that was one of the least painful things you could do to a naked human with electricity. A wet, naked human. He asked Karsch, "How?"

Karsch took a paper bag from the floor beside the desk and put it on the desktop in front of Caleb. "Go ahead. Look."

Caleb walked to the desk and extracted a fifteen cc syringe, cotton balls, and a small bottle of alcohol from the bag, along with a black Velcro tourniquet and a vial labeled PENTOTHAL. His fingers left damp impressions on the label, and he found himself breathing faster. A sort of light-headedness was setting in. Hyperventilation.

"I'm sure you've used it in your work," Karsch said.

Caleb said nothing.

"Sorry I couldn't manage an anticholinergic," Karsch added, "but considering the circumstances . . ." He shook his head. "I think you ought to relax a bit, Doctor. You wouldn't want that vial to break in your hand."

Caleb willed his hand to relax. He reached for the tourniquet. When he brought it to Thinnes's arm, Thinnes lost control for the first time.

"Jack, you're gonna *help* him kill me?"

Caleb met Thinnes's incredulity with his own dismay. "I'm sorry. He's right about electricity being effective. But that's Pentothal—'truth serum.' It won't hurt you, and he'll believe what you say."

"It's on its way to the state's attorney. He's racking up two more murders for nothing," Thinnes said.

"And I'm the King of Siam! Doctor, you've got fifteen seconds."

Caleb looked at Thinnes. "I'm sorry, I can't watch . . ."

Karsch made a sound that was almost a laugh and said to Thinnes, "And you thought *he* killed Crowne and Finley!"

Thinnes didn't reply. He stared at Karsch while Caleb fastened the tourniquet above his right elbow, and filled the syringe from the vial. "My fault," Thinnes told him as Caleb swabbed his forearm with alcohol.

Caleb felt the sweat trickle down his neck. He noticed he was breathing as hard as if he'd just climbed eight stories. His hands shook. He said, "What is?"

"I put him on to you. When I found out Ray'd been murdered, I told him everything I knew about the case."

Caleb shook his head. He didn't look at Karsch. "He'd have come after me anyway, because he's smart enough to know I wouldn't believe it was an accident or suicide if you turned up dead. Any more than you would if I disappeared."

A little shock of discovery seemed to illuminate Thinnes's face. "If we killed each other, the department has a dead suspect and a dead hero, and there's nobody left who gives a damn about Finley. And Karsch is left to redirect any investigation."

Karsch said, "Congratulations. Get on with it, Doctor."

"One question, Karsch," Thinnes said.

Karsch didn't answer. It wasn't going to be like in the movies, Caleb decided, where the protagonist baits his opponent into blurting out the whole scheme, giving the protagonist the opportunity to escape. Karsch wasn't going to explain.

Thinnes asked anyway. "Was Evanger in on this?"

"That horse's ass?"

Thinnes looked relieved. Caleb dropped his gaze to Thinnes's forearm, to the engorged veins crawling beneath the skin like stylized serpents. He put his thumb over the radial vein, raising it even further. He'd started to thread the needle into the vein when its reptilian likeness evoked a line from the *Anaeid* about the snakes that swallowed Laocoön *to keep him from telling the truth!* The image jarred him.

"You see," Karsch was saying, "Skinner was right. All you have to do is find the right stimulus."

Caleb withdrew the needle with a quaking hand. He'd come so

close! He shifted the syringe in his hand until he held it, needle outward, in his upturned palm. He began to shake.

"What is it?" Thinnes demanded.

Trembling violently, Caleb said, "It's *not* Pentothal." He took a deep breath and let it out slowly, controlling his rage. "My guess is that it's a highly concentrated barbiturate." Turning to look at Karsch, he told Thinnes, "After you're dead, he'll strip and shoot me, make it look as though I drugged you so I could sodomize you, and you died trying to defend yourself."

There seemed to be nothing to say. Thinnes closed his eyes and let his head fall back.

Caleb said softly to Karsch, "I *won't* kill him for you."

His eyes widened as he stared at Karsch. His breaths came faster and closer together, and a violent trembling caused him to sway slightly from side to side. His hand fisted around the syringe until he was holding it like a street knife, point up.

Karsch said, "Pity."

Suddenly, Caleb lunged, stabbing at Karsch with the syringe and grabbing for the gun. Karsch fired, but Caleb kept moving. The side of his shirt puffed out and darkened as the bullet barely missed him.

Thinnes jerked spasmodically as he felt a blow like a fist striking his abdomen. A small, dark spot appeared to the right of his navel. He looked down and was mesmerized by the blood beginning to trickle onto Caleb's jacket. Probably won't kill me, he thought. Probably just means several weeks of nonfood in recovery and another reason for Ronnie to call it quits. And Caleb will have to get a new jacket. Funny the way your mind works in shock.

Karsch tried to aim the gun again as he put his free hand out to stay the approaching syringe, but Caleb jammed the needle beneath it and rammed it in just above Karsch's groin with all his strength. Karsch went crazy, kicking and thrashing around. His right hand convulsed. The gun discharged three times.

Three bullets struck the wall behind Thinnes. Karsch grabbed at Caleb's left hand with his own, and Caleb let go of the syringe to grab for the gun with his right. The wrestlers balanced, deadlocked, for a heartbeat.

Then gravity took over. The locked bodies struck the floor with a double thud and rolled across the claustrophobic space until they hit the metal desk with a tinny bang. They rolled back toward Thinnes, and the battery toppled floorward from the desktop, splatting onto the wet floor with an electric sizzle and a crackling of plastic shell. Searing steam wafted outward as acid seeped from the case.

The gun discharged again.

Thinnes groaned.

And Karsch took leave of life with an obscenity.

His body fell away from Caleb's with a sound like a sigh. Caleb pushed himself up from the floor, pale, chest heaving. He dragged the corpse clear of the acid and crawled over to Thinnes on his hands and knees stopping with his eyes fixed on Thinnes's naked shins.

Thinnes recognized the slack-jawed glaze of shock on his friend's face. "*Jack!*" he said desperately, "Don't piss out on me now!"

Caleb seemed to come back into focus.

"Jack, did he shoot you?"

Caleb sat down and felt his sides absently, as if forgetting—halfway through—what he was feeling for. "I think I killed him."

"Christ! I hope so!" Caleb started to fumble with the rope holding Thinnes's feet. "Jack! Did he shoot *you?*"

Caleb shook his head, a gesture that made his body sway slightly from side to side. He said, "Where're your clothes?"

"I don't know. Look in those cartons."

Caleb grabbed the desk to pull himself upright and lurched forward over Thinnes to work on the ropes binding his arms. He looked at Thinnes's wound. The blood flow had slowed to a drip. "That hurt much?"

"I'll live."

"Good. Just sit here a minute."

He searched the cartons, staggering a little, pausing to check the remains of Karsch for signs of life. He found Thinnes's clothing in the second box and used Thinnes's undershirt to dress the wound. "Best I can do in the field."

"Thanks," Thinnes said. He gestured toward Karsch's body. "He killed Ray Crowne hoping I'd think Ray murdered Finley, and

Ray's death would end the investigation." As Caleb helped him into his pants and shoes, he added, "He sabotaged my car just because I *suspected* Finley'd been murdered."

"He was blackmailing Margolis," Caleb said. "It would've ruined Margolis and canceled Karsch's meal ticket if anyone found out."

"The department referred some of the guys to him around the time young Margolis was arrested. That must've been how he found out. Probably heard about Berringer that way too—from the cops he was treating." Thinnes shook his head and winced at the stabbing pain the movement caused. "I heard him say working for the police department had its compensations. I thought he was talking about job satisfaction. He never seemed like the kind of arrogant bastard that would kill for money—always seemed so eager to be helpful."

"Most of us become therapists to work out solutions for our own problems, but a few do it for the power it gives them to manipulate others." Caleb glanced around the room. "I think we oughta call the cops."

"No phone."

"That's par."

"Get me outta here."

Caleb nodded and offered him a hand up. Thinnes grunted as he stood. He put an arm around Caleb's neck.

Reaching for the doorknob, Caleb asked, "You sure you know me well enough for this?"

"Well, anybody'd let a man bleed all over him . . ." Thinnes trailed off as they shifted around to squeeze through the doorway, then added, "You can't get much more intimate than that."

"You have a point." He stopped to pick Thinnes up, lifting him with a little grunt.

"Looks like we have an opening in the department for a shrink. Interested?"

"Perhaps." Caleb's voice grew softer with the exertion as he carried Thinnes toward the exit. "And maybe I could interest you in a cat. . . ."